Tethered
to Darkness

Tethered to Darkness

by
Justin Holley

www.silvershamrockpublishing.com

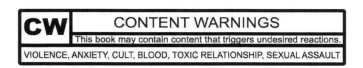

To my wife, Ali, for your love, patience and never-ending support of me chasing my dreams. You rock.

CHAPTER 1

The most beautiful of surroundings can harbor the vilest of occurrences, like rain at the Rose Parade if you really dig that sort of thing, a knifing in the downtown art district, a clown wearing white face paint and an enormous claret grin. Precursors, all—a harbinger. Mia should have seen it coming, but it happened too slowly, gradually, its momentum building like a rock rolling downhill through mud.

He held the cigarette between his index and middle finger. It wagged back and forth as he talked, punctuating his main points, ghost-like wisps of smoke reaching into the branches of the white oak above. The old Siamese cat on his lap looked comprised of nothing save skin, bones, and claws. It peered at the small crowd like they were dinner. In no small terms, the professor and the ancient cat both made Mia anxious. The professor's crooked grin appeared smug and sacrilegious, his eyes shiny—flat and soulless, yet not vacant. Like the faintest outline of sharks beneath dark-blue water. The smoldering cigarette wrangled with her sensibilities.

I'm gonna burn in hell just listening to him!

The leader of the parapsychology club's voice sounded rich and vibrant, yet scratchy. "Our souls, for lack of a better word, are tethered—moored, if you will—to our bodies by a silver thread of energy. At least until we die, at which time it dissipates and allows our soul to return home."

"Where's home?" a guy with black curly hair asked.

Mia thought she remembered him introducing himself to her as Rudy. Or maybe Brody. Her recent irregular acquaintances at state college were still somewhat nebulous. Her father would have called them alternative while condemning them to hell.

"Ah," the instructor grunted.

He jabbed his cigarette at Rudy (or Brody) like a pointer. The cherry broke off and dropped to the lush grass. Mia fought the temptation to go stomp it out. The cat's eyes flickered to the ash, then back to the crowd. It looked perpetually upset.

"Now isn't that the million-dollar question. Where, indeed?" He ran a hand over his black-stubbled chin, then quieter yet, whispered, "Where, indeed…"

"Heaven?" Mia offered. She felt pleased with herself but wondered what the others thought. She often worried about such things. Mia wiped her palms on the dry grass.

The instructor looked to her with his intense eyes, head tilted like a bewildered dog. He smiled, exposing tiny white teeth. "How precocious. A Christian at my proceedings then, is it?"

Sheltered from outside influences, Mia didn't think she would ever get used to viewpoints different from hers. They always shook her on a fundamental level, made her feel naïve. Afraid. She felt her hands tremble.

"Yes," Mia said steadily, even if she didn't feel so certain.

So far, so good. No tears! She didn't want to weep in front of an instructor, but sometimes admonishment by her peers could lead to the issue.

He nodded, the small predator-like smile never wavering. "Very well. You may find yourself in the minority, but that's neither here nor there." He placed a hand over his mouth and appeared to consider Mia's remark further. The cat stared in feline fashion, which now focused in on her like she had offended it. "You may call the home of your soul Heaven, if you wish. I prefer the *spiritual realms* or the shadow lands. Six of one, half a dozen of the other, I suspect."

Mia let out a breath, relieved that Frank Colista seemed to accept her, and no fellow learners mocked her idea.

Chastity, Mia's dorm-mate, leaned over to Mia, black hair swinging over her bony shoulders. Her breath smelled of lemon juice and tobacco. "What would you expect him to say? He's a parapsychology professor, not a preacher." She leaned in closer. "And he's a hardcore hottie."

Mia considered the irony of Chastity's name as Rudy/Brody rubbed Chastity's bare shoulder, closer to her roommate's exposed black bra-strap than Mia felt comfortable watching. Not that Mia completely avoided sex. She had done it twice now, neither time pleasant. Once, the night after their senior prom last March, and again before her parents brought her to state college in August. Jack had wanted to do it more over the summer, but she had always refused.

Don't wear it out, mom always joked, even though Mia knew she wasn't kidding. Her mom got knocked up with Mia before she'd gotten married. *Hypocrite.* Her parents had been wilder than they cared to admit prior to raising the cross and meeting Pastor Matt. Mia felt a chill wrap around her neck despite the warm weather.

"He can believe what he wants, and I'll believe what I want," Mia mumbled, keeping a careful eye on Rudy/Brody's hand. "No big deal." She hoped she sounded strong yet reserved.

Chastity rolled her dark brown eyes as if such a flexible attitude went against her own beliefs.

Mia tried hard not to judge. She hated it when people in her church judged her. The world took all kinds.

"The silver cord," the professor went on, "keeps us tethered to our bodies while we're alive, even if we leave our flesh bag for a time and have a walkabout."

"Gross," Mia whispered, then ran a slender hand through her long blonde hair. The word *flesh bag* made her think of dead, bloated things. Things that stunk.

"What's a walkabout?" another student asked.

Mia's butt hurt as she sat on the grass, so she curled her left foot back and beneath. Her lanky frame was always a problem when it came to comfort. Maybe she shouldn't have come to the parapsychology club with Chastity, but she needed something to do. Regular classes hadn't started, and she didn't know many other people. She'd met Chastity's friends at orientation, but she had not grown close to them yet.

Professor Colista took a big drag off his cigarette, then pointed it at the student as he blew a stream of smoke out his mouth. The cat lowered its ears. "I'm glad you asked. How many of you have heard of astral projection?"

"Like an out-of-body experience?" Mia asked, despite herself, more interested than she thought she should be. Her leg fell asleep and started tingling.

Colista grunted something Mia couldn't understand, then said, "Well…when it's by accident, like near-death or some drivel like that, then I suppose we may refer to it as *out of body*."

"People would leave their bodies on purpose?" Mia murmured, not intending for Colista to hear.

Again, she felt shocked and ill-prepared for the open-mindedness of the college experience. She liked to blame her parents for this sheltered existence but supposed she should shoulder some of the blame on her own. Strong independent women made up their own minds, didn't they? Her cellphone vibrated and she checked it. *Jack. Ugh*. Mia ignored the call.

"Certainly," Colista said, having heard her. "It's liberating." The cat yawned, as if bored by the professor rubbing the fur between the thing's tattered ears. Colista scanned the diverse group sprawled before him on the grassy slope. "In fact, for those who are interested, we'll conduct practice sessions at Parapsychology Club meetings."

"You mean astral projection is for real?" Mia asked, out loud this time. It just kind of blurted out, and she felt her face turn red despite the swell of curiosity overruling her skepticism. Her question elicited a few laughs this time.

"Very funny," Colista said. "Of course, it's real. I've been outside my flesh bag on several occasions. Like I said, I find it liberating."

"How do you get back in once you're out?" Chastity asked.

Mia knew she sang in a band and figured that voice probably came in handy when she sang Jagged Edge songs and other vocal-cord-busting covers.

"Well," Colista started with that bewildered look again, "you just reenter your goddamn body, Chastity. I mean, it's not rocket science. I'll show you. That's what I'm here for."

"You're here to look pretty and be my eye-candy," Chastity said. "You can leave your mouth shut if you're gonna cuss at me." A group of girls with dark eyeliner and lipstick laughed.

Mia slumped down, attempting, as she always did, to stay invisible when something made her uncomfortable. This time it was the professor's language, and she wondered how he kept his job.

The cat lowered its ears again, then hunched its back. Colista pushed it off his lap and onto the grass where it lay down, but not before a lengthy bout of deliberation.

Mia noticed Rudy/Brody had turned red and figured Chastity's remark made him jealous.

Colista winked at her, took a drag off his smoke, then blew it out above his head. The cat hissed for no apparent reason. "That's it for today. Go party, or whatever you all have planned. We'll meet again next week. Prepare to experience *the nether*."

Then he got up and ambled crookedly toward the Psych building. He did not even look back, as if the throng of students were not worth the effort. The cat fell in behind him, yowling at his feet, requesting a lift.

"Nice guy," Mia said. She knew she sounded insincere but meant it.

In fact, he scared her on a fundamental level, caused her to feel…unhealthy. That always proved true when introduced to something her childhood church would find unsavory, like the well-meaning yet pushy parishioners who seemed to travel inside her head with her wherever Mia roamed. This also made Mia uncomfortable. She wanted to live as good of a life as possible, but she also wanted freedom to make her own choices. Her old congregation was full of very pleasant, God-fearing folks, but Mia wanted some fresh experiences and to meet a variety of people. To break away from the constant scrutiny of her actions.

Well, mission accomplished.

"Oh, he's fine," Chastity said. She checked her smartphone and then dropped it back to the grass. "Just fine. Finer when he doesn't talk so much, but yeah…fine."

When Rudy/Brody walked off to talk with some other guy Mia didn't know, she whispered, "Does he always flirt with you like that?" She knew Chastity wouldn't know if she meant Rudy/Brody's hand on Chastity's shoulder or Colista's wink. Her response would be a major tell.

Despite the casual wink, Colista left the impression on Mia that he lived his life well above the petty feelings of his flock. Probably didn't give Chastity the time of day outside of the group.

"Sure," Chastity said. "Sometimes Colista even comes over and listens to the band rehearse. Sometimes…"

Bingo! But Mia found she didn't want to know about *sometimes*. Okay, Colista interacted on some level, but knew anything further would prove wishful thinking on Chastity's part. He'd never sleep with a student. Something about Colista's demeanor told her the professor would never consider it.

"He's just gorgeous is all," Chastity said. She nodded her head, eyes squinted. "Don't worry. You're a bombshell, nice bod, pretty blue eyes. And they always look sad, too, which is great. Guys eat that shit up. If they think you're sad, they'll do anything for you." Chastity fanned her face, then scrunched it up in a knot. A tear slid down her cheek, and she smiled. "If you master that little maneuver, you'll never have to worry about a thing."

Mia gasped, just a slow intake of breath past her thin lips. "I— I can't manipulate folks. I just can't. It isn't right." Mia didn't understand what this latest discourse had to do with Colista, or anyone else. No, Mia would never stoop to that level.

"You can to," Chastity said. "Whatever. You'll learn." And before Mia could respond, she asked, "Gonna come watch us tonight?"

Mia knew Jagged Edge rehearsed most nights in the storage shed associated with her and Chastity's dorm room. Good thing neither of them had much to store. "Maybe. I'm gonna hit the library first, then we'll see."

"There'll be guys," Chastity said. "And hardcore tuneage."

"I have a boyfriend," Mia reminded her.

"That'll change," Chastity said, then grinned over her shoulder as she walked away.

Mia watched as she sneaked over, reached around, and then twisted Rudy/Brody's nipple. He squirmed. She whispered something into his ear that made him smile. Probably a placation.

What had Mia gotten herself into? She found Chastity more distasteful than Colista, despite considering her a friend. Her only friend so far, in fact. This realization surprised her.

Colista talked somewhat rough too, but not like Chastity. He kept at least a modicum of decency. His wink at Chastity hadn't been anything more than a hint to keep her roommate coming to his proceedings. A placation of his own. Of this, Mia felt sure.

She hated to admit it, but she had found Colista's talk about astral projection and a tether of energy fascinating. Dangerous, but exciting in a strange new way. Besides, didn't this bit of information jibe perfectly with her beliefs? Mia believed in an afterlife, and what Colista talked about extended that train of thought. It wouldn't hurt to listen to what he had to say. In fact, Mia felt hungry for more information.

Colista gave her butterflies, but not for the reasons Chastity would think. The man held the key to something more—more than she could learn from the pastor at her church. More than she could garner from the close-minded circle of church friends her parents had carefully handpicked for her.

Mia suddenly felt triumphant in having avoided the Bible-college her dad had selected for her. She had made her own mind up, picked her own college, and would also choose her way through the rest of her life. She smiled and hoped she was up to the task of spreading her wings.

CHAPTER 2

A waft of cool air hit Mia as she entered through the double glass doors of the library; her cargo shorts and cotton t-shirt did little to protect her from the chill. Marble floors stretched away from her until they transitioned to carpet where the stacks and study nooks started. Despite the hum of activity, the place sounded subdued, respectful.

Like a library ought to.

The invasiveness of the last hour washed away when the scent of old books hit her nostrils. A familiar scent, like an old friend. Mia felt at home here.

Behind a horseshoe-shaped reception desk, a shaggy-haired boy looked up from his paperback with a toothy smile plastered on his round pale face. He stared a bit too long. "Help you find anything?" he said overly enthusiastic.

"First time here," Mia said politely. "Just checking things out."

"What's your flavor?" the boy asked. "Oh, and I'm Bruce."

She noticed Bruce wore a black and white checkered flannel shirt, sleeves rolled up to his elbows. His right elbow looked raw and inflamed, where he probably suffered from some mild skin disorder. Beneath the flannel, the boy wore a black t-shirt, and Mia could just make out the Star Wars emblem.

"Young adult, mostly," Mia answered, trying to be polite without hovering anywhere close to being flirty. It seemed all any of the boys were on the lookout for was a one-night stand or a long-term girlfriend. "You know, like Anita Grace Howard's *Splintered* series, or Eric Devine's *Tap Out*."

"Oh," he said, thick lips forming a circle, brown eyes suddenly large and bright. "We just got a copy of Kerri Maniscalco's *Stalking Jack the Ripper* in. I think you'd like it."

"Maybe," Mia said, and she couldn't help letting the hint of a smile curl her lips. "I've heard it's kinda scary, though." What would her parents think? And her church? These questions always intruded on her thoughts, but she steeled herself, determined to expand her base.

"Scarier than *Tap Out*?" he asked. "Shit gets *real* quickly in that one." He covered his mouth with a large-knuckled hand. "Sorry. Sometimes I cuss when I get excited."

Mia smiled bigger. With her face on autopilot, she pushed the tip of her small pink tongue just between her teeth. This was a mistake, realizing he might find the gesture cute.

Stop flirting!

She calmed herself mentally. "I know, I know, but Jack the Ripper? He's a serial killer. Kinda darker than I normally read."

"Not as dark as this," he said, and lifted the paperback by his elbow. "I'm really into Brian Keene right now."

"*Darkness on the Edge of Town*," she whispered. The cover looked frightening. She looked up at him. "Horror?"

"Yep," he said. "Started with King and Koontz, then moved on to Laymon, Keene, and Ketchum. I'm kinda into Janz and Rufty right now, too."

Mia felt herself frown.

The boy smiled. "I'm kinda used to that reaction. Don't worry, I'm not a psycho or anything. Just like escaping into an author's dark world from time to time." He frowned too as if in response to Mia's. "You know, you're even cute when you frown. There's this little dimple at the corner of your mouth that forms no matter what you do with your lips."

Mia's heart sped up. She knew she should not accept the compliment. Mia had a boyfriend, but she couldn't quite bring herself to take evasive action. She felt her lips betray her with another smile, and even flipped a hand through her hair. What was wrong with her?

"Aha!" he exclaimed and pointed. "Made ya smile. How can you not like a guy who can make ya smile? Hey, I'm not exactly Prince Charming, I realize, but we would always have books to fall back on as our common ground."

"I have a boyfriend," Mia said. Her heart was beating a mile a minute.

There was something about him. He wasn't super cute in a conventional sense, but his personality—Mia dug it. And he wasn't unattractive per se...just ordinary. Not a jock like her boyfriend, who never wanted to talk about anything but baseball and football, and how good he was at those activities. And...

Oh no.

She realized Bruce knew that she was at least a little interested. Now he'd never leave her be, and this campus would prove too small to avoid him forever. The thought of rebuking him was overwhelming.

"They all do," he sighed. "At least for the first couple weeks. Then they realize just how big college life really is."

Mia stared at him, frozen by the bold statement, and tried to think of an argument against it. She decided to try for a friendly tone. "And how do you know so much about what girls realize and don't realize?"

"Please don't take that the wrong way," he said. "Sometimes I'm an idiot when I'm nervous. Um…well, you see, I'm a sophomore. I've seen some things. And it's not just girls. See, freshmen come in thinking they're in love with their high school sweethearts. And they might be, occasionally, but often it's just that they haven't been around a lot of other guys or gals. Then, when they find someone they have more in common with…well, kaboom! Fireworks."

"And this dynamic has worked out for you?" she asked.

Mia felt conflicting emotions about the remark. First, she was scared this phenomenon was working in his favor, that he had so many options he wouldn't be interested in her. Secondly, Mia hated that she couldn't completely deny what he said. Neither of these worries, however, changed the fact she had a boyfriend.

The boy frowned and looked down at his paperback. He sighed. "Not for me." He looked back up at her, his lips blossoming into a grin, revealing crooked eye teeth. "But I have hope."

A laugh burst out from between Mia's pursed lips before she could stop it. "Oh my God," she whispered, but felt her grin widen. She immediately felt guilty for the curse.

"Can we start over?" he asked, extending his hand. "I'm Bruce Monroe, creative writing major. I know you already knew my name, but we're starting over here, and…and I'm rambling."

Mia shook her head and knew her sad eyes would turn him on like they did Jack and other boys from her youth group. It never failed, but she couldn't help herself now. This clumsy boy was a colossal doofus, but she liked him. Yes, she could admit that much. She grasped his hand and shook. "Mia Hollenbeck, undecided."

"Nice to meet you, Mia," he said with a sincerity which made Mia's stomach flop with butterflies. "Not many girls read fiction anymore. Like, they might read the mainstream manufactured garbage, but not like… the cool stuff." He paused with a wistful look in his eyes. "Wanna do something later?"

"I do have a boyfriend," Mia said, voice soft so as not to offend. "You might be right about freshmen, but that doesn't mean I have to be a lousy cheater."

"Of course," Bruce said. "I wouldn't want you to be a cheat, either. Can we just hang as friends and see what happens?"

"Nothing's going to happen," Mia assured him. "You'll find me a boring stick in the mud."

"We'll just hang out," Bruce agreed. "Talk about books, maybe music. We could go to the art gallery downtown. They have some great local talent in there right now."

Mia thought about Chastity's rehearsal this evening. It sure would be nice to have a friend of her own there, one that wasn't trying to get her involved with the scummy underbelly of dorm life. "Speaking of music…"

"Music, sure," Bruce said, his smile wide now. "I know all kinds of places." He waved his hands in a nervous gesture. "Not the bar scene. I mean real nice, classy places."

"What I have in mind is probably far from classy," Mia said. Before he could get the wrong idea, she added, "And far from refined. In fact, it'll take place in a storage shed."

Bruce tilted his head in a bewildered gesture. "Okay?" he said, as if waiting for the punchline. He ran a hand through his curly hair. "You sure? I mean, I can get us into the *Horns* concerto tonight at Bangsberg Hall."

Mia shook her head and felt her flowing hair swish around her shoulders. "As fun as that sounds, I promised my roommate I'd stop by and listen to her band rehearse."

"*The Empire Strikes Back* is playing down in the Union tonight," he said, brown eyes wide with hope. It had come out as a question.

"Sorry," Mia said, and meant it. "And just for the record, you're a nerd." She nodded, jaw set. "It's official."

Bruce giggled, the sound a joyful barrage of staccato syllables. "That, Mia, has been official for quite some time." He put his hands together and braced his forehead, elbows on the table, and eyes peering up at Mia like a lost puppy. "Garage band it is, then."

"You sure?" Mia asked.

He shrugged. "The important thing is spending time with someone nice."

Mia pursed her lips. Her boyfriend, Jack, would never have agreed to go. Unless, of course, he might score a beer, or some other guys would be there to talk sports. She nodded. "Okay, I'll see you tonight." She added, "Friends."

"What else?" Bruce said. He reached behind the counter and returned with *Stalking Jack the Ripper*. He handed it to her. "And enjoy."

With a scowl, she grabbed the book. It wouldn't hurt to try it, even if it turned out scarier than she normally preferred. Mia tucked it under her arm. "Thanks." Then she walked toward a reading nook. She glanced over her shoulder. "Birch Hall dorm parking lot. Six O'clock. You'll find us." Had she just made plans with another guy?

Bruce's head continued to bobble up and down as Mia trundled around the corner of a stack and picked a nook. She glanced at the cover of the book and shuddered. First, an occult club. Now, serial killers. What would come next? She wasn't sure she could take much more change, but then she thought of Bruce, and despite her reservations, a smile bloomed on her face.

CHAPTER 3

A bevy of mixed emotions fluttered around inside Bruce's head.

Like a belly fulla butterflies.

He liked Mia a lot. Sure, her looks would turn any guy's head, which would likely end up problematic for him. Bruce realized he wasn't exactly a heartthrob. Kind of pudgy and nondescript, but he also understood things he had in common with her that could enhance his looks or render them nonconsequential.

Bruce opened the lid of his silver laptop and plopped down at his light-birch computer desk. His rough work in progress glared like the smile from a barker at the carnival, missing teeth and all. He cursed at the sight. Once again, he'd forgotten to close out and send it packing back to his cloud service. A horrible habit. He just knew one of his roommates would find it open one day and hit delete, just to screw with him. Then he'd fail Genre Fiction 201 with Rachel Deneen if he couldn't recover the manuscript. In fact, she'd bust his balls if she knew he hadn't closed it out. Bruce sighed.

Well, might as well work on it now that I have it open.

He'd feel guilty otherwise. With reverence, he read through the horror of what he scribed yesterday. When thoughts of Mia distracted him, he started over. After he'd done this three times, he finally sighed, then gave Mia his undivided attention.

What a sucker I am.

What did it matter, anyway? Mia made it clear she had a serious boyfriend. Sure, they would probably split up, eventually. In the meantime, could he trust himself to keep things friendly and casual? Anything else would push her away. A quandary. Bruce needed to act interested enough to hold her attention while nature took its course, but not so ultra-focused to send Mia running away into the arms of another. God knew that had happened before.

"Bastard!" he mumbled and deleted the word *which* and created two sentences. Deneen had warned him about his propensities, his horrible cancerous habits.

Bruce sighed, then placed a hand on his shaggy head. He wondered whether he should use hair product for the rehearsal, create some alternative look.

No, bad idea.

Pretending never worked.

Just be yourself, Bruce.

The thought sounded like his mother—long deceased yet still instrumental to his life. Okay, this time he would just be himself. Let the chips fall.

Pretending.

Since his mother's death, he had formed the habit of making up his life so it sounded more interesting, tried to adjust his looks, whatever it took to fit in. No more. For God's sake—no more. Mia would like Bruce for who he was or she wouldn't.

Mia. A girl who read something besides textbooks. So hard to find, but now that he had found her, he'd have to play the cards just so.

Friends. *Just be her friend.* He said it over and over until he meant it. Nothing more, nothing less. Let Mia see what kind of fun she could have with him. Things would progress, maybe.

Bruce turned on his cam so he could see himself. "Okay," he whispered and checked his teeth. Slightly askew in front, but they were white-ish at least. He'd taken to walking on his treadmill, and Bruce thought his cheeks might look the slightest bit less full. Unsatisfied yet resigned, he turned it off and returned to the WIP and typed a few sentences.

He smiled. Not too shabby. Bruce checked his word count and cringed. He deleted one of the sentences which didn't add to the story.

Better not to overdue things.

Writing and women, Bruce mused. Neither pleased his old man, who thought he ought to major in business or engineering. He'd also voiced his opinion that Bruce shouldn't date until after college. Girls were nothing but trouble. That was just because his mom left, though. His dad hadn't been so anti-women prior to that. In fact, his old man used to lay on the charm plenty thick until she ran off and married an investment banker from Portland.

Then she died. *Irony.*

He thought about his mother, remembered playing Scrabble with her as a kid. Nostalgia took over until he remembered that she abandoned them long before she left this world. He hoped it wasn't the destiny that awaited him. A lifetime of women who wouldn't pass up the opportunity to trade up. Ugh! Bruce didn't think Mia would turn out that way. Maybe just the opposite. But none of his past love interests had panned out, so what reason did he have to believe this one would?

One can only keep on hoping.

Bruce noticed the time at the bottom right of his screen. Four o'clock on the dot. A couple more hours until the rehearsal started.

He'd probably go find Mia a little early. "Being on time means you're late," his old man always said. He'd have to decide how to dress, eat a quick bite, and probably figure something out with his hair. After freshman orientation a few weeks back, Bruce remembered the band Mia mentioned opening for Johnny Holm. Well, the Johnny Holm band, anyway. Old Johnny hadn't been there in the flesh. The band had dressed kind of alternative. Wild hair and bright colors, lots of piercings and ink. They seemed to enjoy the occult—used fake human skulls on stage, pentagrams. Things like that.

That didn't mean he needed to dress simpatico, but Bruce enjoyed wearing appropriate attire for any situation.

Ready for anything, that's my motto.

An incredible lie. He sighed. The new AC/DC t-shirt would work. He'd lucked out and got to see the last concert with Brian Johnson at the helm. Thank God for small miracles. He'd scored this sweet shirt, one exclusive to the concert and his VIP-ticket status. Yes, that and black jeans and his black combats would work nicely. Concert-ish, but not over the top.

Closing out his WIP this time, Bruce slammed the lid on his laptop, stood, and made for the bathroom mirror. He was relieved to have scored a campus apartment versus a dorm room. At least he had some privacy in which to lament in.

Yes, you're a full-blown king of geekdom, Bruce Monroe!

Complete with a couple of burgeoning pimples beneath the unruly shock of hair draped over his forehead.

"But of course," he mumbled.

He poked at the red mounds, then stared with a discerning eye. He knew he shouldn't care, but he did.

Friends.

If anything ever blossomed (besides his zits) he needed to concentrate hard on not overdoing things. It'd be difficult because she would be a breath of fresh air to his aching lungs and the heart betwixt them. Bruce could almost feel Mia's scorn now after she found out he couldn't mask how he really felt about her.

Sometimes, Bruce knew things, sensed them, regardless of what his dad said about him. He'd cultivated his intuitions and what they meant for the world around him. He knew meeting Mia was destiny. That might not mean a forever type situation. She could be a friend for a reason, a season, or a lifetime. One just never knew. He'd spent his entire life helping others find happiness and hoped for his turn for something good—a return on investment from the universe. Hadn't he always been the giver, the helper, the one who solved problems for others? His dad had always leaned on him for everything: cooking, cleaning, and pretty much everything he would have thought of as *her* work. Even the librarian at his high school leaned on him to set up computers and AV equipment for no compensation. Not even a credit toward graduation.

"Just this one time, please," Bruce mumbled, "let me be on the receiving end of something special. Please."

With a swipe of his beefy right hand, Bruce clicked the bathroom light off, rambled out into the hall, then entered his bedroom. He donned the t-shirt and jeans, gave himself a nice spritz of Tag, then headed for the door. Maybe—just maybe—tonight would be the very beginning of the rest of his life.

The door clicked behind him, and it sounded like forever.

CHAPTER 4

Mia's graceful legs powered along in a casual gait, her hands folded behind her back, her nose taking in the sweet scent of the well-pruned yet filled-to-overflowing flower bed. Bees droned in the background, hovering and bouncing from plant to plant. Ants crawled over the large puffy white and pink Peonies. Other students walked hand in hand with newfound friends, or they strolled alone, like her. One girl sat on a large rock. A bushy-haired guy sat on a bench reading a book. Another typed on his laptop.

One perk of state college was the campus. It bordered Diamond Point Park and the lake. Both the park, with its flowerbeds, and the deep-blue lake were beautiful. At least now in August. With the onset of autumn, the weather would change for the worse when the cold set in. She didn't even want to think about the winter months with the snow and ice. For now, however, it seemed like a small slice of heaven had fallen away to Earth, warm rays of sunshine on her skin, and the beautiful fall colors ripening the leaves.

Mia carried a bag over her bony left shoulder, filled with lots of the artsy stuff she liked. The bag bulged with yarn, several vibrant colors, along with her knitting needles of various design, each with their own distinct purpose. How she loved fibers and the beautiful things she could create from them. Her relatives were used to getting hand-knitted sweaters, mittens, colorful afghans, and other items as Christmas gifts.

With plenty of time to kill before Chastity's rehearsal, Mia sat on a wooden-slat park bench next to the fragrant flowers. The strategically placed bench was the best spot to enjoy the beautiful view of the water. She unfurled her latest project, a scarf for her mother, made from a blend of pastel threads. Needles next. They felt like an extension of her long skinny fingers as they weaved their magic. Too bad she could easily think and knit at the same time.

Bruce Monroe popped, very much unbidden, into her mind. Mia knew she should concentrate on other things like her boyfriend, Jack, or about her classes, which started next week, or even about finding some part-time work. Her fingers flew over her knitting, yet thoughts of Bruce still intruded like a thief in her mind. She shouldn't have invited him and only had because it wouldn't be horrible to have a friend there with her. Especially since Chastity could be a handful.

She told herself this, but was it the truth? Perhaps she should try to analyze why her heart beat so fast, just at the thought of him. Why she could barely wait to see him in a couple of hours.

Her brow furrowed as she eyeballed her work. Not because her knitting looked suspect, but because her thoughts were. "Good lord," she mumbled.

He probably can't even hit a baseball, or fix anything. Does he even know how to treat a girl properly?

That line of thought made her feel better until a little voice in her head said, "He's a good conversationalist, however, and you have lots in common. Kinda shallow of you to think otherwise. He's not even bad looking, in that geeky fan-boy kinda way."

He's an artist, Mia thought. *That's the allure here. He writes and you, Mia, knit and crochet.*

She could just hear her dad. *"You're marrying who?"* And then he'd roll his eyes before saying, *"You'll starve!"* Her dad always worried about her decisions and often grew paranoid about how she did what felt right rather than what might prove the prudent choice.

"Well, Dad," she whispered, "you're not here, and I can make my own choices."

Mia wondered what she'd meant, exactly, by that statement. Because she hadn't even been aware a need for a decision existed. She had a boyfriend—a gorgeous one at that, and very athletic. Sure, she may describe him as an occasional jerk, self-centered, and rude to people he thought were beneath him.

"He'll grow out of all that," she whispered, but didn't really believe.

Deep down Mia knew he'd always act combative and misogynistic, one of those guys who joked about sex like it was some kind of trophy.

Mia raised her line of sight to the lake where the water rippled with the breeze. The previous thought left her with a cold pit in her stomach. Maybe that's all she was to Jack, a trophy. He'd ask her to marry him, so she could be his trophy wife. This made her cringe because she knew *trophy wives* possessed much bigger *accessories* than she did. Not that she cared. Goose bumps formed on her skin when Mia imagined the repugnancy of waiting in line for an enhancement while he traveled with some third-rate minor-league baseball team. *Never.*

"Ugh...gross," Mia whispered.

Not appealing.

She decided that would never happen. If Jack didn't like her body as is, then he could go right straight to H-E-double-hockey-sticks. Her parents would hate it, too. And the church.

Mia picked her needles back up and stitched with a violent cadence. Violent because nobody could get her worked up like Jack, even about issues that hadn't even come up yet. When a girl distinctly avoided her by walking on the other side of the path while staring at Mia with nervous eyes, Mia slowed her frenzy.

Girls know things, she mused. And Mia just knew Jack would pop the question this Christmas.

It felt right. Not that an engagement to Jack felt right, but he'd do it anyway, oblivious to her or anything else. It would mortify Mom. Dad would be overjoyed. He liked Jack because he came across as competent, even helped fix the carburetor on the lawnmower which saved her dad a hundred bucks over at the small-engine shop. He'd been in love with Jack ever since.

Let him marry Jack then!

That would make Mom laugh, for sure. Mom often acted like she disliked Jack. Nothing blatant. Just little things like not answering the door or not striking up even a polite conversation. A stark contrast to Dad's attentions, anyway. Mom and Dad seemed so different and Mia often wondered if they only stayed together for her sake. Or for the sake of appearances at church.

Probably.

That would be just like her mother, to sacrifice her own happiness.

Ice water hit her guts. If that were true about her mother, it could be equally accurate of herself.

Her knitting sped up along with her musings. Mia knew she thought too much, worried about drama that hadn't even happened yet, which often resulted in an upset stomach. Nerves. Sometimes she even threw up or cried. She hated the bawling, considered herself an ugly crier. Some girls, like Chastity, used it to enhance their looks, make themselves appear vulnerable. Not her, though. She ended up looking like a drowned raccoon. Regardless, sometimes it just happened, spontaneous, without her permission.

How she'd played rugby without issue eluded her. It never made her nervous to drive another girl's head into the ground. In fact, it'd been a great stress release over the last couple of years. She'd signed up for the intramural club play here at state college, but that didn't even start until next week.

Nothing left to do tonight but go to Chastity's rehearsal with Bruce. This made her stomach flutter, again. Her first two thoughts: *He's not my type*, and then, *I already have a boyfriend*. Mia knew only the second thought held merit. Bruce could very well turn out as the relationship she always wanted, a guy who understood art and listened to her. Mia's stomach gurgled with anxiety. The thought of Bruce brought joy to her soul, even though she just met him. However, the thought of confronting Jack with a breakup made her want to vomit.

"Deep breaths," she chanted as she closed her eyes, hands continuing to knit like an automaton. *Just one more row! Just one more row!*

This had always been her mantra, the little saying that got her through stressful times. Her knitting felt much like therapy. Between her newfound *alternative* friends, Bruce, and the strangeness of her first-time college experience, her knitting felt like the only thing grounding her. She needed a bigger project—much bigger! Something in line with her unfamiliar world. Maybe she should find a church like Mom suggested. That didn't feel right.

Then it came to her.

Mia jumped to her feet, a smile on her face, the butterflies in her belly flying away into the clear blue sky. Yes, it would give her something to do and would really surprise Chastity. It might also piss her off, but that would prove part of the fun, her own private rebellion.

Mia scooped up her books and her knitting, then headed for the dorms to get the things she needed.

CHAPTER 5

A rush of adrenaline coursed through her when Mia stabbed the tiny misshapen key into the garage-door handle. Once unlocked, she lifted the door upward. Such a cheap door, nothing but white thin-walled ribbed steel with no insulation, but it sure made a commotion when it rattled up and inside the receptacle. The garage would be nothing but cold storage in another month unless Chastity used a space heater for rehearsals.

The moment the door opened, Mia's feeling of elation changed. The bag over her shoulder felt heavier, her feet imbedded in wet cement. The darkness within ate the sunlight which poured in through the opening. She half expected the murky area between the sunlight and complete darkness to spin around like a twister, the light and dark both fighting for dominance. Nothing moved back in that darkness. No sounds, either, yet Mia felt something stir back there.

Just your imagination, she thought, but not convincingly.

Luckily, most of the mic stands stood in the sunny area. Mia puzzled at her feelings of unease, then carefully unpacked the long pre-knitted strands of yellow, red, and purple yarn. One for each mic stand.

They looked like the afghans Mia enjoyed knitting but were much narrower. Just big enough to fit the circumference of the stands. Urban knitting—or yarn bombing, as some called it—always took her worries away like nothing else ever could. In her element, Mia worked steadily to knit the final stitches which would adhere the yarn pieces. She did the same with larger squares of color over the four amps which stood along the right-hand wall. The two knitting needles flashed with bright bursts in the sunlight. She worked them up and down, back and forth, hands moving with a quick grace and charm.

Mia, unsure how much time had passed, stepped outside to examine her handiwork. Not bad. The three yarn-bombed stands and four amps glowed in their colorful garments. She felt both a touch of pride and rebellion. Mia knew most people wouldn't find this particularly rebellious, but to her it felt so, and as far as she'd ever be willing to go along those lines. Just like her mom would never leave her dad, even though she should spread her wings and fly.

A flutter from above caught her attention. Mia glanced at the roofline where black shingles sloped upward toward the peak of the shed. She expected to see a bird or maybe a flag.

Nothing.

The gloomy feelings returned when she glanced inside the garage and into the dark rafters. The ice-spiders crawled up her spine. Wooden rafters, the ones closest, revealed no birds or anything else flapping in the non-existent breeze. The middle ones, darker than the first, also revealed nothing. The wood rafters in the back—the ones within the gloom— lay bathed in too much inky darkness to tell what may lurk within.

Mia stepped forward, curious. Back home, her mother tied hummingbird feeders to the overhang in front of their two-car garage.

Sometimes the pesky little creatures, in their never-ending enthusiasm, flew inside the garage and fluttered about. At home amidst the rafters, they sometimes got above the garage door, but here the shed door rolled up into a circular enclosure. So, the rafters remained visible. Mia didn't notice any kind of bird in the rafters or above the garage door cylinder.

Standing among the mic stands, a colorful mini forest of yarn, Mia stared into the dreary recesses. The back of the shed seemed to absorb the light, as if a black sheet hung back there, obscuring her view. Yet she could still hear the fluttering of those tiny—they had to be tiny, right?—wings above her.

Mia stepped into the gloom, then another step, and another, until she could finally see into the back of the garage. No birds, humming or otherwise, in front or above. And yet they still fluttered. The only thing she could see was dust bunnies, empty beer cans, what looked like—*gross!*—a used condom crammed in a corner, half-a-dozen cigarette butts, and a half-bag of Doritos.

Then something else.

With a wretched flop, her heart staggered for a beat.

It didn't exactly surprise Mia, but to see the Ouija board sitting so blatantly, right out in the open, shocked her a bit. She hadn't seen one for a long time. Not since she and her friend Stacey had found her mother's Parker Brother's version on the top shelf of the hall closet. Those were the days before they got churchy and lived to please Pastor Matt. That adventure ended badly when the planchette had sailed across the room and slammed off the wall so hard a piece broke off. She'd blamed it on Christy until they both heard the growl and ran for upstairs. The only time she'd touched the Ouija board after that was to put it away before her mom caught on. If she ever heard a growl like that again, Mia thought she'd just die.

The fluttering sound grew louder for a moment, built to a crescendo, then stopped. Mia nearly stumbled forward into the noiseless void. She looked around, bewildered, fists on her hips, a mocking gesture of the bravery she didn't feel. Mia wasn't a little girl any longer, but right now she felt like one. Not much different from the little bird she had heard in the rafters at home. Skittish.

The Ouija appeared brighter than the surrounding gloom, as if lightened by an internal glow. The clear planchette lay on top, innocent looking, not guilty of anything more than being created.

Mia glanced upward when the sound of wings returned. Maybe the bird was trapped between the ceiling and the roof, if such a place existed. But Mia didn't really believe that and returned her attention to the back of the shed.

Next to the Ouija, an old, tattered book lay closed on a shelf. It looked like a Bible from her church, but the cover held a golden inverted pentagram instead of a cross. Mia had decided she wouldn't push her beliefs on others here at state college, but she still held with the ideology that consorting with the Devil was bad. Her parents sent her to church and vacation Bible school early and often and dragged her to church, where she went through the motions. She listened to Pastor Matt blister them with his sermons of brimstone. Mia knew some stuff. Enough, at least, to know the Christian version of right from wrong...and to regurgitate the things her congregation friends wanted to hear.

Anxiety picked at her, and Mia's instincts told her to bolt, but she wouldn't. Exposure therapy, the only way to conquer her anxieties and fears. Still, tears roiled behind her eyes and threatened to spill out. The back of the shed felt evil.

Mia swatted at her tears. She hated the Ouija. Not because of what it represented, but because of the anxiety and fear it forced to bubble up. If her dad or Pastor Matt were here, they would swat the board off the table and into the darkness beyond.

No...no!

They would burn the thing, destroy the Devil's tool.

She turned her back on the thing, chest heaving.

The Devil!

Mia took several deep breaths, then concentrated on her colorful creations, allowing her fears to dissipate. She may not share all of her parents' beliefs, but she didn't want to take the Ouija and blasphemous book too lightly. Not after her experience as a kid.

Then a golden angel stepped into the garage opening, backlit by the bright sun. A rather large angel, she noticed. "Mia?" it asked. "What's wrong?"

The lovely and kind concern in his voice forced the brimming tears to spill down her cheeks. Jack would have laughed at her, but Bruce approached her with concern wrinkling the skin around his expressive eyes.

He looked from her to take in the colorful knitting around him, a small smile haunting his plump lips, then returned his eyes back to hers. Bruce approached, and Mia allowed him to place a large pancake sized hand gently on her shoulder. It felt warm.

"What's wrong?" he repeated.

"I— I just thought I heard something weird is all," Mia said, voice dismissive, her small hands now wiping the moisture from her cheeks. "It just startled me... It's nothing."

Mia felt her face flush with embarrassment. She didn't want him to see her like this, upset by a sound and a stupid Ouija board. Damn her anxiety. She hated it. HATED. Mia let out a frustrated breath.

"Don't sweat it," he said. "Being scared...or whatever, I mean. We all get scared sometimes."

How could he be so sweet when he could see perfectly well she was overreacting to the situation and didn't deserve his sweetness? His tenderness almost made her cry more, but she couldn't quite muster the emotion. In fact, she felt her anxiety lessen, then dissipate. Now that he'd joined her in the garage, the back of the shed didn't seem so evil, and the Ouija looked benign. The fluttering, of course, had only been a bird up on the roof. Hadn't it?

Either out of kindness or to distract her, Bruce said, "Did you yarn-bomb this place?"

His smile proved infectious because Mia felt hers widen stupidly with the compliment. "Yes," she said coyly.

"Beautiful," he whispered as he took it all in. "I didn't know you knitted."

"Well," Mia said, "you just met me. Why would you?"

He nodded, a thoughtful look creeping into his features. His eyes scrunched up and his cheekbones rose as he deliberated. "Yeah, true. It just seems like I've known you a lot longer, that's all." He raised his palms in a peaceful gesture. "Anyway, your artwork is beautiful. Can't wait to see the look on Chastity's face."

"That's the idea," Mia said as she wiped her eyes dry. She fought the urge to hug him. "Urban knitting should have a certain flare for the outrageous. Or, at least, the incongruous."

"For sure," Bruce said. He shook his head and smiled. "Didn't know you were an artist. I'm a writer, of course."

"I figured," she said. "You certainly won't teach with a bachelor's in creative writing."

"Nope," he agreed. "I'd considered English Lit, so I could write and teach, but that'd be selling out."

"No, that'd be practical." She wondered why she cared what he majored in. She did, though.

Bruce seemed pleased with himself, his eyes dancing, smile tight on his lips, a blush creeping up his thick neck. "Did you know little blue veins break out on the skin around your temples when you get emotional?" His smile widened.

Mia gasped and looked away. After three years, Jack had never noticed such a thing. Too self-absorbed, she knew. Her heart quickened, even though she wasn't sure if she should consider the comment a compliment.

As if in answer, Bruce said, "And they're lovely."

"Stop," she said.

"It's true."

Mia looked up, considering if she should take a step closer to him. She wanted to, more than anything. Mia wanted to feel closer to him and connect with him on a deeper level, even though she still had a boyfriend. Her breathing felt labored. She took a step.

A female voice exclaimed, "Just what in the holy hell's this shit?"

Mia cringed as Chastity pushed past Bruce. Chastity wore painted-on torn-across-the-thigh blue jeans and a black belly shirt. Her stomach looked tan and flat, a skull with ruby-red eyes birthing from her bellybutton piercing.

"You do this?" she asked. Chastity's hands were on her hips. A little of the black from her lipstick had found its way to her gapped front teeth. Her intense eyes bore into Mia's, but Mia thought she just might notice a twinkle of levity. Hard to tell with Chastity.

"Sure?" Mia tried, positive Chastity would rip her one. But that was the very essence of urban knitting, so she could live with it.

With a slight twitch and raising of the left side of her upper lip, Chastity smirked. "Looks like the goddamn Easter Bunny threw up in here." Then she bent down and looked closer. "Not bad work though...for something so stupid."

"Geez, thanks," Mia said, her arms folded beneath her breasts.

"The very reaction a good yarn-bomb ought to invoke," Bruce said. "You have to admit, the stark contrast between Mia's pastels and your rather macabre taste is striking. Is it not?"

Mia noticed Bruce was careful not to look at Chastity's exposed belly.

"Is it not," Chastity repeated, slow and thoughtful. She shook her head. Then she looked Bruce in the eye. "And you are?"

"Bruce Monroe," he said, hand out, ready to shake. Mia smiled at the lopsided grin on his face, a crooked bicuspid turned nearly sideways. "I'm a student, a writer, and, well, I work at the library return-desk."

"No wonder I haven't seen you around," Chastity mumbled. Then she turned to Mia, the smirk making its return in full force. "You screwin' him or what?"

"Oh my God," Mia said and tightened her arms around her body. "I have a boyfriend..."

"Who you never screw," Chastity finished for her. "Why even bother having a boyfriend? They're a pain in the ass, so why bother with one if you're not gonna get some pleasure out of it."

Mia felt her jaw unhinge and fall open. This was over the top, even coming from Chastity. She usually only talked like this when it was just the girls around. Now she spouted off around Bruce like he didn't exist.

"There are more reasons to have a boyfriend than sex," Mia said.

"Such as?" Chastity asked.

Mia noticed how she rolled the red-eyed skull between her thumb and index finger as if it brought her good luck. "Like companionship?" This sounded lame even to her own ears. Mia cringed, ready for the rebuttal.

Chastity looked around the garage with mocking-wide eyes, then settled them back on Mia. "Well, I don't see Jack here doing any *companioning*. On the other hand," she turned and pointed at Bruce, "he seems keenly interested in being the best *companion* he can be. Am I right, Bruce?"

Bruce's eyes went wide for a minute, then he glanced from Chastity to Mia, then back again. "True that. In fact, I'd say that's a very apropos statement. Not that apropos correlates exactly to the word *appropriate*, but in common conversational English, people generally use it interchangeably, and…"

"Bruce," Chastity said, cutting him off like a knife blade, "shut up. You're rambling now, and I'm starting to lose my affinity for you. Just stand there and look pretty, mouth shut, thank you." She turned to Mia and nodded. "You should really keep his mouth busy with something besides conversation."

"Like kiss him?" Mia said, still not used to Chastity's brusque demeanor. She couldn't kiss Bruce. What about Jack?

"Sure," Chastity said. Then much quieter, so only Mia could hear, "Using whatever set of lips you choose."

Mia felt herself blush three shades of red, then rubbed her hand over her face as if trying to wash the skin clean.

"What'd she say?" Bruce asked, his attention piqued, like he was positive she'd said something about him.

"Nothing," Mia said.

"Oh, c'mon!"

Desperate not to tell him, Mia put on her brightest toothy smile and resorted to a small manipulation. "Some things are better kept a secret...for now."

When she saw his eyes brighten, Mia knew she'd made a mistake. It appeared flirty, even though she didn't mean it that way. There's no way she could have meant it that way. This was a fantastic lie, she knew, because she had. Deep down she'd wanted to convey a message, and so now, whatever happened would be on her. Mia felt butterflies in her belly and knew she'd lost all control of herself. Her dad, Pastor Matt, Jack...they'd all be mad.

"Fine," Bruce said with a crooked, tight-lipped smile. The smile someone gave when they knew they were in, that things were only a matter of time. "I have no problems waiting. I'm a very patient person."

"Just shut up, already," Chastity mumbled and fiddled with her mic stands, touching the pastel knitting lightly as if it might scorch the flesh of her hands.

Mia, caught between several emotions, felt joy at Chastity's reaction to her yarn-bomb, excited about possibilities with Bruce, yet abject fear of upsetting Jack and her father and Pastor Matt. She allowed her eyes to flicker to the back of the garage. No fluttering of wings now, and even the shadows looked less dark and threatening. The Ouija still sat on the little table, but it looked like a toy.

What have I gotten myself into?

"You okay?" Bruce asked. He turned to her as if he may hug her, but stopped short of this.

Mia tore her gaze from the spirit-board. The look in Bruce's eyes made her want to weep. Not the weeping she endured when she felt nervous, but the kind when someone truly cares about you. Never once in the three years she dated Jack had she seen eyes like that. His were hard, possibly even steely, like a snake's. Bruce's were soft and kind.

"Yeah, sure," Mia said. "Just admiring my handiwork."

She cringed inside, because lying to Bruce felt wrong. The alternative, however, made her too nervous to consider. She knew from experience she couldn't tell him about the fluttering noises. If either he or Chastity doubted her, the tears would fall, sure as hell.

Bruce nodded, but didn't look convinced. Something about the creases around his eyes and mouth, the tilt of his shaggy head.

Mia wondered what to say. Before she could mutter a word, a putrid odor wafted to her. It reeked like a combination of spoiled meat and decaying vegetation. She tried not to react, because she'd never been one to acknowledge flatulence. She found the topic embarrassing and best avoided. She glanced at Bruce, but his eyes still held a note of concern for her. He didn't appear to smell what she did, let alone prove the cause of it. Even Chastity still puttered with her equipment. If her roommate detected it, she'd have a rude comment...or twenty.

"If you're uncomfortable, we can go do something else," Bruce said. His voice carried a low, soothing quality. "Hard to believe, but I understand feeling awkward in a situation." He laughed at this, short and clipped.

Such a sweetheart.

Mia smiled. She thought about mentioning the odor, but it was already diminishing. In fact, she barely smelled it at all now. Probably just a random scent from the dorms or the dumpsters.

She glanced at the Ouija board, which sat like a harmless lump, then back at Bruce. "No, let's listen to some music. Maybe we can go for coffee after."

Bruce glanced at the Ouija, then back at Mia.

He'd seen her glance at it. Great, now he'd ask and create a scene with Chastity.

To Mia's surprise, he didn't. Only a nod and a smile as if Bruce sensed her desperate desire to leave the subject alone.

"Sure, sounds great!" he said.

Bruce appeared to want to say something else. He fidgeted with his hands, but kept his mouth shut.

Smart guy.

The stench had dissipated completely, like the foul aroma had never been there at all. Perhaps she'd imagined it. The more important question on her mind: How lucky was Mia to have met such a considerate friend?

CHAPTER 6

Colista sat at a sleek dark mahogany desk, a pile of books next to him. With long narrow fingers, he carefully signed the hardcover edition before him with a crafted signature and depiction of a small toothy demon. Not an activity within his norm, but the university had rules about publication. And even more rules about the things he must do once he checked that line item off the old *to-do* list.

Public appearances and other nonsense drove him crazy. So did writing. "It will add to your credibility," they'd said. The powers that be. Those powers wouldn't think him credible even if an apparition took a rather large ectoplasmic dump upon their framed diplomas.

He threw the finished hardcover aside, and, with a violent yank, grabbed another.

The old tan and black Siamese rubbed against his leg in search of attention, then yowled when Colista failed to respond.

"Go on now, Crowley" he mumbled. "You ate just two hours ago. You'll puke it up, anyway."

Cross now, the cat stalked off, then tipped over onto a blanket that lay inside a rectangle of sun. After a couple of testy licks of his fur, Crowley soon began a soft sleepy wheezing, eyes half-closed.

Colista continued to scrawl, draw, and grumble about things like deadlines and doctorate requirements and the impossibility of meeting either. More books flew. One bounced to the floor, flipped open, and the spine creased in that special way only a hardcover can.

Then two things happened almost at once, and if they hadn't...well, Colista couldn't tell which came first. The cat lifted its over-sized head up off the blanket to stare into an ominously dark patch of ceiling, and an unremarkable knock cascaded down from the same general direction.

There were only a few things that irritated Colista to the point of nausea. The first being the activity in which he now engaged. The second would always include flirtation and, heaven forbid, sexual intercourse, neither of which ever lent themselves to sophisticated merit or efforts of thought. Only once in the proverbial blue moon did he require relief from a tug within his loins, even by his own devices. The third, however, just now manifested and grated against the gift so benevolently given him.

The thought of it as a gift gave Colista a momentary pause, always the academic, but then his attention wavered and finally snapped back to the cat who still stared with wet green eyes into the darkest corner of the room.

He tried to sense if the cat's attention was because of some natural cause, such as a small misplaced curio tumbling from a shelf or cabinet top. He noticed no such item. All looked as he'd left it, shelves of religious items from around the world, masks, tribal heirlooms, statuary with wide open maws and veined eyes cut from dense stone and wood. The voodoo section with its portents and potions appeared ominous, but no more so than usual.

When circumstances produced no such mundane cause, such as the expansion of wood joints, a clever draft, even a rodent, Colista forced his mind to consider his third item of discontent. He possessed a peculiar attribute, for better or worse. Usually, worse. He could communicate with the deceased. And certain members of the deceased enjoyed bothering him just to sate their own greedy need for attention. Not so different from Crowley, he considered, but be that as it may, he disdained the behavior. These clingy revenants already got their whack in this world and just because they failed to return to *the nether* upon physical death shouldn't necessitate an emergency on his part.

He reached for a small plastic gun-type device which sat on a mahogany end-table that matched the antique desk. Colista pulled back a red plastic lever on the cleverly designed gun, aimed it in the general direction of the noise, and pulled the curved trigger. A spray of black and white salt flitted through the air like a flock of tiny birds, then bounced off the far wall and shelves, falling benignly to the floor.

Colista rose from his desk chair and took a step toward where the sound had originated. Follow through with the paranormal went a fair distance toward preventing an escalation. Salt was so often anathema to spirits.

His current book, signed but minus the drawing, slid from the desk and fell to the floor with a dull thud. It laid next to its fallen brethren like a forgotten soldier.

Then he spied his newest acquisition—a fine black and white skull carved from a single stone—purchased from a Mayan elder, an artist so she claimed. However, Colista now suspected a bit of unstated witchery may very well factor into her list of considerable talents. The Mayan calendar adorned the skull's forehead within a map of white lines. As he watched, the skull levitated about a quarter inch and then landed back with a slight bump. Undoubtedly the noise he and Crowley had heard.

On cue, Crowley looked back over his arthritic shoulder to make sure the matter sat well in hand. Satisfied, he rolled back over, making a grand show of his indifference with a yawning of his snaggletooth maw.

"Infernal beast," Colista whispered with a smile.

The cat hissed quietly.

"As for you," Colista said. He walked up to the skull, but not before grabbing a shaker full of a mixture of black and white salts and a clear-glass enclosure off the coffee table. "I didn't give you permission to speak." He went on as if the skull would find his discourse intellectually stimulating. "I know not what element or beast you claim to be, but I assure you that just because I appear approachable doesn't mean I wish to chit chat. I'm sure you are well-aware I will only sit for the direst of emergency. And just because some old Mayan bruja attached you to this skull, doesn't mean you should feel the need to take advantage of my services."

The skull jiggled a bit, as if in protest.

"You've survived this long without me, and I'm positive you can do so without me still." Then Colista poured salt from the shaker in a ring around the skull, and after this, finally placed the glass enclosure over skull and salt both. "That should about do it."

With a breath, Colista looked at his watch. *Damn it to hell!* He only had another hour until his evening alchemy class, and over a dozen books still required his signature and artistic representation. Despite his immense hatred of the establishment, he could not bring himself to—how did the kids say it?—half-ass his projects. Those paying good money for his materials deserved a fine product. Damn his conscience.

Crowley continued to sleep as Colista plopped himself back down and lit a smoke.

The Mayan skull sat quietly beneath its cage of glass.

CHAPTER 7

The short rehearsal was over, and Bruce stood with his arms crossed. Bruce had observed the proceedings through what he hoped appeared as a critical writer's eye, objective, aloof, fly-on-the-wall kinds of stuff. Not lofty or arrogant, just introspective and professionally removed. Despite this desire, he knew complete removal of his own feelings would prove impossible. Not with Mia standing slump-shouldered in the corner. In fact, she now used a yarn-bombed mic stand as a crutch.

The storage shed sat quiet and dark save for one lone unfettered bulb on the ceiling. A couple of ratty-winged moths fluttered about the dull glow in their own private suicide mission. Bruce had heard somewhere that it was nested spiders that actually killed the moths and not the hot bulbs. Despite the quiet, a serious ringing still invaded Bruce's ear. Produced, he thought, by the complete opposite, the onslaught of sound bombarding their senses for over an hour. Screeching guitars via Brody/Rudy and even screechier vocals from the one and only. Throw in the pre-recorded bass and drum machine and it would be no wonder if his ears continued to ring right through the evening.

Hello Tinnitus, here I come.

It was an even bigger wonder that nobody called security.

Self-proclaimed superstar, Chastity, sat against the back studded wall, black hair plastered to her head, body aglow with a sheen of sweat, one leg bent at a provocative angle at the knee as her legs lay akimbo. One of her grimy hands lay on top of what appeared a rather rugged Ouija board. Bruce found he needed to look away before he gave thought to how Chastity looked now. *Sweaty attractive.* He concentrated on Mia instead.

Mia stared hard at the board, as if expecting a ghoul to jump right out and go after her. Her eyes were wide and shiny, slight smudges of red where her whites looked distressed and beaten down. In the best of times, Mia had those beautiful soulful eyes, so when they reflected any anxiety, the impression of intense dissatisfaction radiated off them like heat.

"Can't believe nobody showed!" Chastity pouted.

As if art depended on an audience for its success. Bruce detested this but didn't let the thought register as a physical scowl. From the corner of his eye, he watched her grimace at her boyfriend, flick her gaze past himself, then to Mia. Her black eyes were locked on Mia like a predator on small prey.

"We usually get quite a crowd." Chastity grabbed the plastic planchette and, like a child with blocks, thumped it off the board like a Goblin drumbeat.

Mia flinched as if something reached out and touched her. She'd harbored a similar look when Bruce first arrived, like she'd experienced something frightening.

Those eyes. He could lose himself in them. They glistened with emotion as if she may weep at any moment. If he noticed a river of tears spread down her cheeks, it would not surprise him in the least.

"Brody!" Chastity said with a sharpness that commanded attention.

Bruce noticed Mia's lips hint at a smirk and knew she'd caught on to Chastity's vibe. She made eye contact with him just for a moment, but even that slight gesture sent his heart into gyration.

"Yeah?" Brody mumbled, his eyes downcast as any self-respecting Goth musician's would be.

"Ouija board," she said as a command. "Now."

Brody groaned, got up off the cement floor where he'd been fixing a guitar string, then plopped his skinny ass down on the cement across the small table from Chastity. He never spoke.

Good boy.

Chastity's unoccupied hand played with the red-eyed creature which lived in her bellybutton as if it served as a ward or portent. Bruce thought the gesture provocative and lewd, accomplishing nothing but showing off her flat tanned belly. A narrow line of thin ebony hairs traveled down from her bellybutton and disappeared beneath the waistband of her ratty jeans.

Look at me, Bruce thought, careful not to let it register on his face. He wondered what kind of trauma one needed to experience to turn out so dark and broody. Something heavy, he assumed. It wasn't his habit to shame sluts—because he understood being misunderstood, and the fact of being a geek himself. But sometimes people deserved what they got, especially when it made others purposefully uncomfortable.

Chastity looked beyond caring if she made anyone uncomfortable.

"You have a problem?" Chastity said.

It took a moment for Bruce to realize she directed her words at him.

"The Ouija board, I mean." She grinned with her small teeth like a human piranha.

The thought amused Bruce. "Of course not. Do what you want."

Mia gave him a nervous look, then allowed her gaze to flutter up to the ceiling as if she expected something to manifest above her. When Brody sat down across the board from Chastity, her attention snapped back to the board.

Chastity and Brody both placed a hand on the planchette. Almost immediately, the cheap piece of plastic moved beneath their flesh.

Mia brought a hand to her neck and wiped a bit of sweat from beneath her hair.

So silky and smooth, Bruce considered, before kicking himself for more-than-friendly thoughts. However, Bruce noticed the now over-abundant tears which clung to the bottom of each eye. That was all he could take. Mia was obviously uncomfortable with either Chastity or one of her many behaviors. Perhaps it was the board itself that bothered her. Either way, a gentleman should always recognize when a lady, whether or not on a date, felt uncomfortable in a situation.

Bruce caught Mia's attention and motioned with a nod of his head toward the door.

Mia nodded, a look of relief on her face, eyes aglow, and tears finally spilling down the rosy skin of her cheeks.

Tears of relief, Bruce hoped.

As they walked out into the black night together, Bruce heard Chastity say, "Are you with us tonight?"

From beside him, he sensed Mia shiver.

CHAPTER 8

The coffee shop smelled of fresh-brew and mocha, cinnamon and friendship. Delightful. A few couples and one larger group visited quietly, provided white noise. Mia knitted, bag of yarn at her feet, as she waited. When Bruce headed her way, Mia knitted one last pearl, then stuffed the mittens she was working on and her needles into the knitting bag.

Good Lord, but Bruce is a likeable boy.

She watched him walk back with both their orders, careful not to make too much eye-contact. She still didn't want him arriving at the wrong conclusions. This train of thought seemed important, but increasingly more difficult to maintain. The way he'd led her out of the storage shed when she'd begun her infernal crying had made her feel special. More special than anyone ever had.

Bruce approached with a concentrated look, tongue between his teeth as he gently placed both their chocolate lattes on the table. He sat, a solid thud as he placed himself across from her. His eyes reminded her of the lattes beneath the whipped cream. For all things holy, she needed to stop this. What was Jack doing right now? Probably drinking with his buddies. What would he think if he knew she was at a coffee shop with a male friend? He'd become jealous. Probably cause a major scene and demand she leave with him.

"Penny for your thoughts," Bruce said with a smile.

Her internal conflicts were the last thing she wished to share right now. She settled on, "Just wanted to say thanks for getting me out of there. You know, the storage shed."

He nodded thoughtfully, hair falling over the back of his neck as his head moved. His AC/DC t-shirt rippled slightly from beneath. Out of shape, yes, but somehow still not unattractive. He took a sip of his latte. "Nobody should have to stay somewhere they feel uncomfortable. I mean, the tears tipped me off." He gazed at her patiently, and this nearly made Mia weep all over again.

Mia waved his concern off with a flip of her hand. Her usual reaction to her sometimes-irrational waterworks. She could cry watching an old lady pet a cat. "Hang around me long enough and you'll get it. My tears don't always jibe with the situation. I mean, well, I guess what I'm trying to say is that it's kind of a disorder. My— My therapist, who I don't need often anymore, says the waterworks are an anxiety reaction, not a sadness reaction. Everyone always thinks…"

"That you're really upset because you tear up," Bruce finished for her. "I get it. Sorry if I overreacted."

"Yeah," Mia said. "I mean, I cry over the dumbest of things." She pointed at her eyes. "Anyway, in this case, it was definitely time to go."

"You're anything but dumb." Bruce turned to look her in the eye with a sincerity she'd never witnessed before, not even from her parents. "But I can't help but think something got to you in the storage shed. Something you didn't want to be around. You looked, not just teared up, but maybe a little spooked?"

Mia shrugged. "A little maybe."

"Explain," Bruce said with an even bigger smile. "You can't make a big statement like that and not dish up the goods."

Mia sighed. How much should she tell him? She didn't want to sound like a complete asshat, scared of her own shadow. Her silence must have stretched on too long.

Bruce's hands flew up and waved, as if he tried to wave his mistake away. "I'm sorry. You don't have to tell me anything." He took a breath and appeared to relax. "I just want to be a good friend. And if something frightened you, well, then I'd like to help. And, I guess I can't help too good if I don't know what to help with."

"That's sweet," Mia said, "but I'm not sure I require any help. Just something I need to deal with."

"What kind of something?" he asked with a cringe, probably ready for her to tell him it was none of his business. He'd soon learn that wasn't her style. Especially since he only wanted to help.

Mia sighed. "Look, you'll just think I'm crazy."

She lowered her head and looked at Bruce out of the tops of her eye sockets. She felt an obscuring curtain of hair spill over her face. She'd spoken about this once with her mother, who then told her father, who made her talk to Pastor Matt. She'd felt forced to lie to Pastor Matt because he would have considered her experience sacrilegious, even if it was an accident. And she couldn't have him thinking ill of her.

Then there was the time she'd tried to explain it to Jack. He just laughed, then ignored her, turning back to the Vikings game on TV without acknowledging her words. Now here was Bruce, all elbows on table and palms on chin, attentive, eyes bright. Oh, man, she could almost cry again.

"No, I won't," he whispered. "You can trust me. I mean, if we're gonna be friends…"

"Yeah, okay," Mia said. She knew it came out sounding sharp. She didn't want to hurt him. She said, "It's just something I've had a bad experience explaining, that's all."

"Try me," Bruce encouraged.

Mia took a drink of her latte, then looked back into Bruce's warm chocolate eyes. So different from Jack's cold steel-gray orbs. "Okay, but you gotta promise not to judge me—or tell anyone."

Bruce stayed silent but crossed his heart.

Tears welled in Mia's eyes, stinging, but she didn't care so much this time. Bruce had already seen her cry and hadn't berated her for it. She sincerely doubted he would now. He was so nonjudgmental and kind. Bruce cared about her, not just about her body or her soul. But her—all of her. Screw Jack and the church. And her family, for that matter.

Quietly, she said, "So, a friend and I used a Ouija board once when we were younger. Thirteen probably."

Bruce, just about to sip his latte, inhaled a breath and held it, then nodded in understanding. Despite his reaction, he stayed silent, allowing Mia to continue uninterrupted.

"I know," she started, "big deal, right? I mean, people use 'em all the time and nothing bad happens." When Bruce only shrugged, Mia continued, "Lucky me it did in my case.

"It was my mom's before she met my dad, and they became born-again Christians. Our church frowns on their use—an occult item, they say—but she must have forgotten about it. We found it up in the closet."

"I'm guessing your dad must have been the churchy one, that he talked your mom into the deal," Bruce suggested.

"Probably," Mia agreed. "Grandma said she used to get into some mischief, but she won't tell me about it. Says she'll tell me when I'm older, which is dumb. I am older." She took a sip of her latte. "Dad already thinks Grandma is a bad influence because she drinks alcohol, so she keeps some stuff quiet to keep the peace."

"Sure, makes sense," Bruce said. "I bet I'd like your grandma."

Mia pointed at Bruce's AC/DC shirt. "I'm pretty sure, yeah. She's into all the late seventies, early eighties hard rock stuff."

Bruce nodded and smiled but stayed quiet. However, Mia noticed the glint in his eye and wondered what he was thinking. Probably that he might even have a better shot with Mia if he got along with Grams. Typical boy stuff. Grams hated Jack, thought he was a chauvinist, so there was that. Probably exactly why dad liked him. The church seemed rife with chauvinism, something she never cared for.

"Anyway, my friend Samantha and I got into Mom's Ouija. We didn't use it long. Couldn't. The moment we both touched the planchette, the thing whipped off the board and smashed into a wall. It broke. Pieces of plastic flew everywhere."

Bruce seemed to consider this, right index finger tapping on the table, the other pushing a lock of dark unruly curls behind his ear.

"Look, you think I'm crazy, so…"

"Not necessarily," Bruce said with a grin. "I'm a writer and trained to remain objective."

Born from an undeniable impulse, Mia slapped Bruce on the shoulder, not hard but hard enough. The shoulder gave a little in that muscle-beneath-a-small-layer-of-flab kind of way. The way punching a slab of beef might feel.

Mia giggled out loud and raised an eyebrow in mock aggression. "Not necessarily?"

"Violent," Bruce said. "Nice."

"Not nice at all," Mia said. She giggled again, then forced herself to become more serious, before Bruce got the idea she was flirting with him. "So, anyway, I'm not crazy. And the planchette flew and busted. Then—then we heard a growl."

"Like from a dog?" Bruce asked, still rubbing his shoulder.

"Not exactly," Mia said. "More like a low rumble we could feel more than hear. Does that make sense?"

"None," Bruce said, "but that doesn't mean it didn't happen."

Mia tried to think of the best way to describe it but found she couldn't. Instead, she got to the point. "So, what got me so upset today was that while I set up the yarn-bomb, I heard some things. And, I guess, smelled some things—things associated with Chastity's board. Things kind of like my original experience."

"What kinds of things?" Bruce asked. His voice had dropped to conspirational levels, quiet and thick.

Mia could see the outbreak of goose bumps on his bare arms. Since the coffee shop wasn't cold, she figured these last details had gotten his attention.

"Fluttering of wings," Mia said, understanding full well how lame that sounded. She quickly added, "And a rotting smell." She scrunched up her nose to further communicate the level of gross. "Kinda like a dead animal mixed with rotten vegetation."

"How awful," Bruce said.

It struck Mia how unconventional this boy really was. Instead of an early twenties punk kid, he sounded more mature, less impulsive, more thoughtful. An old soul.

He pursed his lips, and his face took on an inquisitive tone. "I don't want to sound skeptical, but I've always prided myself on debunking strange phenomenon. You know, finding physical root-causes for otherwise inexplicable phenomenon."

"I thought you wrote about scary stuff," Mia said. "Thought you'd be open to supernatural goings on."

"I am," Bruce said. "But I write about fictional stuff, made up. Not actual ghost stories. That said, when folks find out what I write about, well, let's just say I hear all kinds of things. Some not so different from your story."

"Do most people lie?"

"No, definitely not," Bruce said. He leaned toward her. "But sometimes their stories can be explained by faulty HVAC systems, or drafts, poorly leveled floors. Things like that."

When Mia frowned, he added, "Like in your case. There could have been a bird, even a bat. And the garbage bin isn't that far away from the storage shed. Maybe the combination of those two things combined with your past experiences…"

"You really think I hadn't thought of those things?" Mia mumbled, eyes on the froth inside her cup.

"Of course you did. I'm just saying..."

"That I'm overreacting..." She could feel tears behind her eyes and hated herself for it. *Weak.*

"Not necessarily..."

The unthinkable happened. The thing Jack always told her was manipulative because men were hard-wired to feel bad for a crying woman. Her dad, and many at the church, frowned at her tears. Even Pastor Matt had no patience for a sniveling, crying girl. She felt ashamed that she couldn't control her anxiety enough to stop the hot tears from spilling down her cheeks. And now Bruce would rush to her side, take back what he said, and later blame her for being manipulative. Or he'd just get mad at her right away for using her tears to get her way. What a joke men could be.

Bruce didn't do any of those things.

He simply continued, "I was only trying to say that past experiences can shape how we interpret our environment. That could be what happened at the storage shed, nothing but a misinterpretation."

When Mia refused to speak, Bruce continued, "Then, again. You might have experienced the genuine article. Maybe you're haunted. In which case, we should do something about it."

"Do what?" Mia asked through her tears. She wiped at them, trying to make them disappear, will them to dry up and go away.

"Professor Colista has a book signing tomorrow. He'll know things. Wanna go?"

Mia didn't know if she was more afraid of Colista or being haunted. Yet, inexplicably, she bobbed her head up and down. What was she agreeing to? Colista, the man who spoke about "taking a walk outside his flesh bag".

Gross!

She supposed it couldn't hurt to get his take on things, if he'd even talk to her. Why should he? He would probably send her back to her dorm.

"I guess," Mia heard herself say.

Her tears freshened, and she excused herself to the bathroom. She needed to go home and get some sleep. Her anxiety demanded it and tomorrow would be a big day.

CHAPTER 9

Bruce walked up to Mia's dorm-room door and hesitated. He wanted Mia to understand how strong of a person he considered her to be, but he couldn't figure out how to say it without sounding like a man trying to get in a girl's pants. That was the least of his intentions. He thought of her in terms of a potential mate, but sex, he believed truly, should remain a biproduct, not a starting point. Not that he didn't think about it, but just wouldn't act like an asshole.

He'd always felt this way. He felt reluctant to speak of this point of view because then he always got the comments, from both men and women, that perhaps he was a latent homosexual or somehow asexual. Or that he suffered from a real or imagined malady rooted deep in his psyche. Perhaps he'd been an abused child? He'd heard that one before. And all that because he didn't pursue sex like a rabid dog. In fact, he often felt the comments were a slam against people who were homosexual or asexual, and to those abused in some fashion or another.

It didn't help that his mom ran off when he was a kid. In direct response, his old man made it a point to sleep with as many women as possible. Mechanics, he assured Bruce, got lots of pussy. He'd also assured him that writers did not. After two years in writing school, he figured his old man might have a point.

Anyway, he wouldn't change his approach now. He knew he didn't deserve Mia, but he'd pursue Mia in his own way. Even if that meant they never reached a level higher up the chain than friends. She was beautiful inside and out, despite her anxieties and fears. What would a nice Christian girl want with a writer of scary shit, anyway? And why would she dump a great-looking, athletic boyfriend for a geeky artist type?

Bruce shook his head smoothed his grayish blue Minecraft t-shirt over his paunch, then stepped up to knock.

After a few seconds, Chastity opened the door dressed in nothing but a flannel shirt which barely covered her pubic mound. She tugged the material down when she noticed he'd noticed, scowled at him, then shouted, "Mia, Igor Stonehenge is here. Lucky for you, he'll probably be sporting wood." She ran a hand through her already-tousled hair, then stood there and blinked at him sleepily until Mia pushed her aside.

Mia looked like an angel. Especially compared to Chastity, who looked freshly woken and smelled of bed-sweat and stale smoke. Okay, yes, Chastity was attractive, but not his kind of attractive. Mia's long hair appeared groomed to perfection, smooth and straight. Her body held her tasteful jeans and blouse as if she'd stepped right out of the pages of College Life magazine.

When she pressed next to him, Bruce could smell just a hint of something intoxicating. He'd never been one to identify popular fragrances with any accuracy, but he recognized the scent as something he'd smelled before and always enjoyed. Mia's tears of last night were long gone, replaced by a confident rise of her eyebrows as she considered him.

"Ready?" he asked lamely.

"As ready as I'll ever be, I guess," Mia said.

Bruce knew she meant the negative to denote Colista and not him, but he still looked to Chastity to see if she caught the reference.

"Don't sound so enthusiastic," Chastity said. Then to Bruce, "She couldn't stop talking about you when she got back last night. I had to fall asleep to get her to shut up."

Mia looked to Chastity with wide eyes, then to Bruce.

He could tell she was trying, perhaps desperately, to think of something to say that wouldn't sound horrible. "Oh, my God," she whispered. Mia glared at Chastity, then smiled with a curt twist of her lips at Bruce. "C'mon, you." Her voice sounded like an odd combination of irritation and coy absolution.

Bruce shrugged at Chastity, who, of course, smirked at him. Then he turned and followed Mia toward the stairwell. He didn't catch up until they got outside and only then noticed the blush creeping up Mia's neck and into her high-boned cheeks.

Mia whirled on him with wide eyes. "I just wanted to say..." She twisted her lips. When Bruce only stared because he knew better than to do anything else, she continued, "That is, well, yes, I did talk about you." She smiled and shook her head.

Bruce watched her naturally sad eyes. Her mouth moved as if she played with words in her mind, trying to find the correct ones.

"Look, I enjoy spending time with you," she said. "I won't deny it. But the fact remains, I still have a boyfriend. So, I guess what I'm trying to say is, please don't read too much into things." In a whisper, "At least, not yet."

"Just glad we can hang out," Bruce heard himself say, although his brain was still processing what she just said. *At least, not yet.* The words smacked of possibilities.

"Thank you," Mia said with a look Bruce couldn't quite interpret. She placed a hand on his shoulder and gave it a shake.

"It's like an adventure," Bruce said. "Like we're trying to solve a small mystery, sneaking around like private eyes."

"Ghost hunters," Mia said with enthusiasm, voice sharp and excited. Bruce could tell she enjoyed the direction he'd taken things. "We'll gather intel from Colista, then see about what needs to happen next."

"Exactly," Bruce said.

The joy in her voice elated him, because she deserved that. A warm and thoughtful girl who seemed, despite appearances, to have endured a rough episode or two in her life. He'd read on the internet about spirits and Ouija boards before he fell asleep and hoped she hadn't picked up a nasty spirit attachment like one site suggested. Apparently, these kinds of things could linger throughout one's life if left unfettered. The information had proven either nebulous, or involved too many opinions and scenarios that made very little sense to him. Mia didn't appear possessed or anything. Hopefully, Colista would know.

They walked side by side. Even though their hands never touched, Bruce felt that kind of energy between them. *It's just like we're...together.* He knew anyone who observed them would assume this.

"Where are we going, exactly?" Mia asked.

"University bookstore," Bruce said. "It's the biggest bookstore in the area. Lots of academic types and even a few fiction authors have signed here. Not exactly Barnes and Noble, but as close as we're gonna get."

Mia smiled at him. *Beautiful.* Two full lips and white teeth. Her eyes gleamed, ultra-brilliant whites with vibrant blue middles. "Is it hard or inspirational to go to someone else's book signing? You know, since that's where you envision yourself someday."

It was a brilliant question, Bruce thought. "Definitely inspirational." Not wanting to sound petty, but to explain things, he added, "But his type of writing is a lot different from mine. The world of academic publications is a whole other beast."

"How so?" Mia asked. She really appeared to want to know, and this made Bruce's heartbeat race.

"Well," Bruce started, "you see, they require professors to publish the results of their time in the field, to lend credibility to their status as an educator at a prestigious university. They are under enormous pressure to do so, whether or not they can write. Sometimes, professors use what they call a ghostwriter."

"How appropriate in this case," Mia said, the words encased inside a beautiful giggle.

"Ha! For sure. So, anyway, that fact doesn't take away from the information within the book. It's just different from other kinds of publishing. It's rarer for a fiction author to use a ghostwriter, but some do, I hear. The big ones who want to pump out lots of books."

"Seems silly to write a book and not get your name on it," Mia said.

"Money talks, I suppose," Bruce said. "If it was the only way for me to write for a living, I'd do it. It's still art. Practicing the craft, if you will."

"I suppose," Mia said.

She didn't exactly sound convinced, but they were at the large double doors of the campus bookstore before he could reinforce his position on the matter. A line of people milled about. She stopped in her tracks and Bruce bumped into her on his way to open the door.

"Sorry," she mumbled.

"Everything okay?"

Bruce watched her shoulders slump, just a slight lowering but noticeable. She said, "Colista frightens me a little. His beliefs are just so different..."

"Different from what you're used to?" Bruce asked.

Just like me, he considered, but kept the thought to himself.

Lives changed, people changed, he knew. College had a way of bringing this transformation about. How much had he changed in the last two years? Transformed in increments from an easily intimidated kid to a confident young man, more or less. He, at the very least, recently conquered the fear of what others thought of him and his life choices.

Except Dad's!

"Yeah," Mia said. "Different from my family's world-view. I've— I've been told for so long that any other point of view is the Devil's work."

"There's a difference between different and evil."

Mia's shoulders shook. Bruce wondered if she'd tear up, again. If so, fine. She couldn't help her body's response to stressors. He would help her through it, even if all she allowed from him was to remain by her side. He'd never pressure her for more. At least not a lot more.

"I know," Mia said. "My brain knows. My heart is a different story. I've been told to keep Jesus in my heart and nothing else. *What Would Jesus Do?*"

"Does it matter? Do we even know the answer to that?"

She shrugged.

Bruce waited.

Finally, Mia turned to him. "Thanks for your patience," she said with a shy smile. She opened the door.

With a swift move, Bruce grabbed the door and held it as Mia slipped inside. It made his day when she smiled her thanks. He could never be certain how a woman would feel about chivalry, but had decided a long time ago to err on the side of being helpful. If someone got mad at him for kindness, then okay—he could live with that.

Bruce followed her in and tried not to enjoy the way Mia's body swayed like a willow in a slight breeze. *Out of my league,* he thought. *But not out of the realm of possibility.* They had certain things in common. For the art, he remained grateful, because it was the glue which held them together, either as friends or more, should the universe allow.

Folks spoke in hushed tones as they waited. A sign with Colista's name and likeness stood next to a black table. A stack of hardcovers sat on the table. He glanced at Mia, and she stared at Colista's photo with some trepidation, her eyes squinty, tongue darting to dry beautiful lips. Her eyes fluttered as if to ward off tears.

He cared about her. Or, at least, the precursor of such stirrings.

The crowd murmured when Colista stepped out of the restroom, the first time Bruce had ever seen the man in a jacket and tie. His dark short hair lay parted on the side, bangs sloping downward over half-lidded eyes. His cheeks appeared sunken, but not to an unhealthy degree. Slight lines above his upper lip denoted his smoking habit.

Bruce wished to club this man over the head and assume his identity. A writer on the way to the signing table; Bruce's dream within a dream. The thing he would give up all else for. He gave in to a daydream in which he himself walked up to a table, fans lined up, Mia sitting in a chair just off his right arm. She glanced at him lovingly before smiling at the first person in line who was none other than Brian fucking Keene.

"Bruce?" Mia asked in a whisper. "Earth to Bruce?"

"Sorry." But he wasn't really. It's like time didn't exist.

Colista walked toward them in slow-motion, like a model on a runway. But Bruce was here for Mia. She needed help, and he knew he should concentrate on her. This wasn't about his petty desires and dreams.

"Professor Colista," Bruce said as he grabbed Mia by her forearm and pulled her toward the man. "Can we speak with you a moment?"

Colista's eyes went wide, probably attempting to comprehend the situation. He glanced at the line forming before his table, then back to Mia. "Ms. white-bread Christian, if I'm not mistaken."

Bruce watched as Mia's face performed its rendition of a blush. Instead of blood running closer to her skin, it appeared to shrink away. The anomaly seemed to cause the blue-veined smudge beneath her eyes and temples to grow.

"We don't mean to bother you," Bruce said. He glanced at the line of fans. "It's just that…"

Mia's head tilted toward the ceiling as if she'd heard something way up there among the exposed wooden beams and black powder-coated hangers which held them. Mia seemed to shrink toward the ground as if to escape whatever had caught her attention.

Colista followed her gaze, frowned, then looked at Mia. "Priorities. Even I have priorities."

Bruce wasn't sure if he was speaking to them or to himself. Then Colista put a hand on Mia's shoulder. His voice hushed, he whispered, "I've been at this a very long time, Mia. A simple—most likely benign—attachment. Something which follows along now and again, but never always."

"What are you…?" Bruce began.

Colista put up a palm to stop his question.

Mia seemed frozen, her gaze now fully on Colista. A gazelle and her cheetah…or her savior? Bruce couldn't tell.

"Let me guess," Colista murmured, his piercing eyes unreadable and deep. "Early Ouija board use. Afterword, a series of inconsequential—yet to you, terrifying—paranormal events. Now, exacerbated by a novel environment, the events have returned." He picked at his left cuticle. "Especially considering a roommate who dabbles in the occult like a drunk drinks a pint." His smile appeared warm, and Bruce thought, protective. "She may dabble in that, too."

"Yes," Mia said. She said no more, but Bruce watched the tears—always those tears that ripped at his heart—accumulate in the lower part of her eyes.

Bruce wished to take her away to a place where Mia could find herself free of whatever plagued her, whether paranormal or imagined. He would write as she knitted, words and fibers used to create masterful works of art when their energies entwined and fed off each other.

"No need for tears, I'm sure," Colista said, somewhat louder. "Allow me to propose a yoga session with a colleague of mine. She is a fine practitioner who can not only cleanse the body, but what you would call the soul. It will take care of your little problem. Not only will your body thank you for the experience, but you will find yourself—to what extent is possible—spirit free. It's quite simple, really. And natural, what you're experiencing."

The line in front of the signing table grew louder, more vocal, as they waited impatiently for Colista. The bookstore manager stuck his head out to see what the delay may be. Bruce thought he looked annoyed.

"Pastor Matt says yoga leads to possession," Mia whispered. Her face held a note of pain, eyes pinched, lips pressed firmly together. She glanced at the ceiling again.

"Ludicrous," Colista said as he also glanced upward, just for a moment this time. He frowned, then took a step toward the awaiting table. "Don't you see? Christianity is a fabulous way to interact with the spirit world. Faith and intention galore. Why, I've seen demonics tremble at the mere mention of Christ. The problems arise when zealots recognize no possibilities beyond their own narrow scope of reality. You haven't figured everything out, yet. Perhaps you believe the only way for your soul to reach Heaven is through your Christ. Fine. I understand and believe what you say has merit. At least, I believe you feel convicted toward this eventuality. But don't think for a moment that Christianity is the only way to approach the spiritual realms." He took a step toward the table, "You'll be disappointed."

Bruce watched Mia cringe at the word *convicted*, as if the word held power over her, or some kind of rapture.

Mia said, "You *have* been to the storage shed, then."

Colista nodded. "Once, yes. I had hoped to enjoy a pleasant Irish ballad, as promised. Instead, I received a headache." He walked toward his table but glanced over his shoulder. "Not to worry. I noticed her board. Just go to the yoga session." Then he left, taking a seat at his table.

The throng of people edged closer as if cramming toward the table would get their books signed any faster. One guy edged around the table and right next to Colista's chair. Colista scowled, and the man retreated.

Mia glanced at the ceiling, then pulled Bruce toward the exit. She seemed all arms and legs, he all middle. They spilled out into the sunshine and both stood staring at each other. Tears streaked her face as Mia absorbed the sunshine, as if it gave her strength. The blue smudges on her temples and beneath her eyes receded, but not entirely.

"He scares me," Mia said, but she'd straightened to her full height and the tears had not freshened.

Bruce nodded, stayed silent as he sensed he should, then picked nervously at his t-shirt. She, despite falling apart, looked so put together and natty, beautiful. He would prove just the opposite, Bruce knew.

"I heard the fluttering of wings again," Mia said after a pause. "In the rafters. Colista heard them, too. Did you?"

Bruce shook his head.

"He knows," Mia said. Her eyes bored into his. "I know I shouldn't, but I'm going to the yoga session. I— I don't know why, but I trust him. Even though he scares the piss out of me."

"I'll come with," Bruce suggested, because the thought of leaving her alone seemed unpleasant. He wanted to help her, be near her.

"No," she said. "I need to do this alone." Mia fussed with Bruce's t-shirt, adjusting a collar that was already straight. A gentle grooming gesture which made Bruce's heart swell.

She rubbed his shoulders and smiled. "Go get a signed book. You know you want to. Ask him all your writer questions."

Bruce nodded. "Will you meet me for supper?"

"Of course," Mia said, then walked away, peering over her shoulder with a bright smile. Soon she was jogging toward the rec-center.

Bruce felt the thread that connected his heart to Mia's stretch thin and taut as the distance between them grew. Soon she disappeared around a corner, and Bruce's heart felt...alone.

You'll see her for dinner.

He turned, took one last long look back, then finally made his way inside.

CHAPTER 10

Mia couldn't decide how she felt. Violated? Cleansed? So many conflicting emotions battled her mind that she couldn't pick one. The session itself had seemed benign and friendly, like a stream of consciousness between she and the instructor that Mia couldn't shut off. In the midst of a Trikonasana pose, Mia imagined her congregation there with her, frowning as she stretched and made noises which sounded suspiciously like devil worship.

The Devil? Mia wasn't sure why she felt that way. Probably a subliminal prompt long ago burned into her subconscious regarding the evils of yoga and other meditations. Ironic thing, prayer, a meditation all onto itself.

The good: her body now lay bathed in sweat, a workout worthy of any fitness video she'd ever chanced to use. Her yoga pants and tank-top felt as though they clung to her frame like a second skin. She could smell her body, pungent yet exhilarating. Something she knew would turn Jack on, which she didn't want. She often found herself wearing more clothes than necessary around him. What did that mean? And what did it mean when she thought of Bruce instead?

Mia shook the emotions off. She refused to allow bad thoughts to pick at her brain. Things like how she'd felt the incense cling to her skin like dust, running off with the little rivulets of sweat. The chants still echoed in her ears as if demons lived inside her head and rejoiced at her foolishness. Even her thoughts of Bruce felt evil and too much like giving in to the serpent in the Garden of Eden.

The congregation inside her head pointed and frowned, brows furrowed with concern for her behavior. In some ways, she hated them. In others, she felt loved and cared for.

So confusing…

Despite all of this, Mia trusted Colista to an extent, if for no other reason than because he'd also heard the flutter of wings in the bookstore. They were simpatico in that way, in collusion. The second word, she knew, would be the one her church picked. She knew how they'd feel about him. *Sacrilegious. Evil.* Only he wasn't. Mia knew and understood that he'd wanted to help her. Offered a solution, in fact. The congregation would offer no solace save for lectures on avoidance and prayer. Boatloads of prayer, which hadn't saved her from the experiences of her youth. No, she would never turn her back on her faith, but it was her faith, not her parents'. Certainly not the congregation's. And her faith contained room for the viewpoints of others.

Mia nodded to herself, then ran her fingers over the crucifix beneath her tank. It felt cool to her touch, comforting.

"Will Colista have you here more than once?" the instructor asked.

The woman appeared in fantastic shape. Almost no body-fat, like Mia but with much more muscle definition. Her short-cropped raven hair clung to her head, wet with sweat. Her green eyes shone like a cat's.

Mia didn't know what to say. It wasn't only Colista's decision. She decided to keep options open. "Maybe." Mia used a towel to wipe sweat from her face. "It felt great to get such an awesome workout."

"Did you experience anything else?" the woman asked.

Mia didn't know exactly what the instructor meant and didn't wish to ask. What was Mia supposed to feel, the release of energy? The detachment of the spirit Colista said haunted her? Mia didn't know and didn't want to. This was a lie.

Mia decided on, "Not sure. Maybe? I guess time will tell."

She'd explained, ahead of the workout, why Colista sent her. The instructor had shrugged and smiled as if this kind of thing happened every day. Made sense she'd follow up and ask Mia about it.

"Come anytime," the instructor said, eyeing her with a suspicious gaze which told Mia she indeed thought she'd see her again quite soon. "It's included in the cost of your tuition, of course."

"Thanks," Mia said.

"Oh," the instructor said as Mia turned to walk away. "Keep your focus on the image you used for meditation. It's a very personal thing, very important. You need to carry the benefits of the meditation with you for it to stick."

Mia nodded and fingered the crucifix beneath her spandex tank top. "I will." Then she turned toward the glass studio door, pushed through, and finally walked across the area filled with indoor tennis courts and a green running-track. A mixed-gender group played a rigorous game of basketball further down the complex.

Mia passed the rooms which housed the individual racquetball courts. The sounds of small blue balls smashing against wood walls cascaded from one of the rooms, along with the grunts of two opponents as they strove to win. The sounds reminded her of Jack, so she hurried along.

These negative thoughts of Jack were new to her college experience but coming on strong. Or had she always harbored them and not wanted to acknowledge the facts? So many girls would love to take her place. Secretly, she now wished they would. He'd been an okay boyfriend for the Winter Formal and Prom, the kinds of things she wouldn't have wished to miss. But those things seemed so juvenile now, from another, earlier, time in her life. A time when nothing mattered save glamour magazines and shopping at the mall. She wanted more than this now. Something richer, more fulfilling. Meaningful.

Artistic and beautiful.

Just because that's what she wanted for herself, it wouldn't stop Jack from pulling that ring box from a hidden coat pocket and proposing, probably in front of her family so she would feel uncomfortable with the words she knew she would utter. Contrary words—words he wouldn't want to hear. Words her father wouldn't want to hear. However, they needed uttering. They needed saying so that she could avoid the existence her mother clung to only because she knew no other. Her father always made sure of that.

State college was Mia's rebellion, an escape. One step toward freedom from her father, a repressive church she no longer wished to attend, and yes, from Jack. Freedom from the man-child who would try and drag her down, just like her father had done to her mother. He would talk her into transferring to his school as his fiancé.

Not in this lifetime.

Mia opened the heavy double doors with a frustrated burst of energy. The shock hurt her narrow wrists, but the pain felt glorious, something with which to channel her angst with Jack. However, when the doors shut behind her, she felt as if she'd entered another world.

The sounds from the rec center were reduced to a slurry of white noise. The white-tiled tunnel before her contained more shadows than she felt it should. Mia's anxiety flared. The space in her brain where her rebellion lived filled with a cool dread. The growing seed of fear started in the base of her neck and traveled outward to her limbs. A strange tingling sensation made her arms shake. To stop them, Mia wrapped them around her torso, as if to warm herself.

The fluorescent lights never flickered as she half-expected them to, but appeared subdued and dimmer than she'd ever noticed before.

The hall she traversed in the gloom sloped downward in a gentle grade and led to the locker rooms. Mia could just make out the wood doorways down at the end. She suddenly wished the game of basketball to finish up so someone, anyone, would join her. Her footsteps echoed up off the floor, then scurried around her head and ears as if after her undivided attention.

Better than the sound of fluttering wings!

The thought made her stomach clench and her shoulders bunch. If she heard the wings now, she'd seriously flip out, probably run out without showering. Mia half-contemplated the notion but just as quickly discarded it. She didn't enjoy it when her body felt sticky or otherwise unclean. No, she needed a shower before she could properly interact with humanity.

The downward grade propelled her forward with its own powers. Inertia and other properties of physics caused the sensation. Mia knew this, but she could imagine a scenario where a spirit pushed her along from behind, cold hands on her back as it guided Mia toward its ghastly ends. She could see the door to the locker room now, and also the door at the end of the passage which led to the tunnel system connecting every campus building.

Don't be dramatic! Mia thought the words, but the voice belonged to her father, or perhaps Pastor Matt.

She reached the heavy wooden door to the women's locker room. Her downward momentum over the slick tiled floor caused her to bang her shoulder into the door with a meaty thud. Mia took a deep breath, regained her balance, then yanked on the heavy door. It opened slowly until enough space existed for her to slip past. Once inside, the door closed behind Mia with a whoosh of hydraulics.

Like a crypt door!

Mia hurried along, black duffel bag with a change of clothes balanced on her slender shoulder. A brick privacy wall extended outward, then Mia swept past it and into a room with lockers and benches. Just beyond the reach of the fluorescents, two dark rectangles loomed like doorways to nowhere.

Nowhere you want to go, her mind finished.

For once, she wished to find comfort in remaining smelly for the duration of the walk back to her dorm. People did it all the time, just threw on some sweats and a hoodie and went for it, showered when they got back. But not her.

Cleanliness is next to Godliness.

Before she removed a lick of clothing, however, Mia needed to get her bearings. She walked toward the first rectangle of darkness. As she approached, the auto-sensor clicked, and the waterproof half-shell sconces burst to life. They illuminated blue tiled floors, along with stainless steel pylon-style shower stations. Dark grated drains lay scattered at strategic intervals across the one large room.

Satisfied that nothing sinister, paranormal or otherwise, waited for her, Mia peeled off her sweat-soaked clothes. She left them in a heap on the floor beneath one of the benches, then padded into the shower room. Her crucifix bounced against her chest. The lights immediately dimmed, burst quickly back to full-strength, then faded back to a creepy half-light.

What the hell? She longed for the full ration of light to return. It didn't. *No big deal.* She just needed to hurry, wash up and get the heck out of here. Mia hoped to all things holy that the lights didn't go out altogether.

Mia reached for the shower handle and started the water. She stood outside the stream until the water turned warm, then stepped beneath the stream. The jet felt like little needles on her skin, and she imagined it peeling the flesh off her muscles.

Gross!

Mia quit with the horrid imagery and turned her back to the stream. She bent her long neck back and allowed the water to soak her hair and cascade down her face. She imagined her sweat sloughing away and down the drain.

A scent like rotten eggs filled her nose. *Hard water*, she thought. Perhaps the school failed to recharge their industrial-sized water softener. She imagined her hair turning orange from the minerals. A sharp clip of laughter erupted from her mouth. *Yeah, right.* State college used city water, pre-treated. Nothing to worry about. She'd rinse a bit longer and get on her way. The scent then morphed into the smell of something long dead.

Mia's eyes flew open, and she raised a hand to her mouth as if the horrible odor might try and get inside her. No possible origin for the scent presented itself. No dead bodies of half-decomposed mice. Her eyes scanned the shower room floor until something above caught Mia's attention.

You've got to be kidding. Gross!

A large spider crawled toward her on eight longish legs which stuck out of a fat gray body. She just knew it would drop on her first chance it got. It approached, closer and closer, in quick twitchy movements.

Then, the worst of all happened. The unthinkable. As if whatever plagued her knew what her mind would not want. The fluttering of wings. *A hummingbird above Grandpa's garage door!* The lights dimmed further, casting the edges of the shower room into deep shadow. The wings, from within those shadows, fluttered louder. And louder.

Mia ran. She stumbled toward the door to the shower, arms covering her body from whatever eyeballed her nakedness from the dark. She glanced back once, just in time to watch the large arachnid slide downward on a silky thread.

It's coming for me!

She stumbled over the lip of the shower room and into the locker area. Mia stood still as a statue, listening for the wings. Watching for the large spider. Both would come for her, although, neither seemed to plague her now. In the diminished light, the shower-room opening appeared as a cave of almost perfect darkness. Nothing stirred.

But the cold! Mia shivered, her arms still wrapped around her nude body.

On the surface of her skin, she could still feel the cloying warmth of the hot water she just abandoned. But, beneath—beneath her skin, between the red mass of her musculature and her flesh, Mia felt a stinging cold layer, like someone had stuck her with a needle and injected her with a frigid liquid. Within that cold, little pinpricks of pain poked at her from inside her body. Paranormal or nerves, Mia didn't know, but it became too much. Her nervous, anxiety-driven tears flowed down her cheeks. She shrieked from sheer terror and from the desire to just be left alone.

The lights went out completely, but only for an instant. When the fluorescents returned, the blinding flash nearly knocked Mia to the ground when, in her panic, her foot caught the leg of a wooden bench. She stumbled around, trying to regain her equilibrium. Her breaths came in panicked gouts. The spider and the wings were coming for her! Next, the door to the outside hallway banged open and three women with duffels over their shoulders walked in with concerned looks.

A pretty woman with dark curly hair and toned lean muscles looked at Mia as if she'd grown a third eye. "You okay?" she asked, then looked around for any signs of danger. "We heard you holler."

Mia, used to the anxiety attacks and sheer panic, regrouped almost right away. She pointed at the shower room. "Spider," she managed. "Big ass spider." She took a big breath, smiled a sheepish grin at the girls. "Sorry if I worried you. I just hate spiders."

All three looked in the direction of the shower room and scrunched up their faces.

"Gross," one said. "Can't blame ya there."

For a horrifying moment, Mia thought they would walk out, decide to shower at the dorms, leave her here alone with...the fluttering. The cold. But then they entered and pulled off their sweaty workout clothes.

Mia took a big breath of relief, then wiped down and dressed. After, she hurried out and headed to the dorms.

Mia stood in the hall, out front of her dorm-room door. A pair of black panties hung from the doorknob; they looked clean, but she wasn't about to find out. From inside, bass thumped from Chastity's stereo, and she could hear two people having a conversation. Muffled tones and muted words. Then Chastity giggled.

Great, Mia thought. *Chastity and Brody are gonna go at it.*

She remembered what panties on the doorknob meant, Chastity not one for subtlety. That was her style, and Mia wouldn't judge her on it. No, that's what her church did—judge. It often did more harm than good. Everyone was different, so she'd leave it be. Despite her feelings of inclusion, Mia had zero desire to walk in on the couple.

Some things don't need to be seen. She pulled her cellphone from her back pocket and texted Chastity. "You busy in there?"

Seconds ticked by before Chastity answered. "I'm banging Brody go away".

Holy hell! Mia stared at the screen a moment, then pocketed the phone.

As she decided what to do, she grinned and quietly laid her duffel on the striped hallway carpet. Several years of hall sports and general traffic had left it faded and thin. Careful to remain quiet, Mia unzipped the zipper of her duffel, rummaged inside a moment, then pulled out a sign covered with a fair amount of red and black yarn. The shape of the sign was the best: a circle with a line through it. Inside the circle, yet behind the line, was the universal shape of a penis. The sign was adorned with a hook from an old coat hanger to attach it to the doorknob. With a wicked grin, Mia placed the sign over the panties.

Message sent!

Fun as that was, Mia still needed another place to go. *Where then?* The decision she arrived at frightened her more than walking in on Chastity and Brody. But what other choice did she have? Either that or go spend the night in the lounge. The lounge was dark and quiet this time of night. Nobody would be studying. Plenty of quiet for those fluttering wings to make an appearance.

Okay, she would go. She took a breath which swelled her chest. Mia knew she wasn't going because of Chastity and Brody screwing or the fluttering wings. She was going because that's what she wanted.

Oh, God, you're gonna burn in Hell, Mia!

She remembered they'd agreed on a late supper anyway, so she could pretend that was her only intention. It relieved her guilt a little, but deep down she knew she'd ask to stay over. *On his couch, Mia. On his couch!*

CHAPTER 11

Bruce sat at his computer desk and tried to think of a sentence. Any sentence. He'd been on a literary roll with his horror novel earlier, but the stream of words dried up whenever he thought about Mia. She'd be a great muse, but right now, she was proving to be more of a distraction.

Not her fault. Mine.

He enjoyed thinking about Mia. Her artsy ways and awkward demeanor really appealed to him. Her looks certainly didn't hurt, but he didn't want to dwell on those attributes. Some qualities were much more important to him.

Bruce wondered how her yoga session went, then figured she'd tell him all about the session at supper. He looked at the time on his computer. Already just before seven o'clock. He'd been writing longer than he thought.

Shoving away from his desk, Bruce got up and went in the bathroom to freshen up. He sure hoped, whether real or imagined, Mia could find relief from her worries. He would help as much as possible, be there for her when she wanted him to.

In the mirror, Bruce noticed a horrid red pimple in mid-rupture, rearing itself up like Mount Vesuvius on his upper cheek.

"Great," he murmured, then fussed over it with an acne wipe, which only seemed to make things worse.

That's all he needed, already outside of Mia's class looks wise. If she hadn't ditched him yet, maybe this wouldn't make any difference. She wasn't a shallow person, though, so there was that.

Shallow.

The image of a packed U-Haul crept unbidden into his mind, red and white painted steel taunting Bruce's family like a meddlesome demon. His mother had loaded it up with her belongings while he'd been at school, while the old man was turning wrenches over at Southside Towing and Repair. That's how big of a coward she'd become, having slipped out with her new upgrade under the cover of a silent, empty home. She hadn't even bothered to say goodbye to Bruce. No hugs. No assurances that she'd send for him to visit once she settled.

His old man had raised him best he could, having tried hard most of the time, but there was only so much a life-weary old grease-monkey could teach Bruce. After mom left him for a rich banker, the old man had found himself at the bottom of a cheap bottle of whiskey. Bruce had been forced to find out about life in the most unconventional ways, either through school, his few friends, or the yellowed pages of the used paperbacks being sold at the local pawn shop.

His thick fingers continued to poke at the pimple. When the thing didn't go away, he settled for trying to flatten out his always-frizzed brown locks. When none of his efforts produced results, Bruce threw on some pit-stick and thought about changing his clothes. When he noticed he'd need to do laundry tomorrow, Bruce decided one could never go wrong with Minecraft. He patted the picture of a cube-looking zombie on his chest with affection.

A series of knocks erupted from the front door, robust at first, then rescinding into gentle taps. Then came a period of waiting calm. When Bruce hesitated for too long, the silence morphed into a frenetic burst of fist-beats.

"Coming!" Bruce yelled. "Calm the H-E-double hockey sticks down."

Without more time to primp, Bruce decided he looked, sadly, as good as he ever would. *Let in the world.*

On the way to the door, Bruce made sure he closed out then pushed the screen of his laptop down, and stormed forward. He swung it open and before him stood Mia, fist raised, eyes a bit bigger and frantic than Bruce felt comfortable with.

"Hey!" Bruce said. He considered asking what was wrong, but decided on, "Come in. I was just finishing up a challenging section of my manuscript."

He moved aside just as Mia darted forward and past him. His heart raced at Mia's presence but sank when the realization sunk in that another tragedy most certainly had reared its ugly head.

"Sorry to barge in," she said, "but Chastity is using our room as a brothel."

"Better than a charnel house," Bruce said with a smile and an upswing of his index finger.

"A what?"

"You know," Bruce said, "a place people meet their violent, and often, bloody death."

Mia frowned, but her eyes held a spark of amusement. "Remind me to never read your writing."

Bruce found the comment ironic when held in contrast to the situation Mia now dealt with. Things such as Ouija boards and flying planchettes were the fodder of many a horror story. Not to mention phantom smells and invisible flutterings.

"I prefer good writing to cheap scares," he announced. "However, what little I know of Chastity, I suppose we can feel lucky about the charnel house thing. I mean, you never know." He smoothed his t-shirt over his belly self-consciously and shut the door. "Should we grab some supper?"

Mia took off her shoes, then sat in Bruce's office chair. She allowed the wheeled chair to come to rest before she said, "Can we order out for pizza? I'm not up to being around a bunch of peeps right now. That okay?"

Bruce could see the worry tugging at the corners of her mouth. She held her arms around her body as if to ward off an attacker.

"Of course," he said. "I think it's a kick-ass idea."

In fact, hanging out with Mia alone excited him, but he needed to remember that she needed a friend right now, not some douche who wanted to get her in the sack. Despite these thoughts, he couldn't help but imagine what it would feel like to hold Mia close, smell her hair, run his hands over her smooth skin. Her cheek on his pimpled one.

"Can we talk first?" she asked. "I'm kinda freaked out right now."

"Something happen at yoga?"

"After," she said, then ran a hand through still-wet hair. "In the women's locker room." She paused as if trying to decide what to tell him first. "The lights were acting funny, dimming and then getting brighter. Then they turned off altogether for a few seconds. Crazy."

"While you were in the shower?" Bruce asked.

Mia allowed a clipped giggle to escape. "I know you mean well, but guys aren't supposed to think about girls in the shower." She furrowed her brow in such a way it formed a wrinkle between her eyebrows. Her best mock anger look, Bruce guessed. "Or at least, they shouldn't admit they did...think about it."

"I— I just meant...well, what the hell else would you do in the women's locker room?" But he knew she was right. Mentioning the shower made Mia think he was imagining her in the buff. Bruce swiped at his t-shirt, again, nervous now. He pinched the fat beneath, his signature self-conscious go to. He hadn't meant to upset her, but maybe he had.

"I'm teasing you," Mia said. She looked at him now with soft eyes; her irises sparkled. "But I like it that you're respectful. That you care how I feel. That said…just be you, Bruce. Be yourself. I want to know who you really are, not who you think I want you to be. Make sense?"

Bruce nodded, but his heart felt like it would beat right out of his chest and plop onto the floor at his feet. She wanted to know the real him. His own mother hadn't even wanted that, so why did this beautiful girl want to? Bruce couldn't make any sense out of the words.

He heard his dad whisper in his hear, "The one you pass up is the one you'll never get. Women like men who are good with their hands… Gotta be useful or they'll run off like your ma."

Lotta good that did ya, Bruce thought, then realized Mia still stared at him with a thoughtful look.

He fought to remember what she'd said, but finally managed, "Yes, of course. Agreed. I want to get to know the real Mia, too. Nothing I want more." He felt a blush creep up his razor-burned neck.

"Nothing?" Mia asked. Her voice sounded lower than normal, husky.

"Well," Bruce said, then didn't know how to finish the sentence up. *So, what's new?* "I mean…you know what I mean."

"Do I?"

Bruce stared at her, senses now a frazzle.

Mia placed a hand on his knee and smiled. "I believe you. You're a great guy; I can tell. But I'm wondering if you're holding back because I have a boyfriend, you're too nervous, or you truly are one of the last gentlemen."

Bruce took a deep breath, then looked Mia right in the eye. A difficult maneuver now that he'd stuck foot in mouth. His heart pounded, and he was having a hard time catching his breath. What was he doing here? *She's out of my league, boyfriend or no.* He figured he'd best be honest or she'd know he was lying.

Bruce calmed himself, then said, "A little bit of all three." When Mia's eyes remained soft and gentle, Bruce continued, "And throw in the fact that you need a friend right now more so than another guy trying to get with you."

"Thanks for being honest," Mia said, a lone tear snaking down her cheek. Bruce knew she just cried sometimes. Not because she was sad, angry, happy, or any other emotion that made any sense to him. Just her body's reaction to its environment.

As if she sensed Bruce's thoughts, she wiped the tear. "I'm sorry. This is just what my body does. It's a nervous disorder. I would— I would never try to manipulate anyone with my emotions...although there's lots of girls who would use something like that to their advantage." She shook her head. "It's a curse, really. These damn sad eyes."

"They're beautiful," Bruce blurted.

"You're beautiful," Mia whispered and hugged him. Her closeness to him, the weight of her head resting on his chest, sent a surge of adrenaline through Bruce

"Thank you," Bruce said.

He lived in the moment as they held each other. The closeness felt heavenly, the heat of another human being, the emotional letting. He cared for her so very much.

From his chest, Mia said, "Jack hates them. Thinks my tears are a weakness, that I need to toughen up."

Bruce chanced a hand over her back. "Screw—Jack." He liked the vehemence in his voice but hoped he hadn't overstepped.

Mia giggled, then sniffed. She pulled her head away. "Yes, quite right. Screw him. I'm starting to warm to the idea of breaking things off." She looked around the room. "Do you have a tissue?"

Bruce stared at her in silence. He couldn't believe what she'd just said about Jack. Then he shook it off. "Yes, of course." He walked over to the bathroom and grabbed the box off the back of the toilet and threw it to her.

"Thanks," she said, then alternated between blowing her nose and tucking stray hairs behind her ear.

Bruce put a hand on her back to comfort her, to let Mia know he cared. "So, you were gonna tell me what happened after yoga."

"Yes," Mia said with a smile, mischief in her eyes. "While I was...in the shower."

Bruce laughed. "Yes, then."

Mia sniffed, looked around Bruce's room. Once her eyes settled on a poster of Star Wars: Rogue One, she spoke in a quiet, subdued voice, "It began, I guess, after I left the rec area and the doors closed behind me. Everything seemed too dark and too quiet. Like I had been transported to another dimension where nobody existed but me." She allowed her eyes to settle on Bruce. "Does that make any sense at all?"

"As much as anything." Bruce hoped it sounded how he felt: committed to her but not giving off a sense of false understanding. He wrote horror stories, yes, but he had never dealt with the possibility of those things being remotely true.

Mia took a deep breath, then reached into her duffel and produced yarn, needles, and a small mass of already-knitted material.

"Do you mind?" she said. "It helps."

He knew Mia meant with her anxiety, so Bruce shook his head emphatically.

Mia's hands took to the needles as if her fingers had merely grown longer and the metal sprouted from the plush flesh beneath her painted fingernails. She kept her eyes on Bruce, not even needing to look as she worked. The moisture at the bottoms of her eyes receded as if someone pulled a plug on the backside of her eye sockets.

"Knitting really calms me," she said. In a louder voice—but not by much—Mia recounted the events of the last hours. The lights, the stench, horrible gray-bodied spider, and finally a telling of the cold sensation beneath her flesh.

After Mia finished with the part concerning the yarn-bomb of Chastity's underthings, Bruce knew he needed to lighten the mood. "You really hung a *no penises allowed* sign made from yarn on the doorknob?" He laughed.

Mia kept her hands moving and a wry smile erupted on her face. "Who wants to look at Chastity's panties...other than Brody? And he was already in the ones she had on, if she wore any."

"I didn't know born-again Christians could have so much fun," Bruce said. "Thought they were all stodgy and judgmental."

"Born again?" Mia repeated. "I really don't even get what that means. You either believe in what Jesus did for you or you don't. Period. Other than that, the rest is all just fluff. A way to make money and control others."

"You really believe that?" Bruce asked.

"Yes." Mia kept knitting, brow furrowed, but no moisture sprang to her eyes. "Like my church. It's never been enough to believe. We are expected to act a certain way. Raise money. Never drink. But what a crock. We're human beings. We're alive."

"That's why you came to state college," Bruce confirmed. "To be you."

"Yes," Mia said. "And even though my dad is okay, I came to escape the control, the ever-watching eye of my father, who is really just an extension of Pastor Matt and the congregation. He's never had an original thought in his adult life."

The next thing out of Bruce's mouth came unbidden. "He enjoys the control the church offers over you and your mother. Jack is also an extension of that control."

Mia's knitting stopped. Her brow furrowed deeper. "That's deep, Bruce. Real deep." She looked him in the eye. "Sometimes it feels like that, yes."

Bruce felt himself turn red, hot on his face and thick neck. "Just give me Jesus, drop all the other baggage. I get it; I feel the same. Not that I've gone to church much, but— I believe in certain things."

"Your beliefs are personal," Mia said. "As are mine. I'm no evangelist, and neither are you. Let's leave it there for now, because the last thing I want..."

Bruce cut her off, even though he knew he shouldn't, "Is to tell me what to believe. I know. And I appreciate that. But what about spirituality? The supernatural? I mean, that's all part of it, right?" The words had shot from his mouth like cannon balls.

Mia shrugged. "I don't know, Bruce. What's happening to me, I don't know."

"I'm under the assumption it's not something you could speak with your family about," Bruce said.

"Absolutely not," Mia said, voice stern. Her eyes scanned the rest of Bruce's sci-fi and horror posters. They stopped on one advertising Rob Zombie's remake of Halloween. "They'd just use it as an excuse to make me come home."

"They can't make you do anything," Bruce said.

Mia shrugged, moisture returning to the bottoms of her eyes. She fingered her knitting but didn't begin any work. She continued to stare at Michael Meyers.

Bruce understood there must be a dynamic at play which wasn't clear to him. He couldn't imagine allowing a church, a congregation, to garner so much control of his life. That kind of thing must happen a little bit at a time, slowly eroding one's ability to break away. Mia was trying, and he'd help her any way he could. He hated to see anyone, especially her, live a life where they constantly needed to look over their shoulder.

"Anyway," Bruce said, to change the subject for now, "the yoga hasn't seemed to help, at least not one-hundred percent."

Mia smiled, seemed appreciative of the reprieve from speaking about her controlled life. "I'd say, not at all. The-the activity maybe even seemed a little worse than in the storage shed."

"Like it's building strength," Bruce said to himself more than to Mia. When he looked up, she was glaring at him.

He wanted to hide in shame from Mia's glare. He'd said something wrong.

"This isn't one of your books," she said. The tenor of her voice held power—power that warned Bruce to watch what he said. "Don't say things you don't know for sure. They'll only frighten me."

"Mia," Bruce said and knelt beside her. "I'm sorry. I didn't mean that. It just slipped out like some stupid monologue. The last thing I want is to scare you."

"I know," Mia said. "But once again, that brings us to what you do want."

"Just to—" Bruce started, but Mia held a finger to his lips.

She stood, her knitting falling to the carpeted floor, and grabbed Bruce's hand and pulled him up to her. She led him to his bed which he had taken the time to make. Mia sat and patted a spot of bedspread next to her. They scooted until both leaned back against his headboard.

Bruce's heart beat so fast black spots danced around his vision. He knew he must look flustered, but he sat next to her.

"Hold me," Mia said into his ear.

Bruce held her. After they sat slouched that way a while, Bruce said, "Do you know what I like about you most?" He felt the words appropriate and, surprisingly, wasn't afraid to spit them out like he would have been in the past.

"What?" Mia asked, voice sleepy and relaxed.

"You're smile." He spoke this directly into her ear, almost a nuzzle. He knew the action probably tickled her, but she didn't even flinch. "I've never had a female in my life who smiled at me like you do. Like I matter."

"Your mother," Mia suggested.

"My mother's a cunt," Bruce said in an authoritative voice.

Mia lifted her head from Bruce's large shoulder to look him the eye. "Don't use that word."

"My mother's a cunt," he repeated. A tear streaked from his own eye. "But out of respect for you that's the last time I'll say it."

"I'm so sorry," Mia said. She smiled at Bruce.

He didn't know what Mia had to be sorry for, but Bruce held her until they fell asleep in each other's arms. The last thing he remembered before sleep took him was that, for the first time, he felt so comfortable around someone, a female. He didn't even worry about things like snoring, flatulence or any other horrendous development. A stupid thing to think about, but he smiled once more before drifting off.

Mia couldn't sleep, hungry because they never ordered pizza. She listened to Bruce breath as he drifted off. His chest rose and fell in a gentle rhythm. She knew, just a few months ago, she wouldn't have exactly picked Bruce from a lineup of eligible bachelors. Of course, she hadn't exactly been looking, either, but still. No, she'd always sought men with more of an athletic frame.

Like Jack. She picked up her phone. She'd ignored several phone calls and wondered what he thought about that.

Mia felt like she deserved more than Jack, and Bruce deserved something better than he'd experienced thus far in his life. Bruce cultivated her artsy side and seemed in tune with her emotions. On top of that, he harbored no fears about expressing his own. Better yet, he didn't seem the type to blow sunshine up her butt just to get in her pants.

Like Jack.

Careful not to wake Bruce, she stood. His room looked comfortable, most of the décor meant to stimulate his muse for writing purposes. Movie and heavy-metal posters hung on the walls, along with bookcases stuffed full of dark subject matter. This didn't spook her or make her uncomfortable, because she knew Bruce. She understood his heart.

She walked over to his small yet tasteful birch writing desk. His laptop lay shut, a yellow notepad next to it with a brief outline and some notes of things only he would understand. Things like, *only The Colossus would understand his pain* and *if he was so damn smart then why did he go back to look for Marcus?* One near the bottom of the page almost made her laugh out loud. *Why would the villain even bother to kill such a gullible and foolish asshat? Should probably rewrite…*

A hardcover book caught her eye. She thought it just another horror book, until Mia noticed the picture of a man in jeans and black shirt beneath a gray jacket on the back flap. *Colista.* He appeared wise and scholarly, yet aloof somehow. Dismissive as he stared off into the middle distance.

Mia picked the book up off the desk and turned it over. She grimaced as she read. *Take A Walk Outside Your Flesh Bag with Frank Colista.*

"Gross," she whispered.

She'd never get used to the word *flesh bag.* She opened the front cover and noticed where Colista had signed it with a flowery script and then personalized the signature with a drawing of a little demon monster. Mia didn't like the look of it. The little thing fashioned from black ink frightened her, especially when she thought about the phenomenon that had plagued her recently.

Further up the page, Colista had scrawled: *To: Bruce. Good luck in your own writing endeavors.* Just beneath this, in smaller letters, like he knew she couldn't resist snooping, he wrote, *Mia, everything's fine. Just fine.*

Mia smiled at that one. *Am I that predictable?*

Careful not to crease the spine, she opened the book past the publisher pages and dedications. Chapter one's title read: *How to ensure success: Preparation.* Mia read about things like focusing on a keyword and repeating it and turning her eye upward to where real sight began, moderation of breaths and states of being. Finally, about the importance of belief. All ambiguous and unbelievable as she would have expected. Just enough substance to sell books and, perhaps, grow a bit of credibility among like-minded people.

Despite her skepticism, Mia sat in the office chair and rested her head against the backrest. What word should she pick? It seemed like an important part of the process, and she wanted to take it seriously, even if she didn't think she would succeed. When the word redemption popped into her head—a byproduct of her church upbringing—Mia decided just to go with it. She repeated the word in her mind, over and over, considering the meaning, as she tried to strain her right eye skyward to where this supposed real sight began. According to the book, she needed to do this until her mind allowed the transition from her conscious state of being to her spiritual. Only then would her flesh bag—*gross!*—release her spiritual energy and allow it to walk free.

Mia tried to concentrate on the word, however, her thoughts flowed to Bruce and then to how dumb she felt for even trying this, and finally to the fact that she didn't really believe. Wasn't that a large component, a belief it would work? Maybe she should have read more of the book first. Perhaps there existed an entire section of something she needed to know before the astral projection nonsense could take root.

Nonsense. A funny word. She should watch her thoughts.

This subject matter was Colista's livelihood. A dizzy spell washed over Mia as she contemplated Colista. His image on the back cover wavered like a mirage in the desert. Her peripheral vision darkened. She couldn't recall falling asleep, so why did she feel as though she was stuck in a dream? Bruce's room blended with a weird yet groovy filter of sleep. She could feel her belly rumble with hunger and a slight tingling in her hands and fingers. She looked around. The effect was as if she peered into a hazy room from inside a perfectly clear one. Just as she noticed the hazy room before her, she was in it, transported by unknown means. Mia stared down at her own body sitting in Bruce's chair. Fear raced through her consciousness at the sight.

It worked!

She looked around, into the haze of this dream-walk world, and noticed a bright aurora in the corner of Bruce's room which looked like a miniature sun. She thought it best to avoid something so unnatural.

Mia couldn't see her energy, or whatever part of her that had achieved consciousness, but her physical form definitely lay sprawled on the chair before her. Her physical eyes were closed, yet she could see. Mia didn't understand how this was possible.

She turned her line of sight and studied the bright sun-like sphere in the corner of Bruce's room with some concern, wondered what purpose it served and why it existed in this state of spiritual being but not the corporeal. What else existed here that didn't when her consciousness only lay inside her body?

The tingling sensation in her ghostly hands and fingers intensified as a strong odor invaded whatever passed for a nose in this new awareness. Fear gripped her. Mia didn't think she was safe.

A breeze started up which Mia thought originated from the miniature sun. It grew stronger and Mia could feel the weight of it push at her spirit form. She imagined her hair blowing back, but when she looked to her physical form sitting in Bruce's desk-chair, her locks remained unmoved. A sudden gust propelled a black, misty form. The form rushed at her from out of the bright orb of light. It seemed aggressive as it approached in increments, as if she watched an old film with some frames missing.

Mia's heart pounded, and she wanted nothing more than to jump back into her body. But she didn't know how. She tried to will her consciousness away from this thing but found she couldn't move.

The dark blob morphed from a diaphanous shadow to something humanoid in shape. It growled, although Mia wasn't sure if she heard it or felt it. Either way, the intent was clear. The entity approached like a predator.

Mia panicked and knew she needed to wake herself. She looked to Bruce, who snored softly from the bed. She'd get no help from that quarter. Frantic, Mia elected for a desperate leap at her body like a cheetah after a gazelle.

Nothing happened. She was trapped outside her body.

The dark, fully formed humanoid figure approached. It growled in a way Mia thought only she could hear. Its eyes flashed blood red as it appeared to consider the trapped human energy before it. The stench of a thousand corpses pounded at her energy, confusing yet visceral. How this thing could project corporeal elements of sense to her, lay well beyond her reckoning.

God, please!

Mia closed her eyes, preparing for the attack. She was helpless. It was like that time as a little girl with her momma's Ouija board. The growl, the sense of helplessness. A memory she thought buried. If the congregation or Pastor Matt knew, they would frown and shame her. Maybe shun her, remove her from the church. What would they think now? Mia felt herself shiver as she waited for the end.

Nothing happened. Mia chanced a look, opening her eyes, sure the dark creature would choose that moment to rip her apart.

Mia breathed hard, as if she'd just finished a marathon. Her eyes darted around the room, afraid the thing would pounce when she least expected. Everything seemed okay, normal. The creature and the haze were gone. Even the bright ball-shaped aurora had vanished. A burst of adrenaline rushed through her.

I'm back inside my body!

Mia lifted her hands and stared at them. She waited until her breathing normalized, then thought things through. What had she just experienced? Had she fallen asleep and allowed Colista's dumb book to influence her dreams? That had to be it. Yet, she couldn't shake the feeling she'd experienced something with no explanation--something she shouldn't have. With a biting certainty, Mia found she craved company, needed to feel the heat of Bruce's body next to her.

With a flurry of motion, desk chair gliding back across the room, Mia launched herself and raced to the bed. It felt fantastic to use her legs. She lay down as softly as she could. If he woke, Mia hoped Bruce would just think she had used the bathroom. She took a deep, shaky breath to calm herself, then lay next to him, enjoying the feel of Bruce. In a compulsive maneuver, Mia turned her head and kissed him on the cheek, the flesh soft beneath her lips. He tasted lightly of salt and some manly-scented soap.

Mia gave the room one last scan before letting down her guard and returning her head to the pillow, finally satisfied they were both safe. As the room blurred with impending sleep, right at the tail-end of consciousness, Mia thought she heard the subtle stirring of wings.

CHAPTER 12

Mia woke. Her cell phone vibrated from inside her duffel. Her arm was still around Bruce, who breathed lightly next to her, mouth open just a little. He looked younger like this, innocent, more like she perceived him.

She had feelings for him. Mia wouldn't lie to herself and certainly not to Bruce, if he asked. But how to deal with these feelings was the issue. Cuddling with Bruce felt right, and good. The dream the night before came back to her as she enjoyed the comfort of Bruce's body. It had to have been a dream, right?

Mia knew she should stop thinking about it, needing a distraction. Then she noticed the skimpy, newspaper thin quilt, stuffing bleeding out from tears in the fabric. A burst of inspiration caught her, and Mia knew what she would get Bruce for Christmas. Mia smiled as she calculated the needed materials.

The phone vibrated again, and Mia slowly extricated her arm from under Bruce's neck. Bruce wiggled a bit, turned his body, then his breathing dropped back into a gentle rhythm.

Mia reached into her bag and found the phone. Her screen read: *Chastity*.

She hit the little green phone symbol and said, "Yeah?"

"You sleep with him? Oh, and thanks for that wonderful peace of fucking art you left on the doorknob. Whatever!"

"First of all, yes," Mia whispered.

Chastity inhaled a large breath from the other side of the conversation, and Mia took a perverse satisfaction in the shock value of her words.

"But not the way your trashy mind thinks," Mia added. "We...cuddled."

"Look, you had me going there for a second. Thought maybe you finally woke up." Chasity coughed, which sounded more like a retch. "I just threw up a little in my mouth."

"Second of all," Mia continued, "yes, again. I found the artwork insanely appropriate. Your smelly underthings needed covering."

"Hey," Chastity shouted. "Those were clean. Hadn't even worn them yet."

"What do you want?" Mia asked, ignoring the banter, wanting to get back to Bruce. "You called me, and I'm sure you didn't wake me just to gossip about your panties and my cuddling."

"Right," Chastity said. "Don't let me keep you from Mr. Writerly Nerd Boy. I called because I didn't want you to forget about Para Psyche Club this morning. We'll be out in the quad like before. Colista's gonna show us how to leave our bodies."

Mia cringed. *Way ahead of ya there.*

She needed to speak with Colista; no way around it. Whatever this thing was—the thing that came at her like a demonic black cloud—needed some attention. Otherwise, it would continue to flutter around her like an invisible bat. Not to mention all the other undesirable stuff. She needed guidance about this astral projection nonsense, too. She'd probably sinned six ways from Sunday by doing it.

"You coming or not? Ten o'clock."

Mia gave the room a good look, saw no sign of the thing. No fluttering noises. No Godawful smells, paranormal or otherwise.

"Well?"

"Yes," Mia said, finally. "I'll be there. I may bring Bruce."

"You asking me for permission?"

"Whatever," Mia said. "I gotta go."

"You have just enough time to get a good roll in th—"

Mia hung up.

Oh, my god! She's unrelenting and has a one-track mind.

She glanced at Bruce, at the bulk of him beneath the tattered comforter. Her heart sped up. She'd spent the night in the bed of a guy who wasn't her boyfriend. Another reason she'd burn in hell. Her stomach flip-flopped with the knowledge she'd have to tell Jack their relationship was over. Even if things didn't work out with Bruce, Mia knew she could never truly be happy as Jack's little trophy. Yes, she would need to end it before he did something stupid like show up with a ring.

"Bruce," Mia said and gave his shoulder a push. The bed rocked back and forth on old springs and made little creaky noises which sounded a bit too much like the flutter of wings. When Bruce didn't wake, she rubbed his cheek with a tender stroke of her palm. "Bruce?"

Bruce stirred, then stretched an arm out and up with a yawn. Then his eyes popped open as if he just remembered something. "Did I snore? Worse?" He cringed.

"No," Mia said. "Not at all."

She affectionately pushed a curly stand of hair from in front of his eye so Bruce knew he was just fine. Mia enjoyed setting his mind at ease, soothing his insecurities. He certainly did the same for her. He understood her tears, her anxieties, her art.

"I just need to get going. The parapsychology group is gonna meet soon, and I want to speak with Colista before it starts. You know, about…"

Then she remembered Bruce didn't know about what happened last night after he fell asleep. She glanced at Colista's hardcover and winced.

Bruce tracked her gaze to his writing desk. "Yeah," he said slowly as if, perhaps, he had put two and two together. "Tell him about your locker-room experience." When Mia didn't answer right away, he said, "Right?"

Mia nodded, then looked at Bruce. She felt the sting of anxiety-produced tears behind her eyes. She could tell there weren't enough to spill out, not yet, and Bruce wouldn't care if they did, but they still bothered her. So many had accused her of being manipulative, using her tears to get her way. Even by people who should have known better, like her dad, Pastor Matt. And Jack. Especially Jack.

"You read the book?" Bruce asked casually, and Mia could tell he didn't mind.

"Yes."

Bruce's turn to nod. "And something happened."

"Yes." Bruce's instincts were amazing, and she wanted to hug and kiss him. Nobody had ever understood her like Bruce, and she'd only known him a short time.

Bruce got up off the bed and wrapped her in his beefy arms. "You should have woken me."

Mia slid her head down onto his left bicep and wrapped her arms around his broad back. Bruce arched to allow the maneuver. He smelled still of his deodorant or cologne. She felt safe—safer than she'd ever felt--from her many worries.

Colista rolled his eyes as the two groups of protesters continued to shout untruths at each other behind him. He wished he'd decided to hold group down by the lake instead of at the quad.

Crowley peered from behind Colista's left leg and hissed at the noisy groups of students. Then the cat plopped its old ass down on the grass and licked his rear-end.

Colista heard someone say, "I have the right to kill my own food. It's healthier."

Someone from the other group shouted louder than necessary, "Sure, but you don't need a full semi-auto to accomplish it."

"There's no such thing as a full semi-auto."

"You know what we mean, the full semi-auto that looks like an assault weapon."

And so the shouting went on and on.

Colista turned from where he sat with his back to a tree and addressed the students. "May I proceed with my university sanctioned group now? Or perhaps you'd rather just pile up in the middle and fight it out? You know, get this shit over with? Because you're never gonna agree."

"Sorry, Professor Colista," a girl with dark curly hair said. "We just don't want anyone else killed by an assault weapon."

"I know you don't," Colista said with what he hoped was a sympathetic tone.

"And I just want to hunt," an Asian kid in green camo said. "That's how my parents fed us, and I just want to continue the tradition."

"Of course, you do," Colista said, trying to sound equally concerned. He pretended to think a moment, thumb and index finger on chin. He nodded. "And I'm positive you can all find some common ground from which to agree. However, would you mind finding it elsewhere? The lake is quite beautiful this time of day, so perhaps there."

Several members of both groups nodded, then wandered toward the water, where the sun reflected like a million tiny prisms.

Crowley hissed again at no one in particular.

Colista turned back to the quad. A few students he recognized strode in his direction. Then he noticed Bruce, the guy who fancied himself a horror writer. Colista had signed a book for him. And the girl who walked with him was the one he'd sent to yoga. By the look on their faces it appeared the yoga hadn't done the trick.

Or her attachment is in her head.

Freshmen had a naïve way of finding problems where none existed. Melodramatic, some would say.

Mia approached, towing Bruce behind her with a hand firmly caught up in his. She was obviously in a hurry to discuss the matter before any of the others arrived.

"Professor Colista," Mia said, "can I speak with you?"

He needed to fight himself not to say, "I don't know, can you?" He settled for, "Of course. How was yoga?"

Crowley flopped to his other side and began to lick pieces of grass off his ruffled fur.

Mia glanced at the cat until Bruce caught up and moved next to her, then looked up at Colista. She seemed to struggle. "Not to say that your advice didn't help at all," she started, "but it seems as if I'm still not rid of my problem."

She went on to explain about the locker-room incident.

"I see." Colista glanced at Crowley. Even the cat had now given Mia its undivided attention. Certainly not a good sign, he thought. "So, your attachment persists." He considered this as more students wandered in his direction like zombies toward fresh meat. "Have you actually seen your little problem? It could appear as a misplaced shadow, or even as a bit of refracted light, a flicker in a mirror."

The girl seemed to think about her answer, so Colista braced himself for some vital piece of information. He'd seen this look before, more often than he wished.

Crowley rubbed its bony, arthritic body up against Mia in a most unprecedented maneuver. *Not in all our years.* He'd never known Crowley to pursue affections from anyone save him, even when in the aid of a client.

"Well," Mia said as she bit her lower lip.

Colista could see tears build at the bottoms of her eyes. Those eyes, so sad she could get a beggar's last coin.

"Actually, I have. But…" Her eyes shimmering like diamonds as she appeared lost in thought.

"Go on," Colista insisted, "you're in good company."

Crowley continued to rub Mia's legs. Was that a low growl he heard rumble from the cat's chest?

"I found your book on Bruce's desk. It was late at night, and…" Mia blushed in her special way, skin turning blue at the temples and beneath her eyes.

"I don't judge," Colista said with a rueful smile.

"Thanks," Mia said. "It was late, but I found your book captivating. I mean, admittedly scary and probably something I shouldn't mess with, but interesting all the same. I didn't think…"

"That it would work?" Colista finished.

She nodded. "I was probably just dreaming."

"Did you see your own body?"

"Yes."

"Then you weren't dreaming," Colista said, greedily. "What else did you see?"

"I saw a bright light. Kinda like a sun, except it looked more like an entrance to a tunnel. Or, at least that's how I felt."

"Of course," Colista said. "Of course, you did. Go on. What else?"

"The light felt so peaceful, until…"

"Yes?" Colista leaned forward.

"Until this black… mass, I guess you could say, rushed at me."

"What did you do?" Colista leaned even closer. Goose bumps had risen on his arms and neck. *It has been so long…*

Crowley also stared at Mia, as if he understood every word.

"I— I leapt back into my body."

Colista nodded, hands interlocked behind his back.

"The sun tunnel thingy and...and the shadow were gone," she explained. "Everything turned back to normal."

"Did you experience anything further?"

"Wings," Mia said. "The flutter of wings."

"Yes," Colista said. "It's how it presents itself to you. A signature move, so to speak."

"Why didn't you wake me?" Bruce said. He looked like he wanted to kiss her cheek but refrained.

Mia blushed with even more blue, if that were possible at this juncture. "I didn't want to wake you. I was fine. I'm— I'm fine." She shook her head.

"I suggest you take a break from leaving your flesh bag for a while," Colista said.

"Gross."

Ignoring her, he continued, "At least until we find a remedy for your dilemma. Probably a harmless little hanger-on, but we should be rid of it." He looked at the cat. "Isn't that right, Crowley?"

The cat answered by again rubbing Mia's leg.

Colista was about to lend an invitation for a session after group when a hand clamped down on his shoulder.

"Hey ya, eye candy," Chastity said. "How's it hanging?"

"Do kids really still ask that?" Colista said. "Thought it went out with the nineties."

"I do," Chastity said. She glanced at Mia. "Why the tears, babe?"

"It's nothing," she said and wiped at her face as if it were streaked with dirt. Then she glanced at Colista. "I'm sorry if my roommate is rude. She considers herself irresistible."

"No worries," Colista said with an earnest tone. "Besides being my student, she's not my type in many ways. If you catch my drift."

"Oh," Mia said. "Oh! I'm sorry, I didn't realize."

"Nothing to be sorry for, I'm sure," Colista said.

"Oh, I see," Chastity said. "You swing the other direction."

"I don't swing in any direction," Colista said. "At least not for a very long time." He decided his past fell outside the realm of anything they needed to know. He shook a smoke out of the pack in his pocket, much needed by this juncture, then turned to Mia. "Why don't you and Bruce come with me after group and we'll see about your minor dilemma."

Crowley backed away from Chastity when she reached down to stroke its fur.

"Your cat's rude, Prof," she said.

Are you kidding me?

Colista lit his smoke with a silver lighter, a gold cherub emblazoned on either side, then inhaled. He held it a moment before exhaling out his nostrils. Twin plumes of smoke poured out then up. Cigarette resting on his bottom lip like a grub, Colista said, "I think, perhaps, Crowley disagrees."

Chastity frowned.

"We'll come," Mia said.

Bruce smiled at her, then at Colista as if he couldn't think of an idea any more wonderful. Colista watched with interest as Bruce placed a protective hand on her arm.

A damsel in distress...or does the fine Sir Bruce possess other motivations? Love, yes, of course. Most certainly. Look at how he coddles her.

Colista could tell the boy's affections rang true with Mia by the way she leaned into him

"Can Brody and I come?" Chastity asked.

Colista pointedly ignored her. Then he noticed a rather athletic young man walk—no, strut—toward the gathering group. He noticed him only because he'd never seen him before, and the boy dressed different than most of the students here at state college. He wore tan khakis and a white button-up collared dress shirt. No tie, but something about the body language suggested that he may, on the occasion, add that to his wardrobe as well. The young man also seemed to be locked in on the little group before Colista, dark eyes intent. He seemed particularly focused on Mia and Bruce.

Shit would now, in near certainty, hit the proverbial fan. Freshmen and their high school sweethearts, and the betrayal of such, were as common as residual paranormal energy on a college campus. Oh, the drama of it all. Lucky him, he'd be privileged to watch it play out before him.

A small gasp left Mia's lips as she adjusted her body just enough to allow Bruce's hand to fall from her arm. The red and blue hues that rivaled each other both began to deepen.

She knows, Colista considered.

Bruce glanced in the direction in which Mia now concentrated, directly at the well-dressed man. Colista watched his mouth fall from a smile to a confused frown. Then Bruce glanced at Mia.

"Who's that?" Chastity asked.

But, of course, she asked, Colista thought. Colista found it telling that nobody answered her most gravid of questions.

Crowley let out a growl, then left Mia's feet to hide behind Colista.

Mia glanced at Chastity with large eyes, ignored Bruce with a perceptible turn of her body which Colista found cold, then managed a small smile for the one who approached.

Colista allowed his smoldering cigarette to hang from his mouth in anticipation, then noticed when the boy raked Mia from toe to head with a bewildered—or was it a disapproving—look.

Yes, definitely disapproving.

"Mia?" the athletic looking boy asked.

"Jack," Mia said, voice hardly more than a whisper.

Jack didn't say another word until he stood before Mia, preferring a resounding pregnant silence. His eyes never left her, not even to acknowledge the others in her presence. Without a smile, he finally spoke. "I've never seen you wear sweats in public before."

Colista couldn't derive the emotion behind his words. The kid possessed a cool demeanor, expectant, in complete control. Colista didn't like him.

"Hey, Jack," Mia said with a nervous quiver to her voice. She glanced down as if unaware of what set of clothes decorated her lithe form. "Oh, this. Well, I worked out, then…"

"Then she didn't have time to change," Bruce finished.

Colista observed Bruce and found the boy wanting in many ways, especially the Megadeth t-shirt, the large red pimple on his left cheekbone, but could appreciate the confident pull of his shoulders, the suspicious gleam in his eyes.

"Who are you?" Jack said. He sounded aggressive, one side of his mouth pulled downward in what Colista imagined must be the boy's attempt at a sneer.

Spoiled youth don't understand how to pull off a proper sneer. The world hasn't yet torn them asunder quite enough yet. He considered the possibility this very encounter may prove a catalyst toward that eventuality, though.

Bruce turned to Mia, an uncertain look gracing his features, as if the responsibility lay with her to answer the proffered question.

Mia stayed silent, most likely with words left unsaid, chest rising up and down as if she couldn't catch a proper breath.

CHAPTER 13

Panic gripped Mia as if her heart had clenched in spasm. She'd come to the realization that something should be done about her relationship with Jack, but now that he stood before her the notion seemed easier thought than said out loud. She could see her father in Jack, and even Pastor Matt. That terrified her. She'd never felt this way about Jack before.

"That's Bruce," Chastity answered for her.

Jack nodded, that serious expression never leaving his face. He turned to Chastity, eyed her up and down. Probably observing her short-shorts and tight t-shirt, knowing Jack. He scowled before turning back to Mia.

Mia glanced at Colista, hoping he might offer some solace with his scholarly wisdom, but the man stood aloof in cold apprisal, cigarette smoldering at his lips. *Just an observer*, Mia thought. She would need to take control of the situation before her life spiraled out of control.

She turned to Bruce. "I'll catch up with you later." She hoped her uncomfortable smile made clear her position. Then she reached for Jack's hand. "Let's go down by the lake. It's nice down there in the morning."

Bruce nodded, but Mia barely noticed before she began to lead Jack away. She relished the fact she could still cool Jack off with nothing more than the opportunity to be alone with her. Yet, Mia still didn't dare turn to look Jack in the eyes. She knew her eyes would betray her.

"You should have called first." Mia hoped she sounded pleasant. "I would have worn something nicer." She hated herself for vocalizing a sentiment she didn't feel in the least. She didn't want to care what Jack thought of her clothing.

"I wanted to surprise you," Jack said in a serious tone.

She risked a glance at him and found his face unreadable, all hard lines and a set of flatlined lips. His eyes appeared dull and lifeless in a way that made her nervous. Certainly, he wouldn't have come all this way to break things off. No, that wasn't Jack's style.

"Well," Mia said, "surprise! Here you are." When Jack didn't smile, she said, "Here we are."

"Yes," Jack said flatly. "I thought you might be a little more ecstatic to see me."

"What are you doing here Jack?" When they were younger, before Jack became more forceful, Mia had possessed the ability to guide their conversations where she wished, and she hoped to in this instance as well.

Jack stopped walking, stopping Mia's momentum and pulling her toward him. "Do I need a reason? Is the fact that I missed *my* girlfriend a good enough one for you?"

He glanced accusingly at Bruce who, Mia noticed, was still looking in their direction. Colista too, cigarette still smoldering. Even the cat was watching, the furball's tail swishing back and forth as if in irritation.

Mia didn't care for the way Jack had taken over control of the situation, especially in front of her new friends.

"I guess," she answered. "But I might consider the fact you only came to check up on me."

Jack tore his eyes away from the onlooking group and riveted her with an icy glare. Then his eyes softened as if her face wouldn't allow him to hold his anger. He began to walk toward the lake again.

"I just figured we had some time before classes started," he said, but Mia thought he sounded as if this may not end up being the whole truth. "And I've been doing some thinking."

"I've always told you not to bother with that," Mia said quickly, before he could blurt out something stupid like a marriage proposal. In a whisper, she said, "It's not one of your strengths."

"Very funny. You may be right about that, but this time I had some help with my thoughts."

Mia glanced up at him, but it was his turn to look away. "What have you done?"

"Just sought out some solid advice," he said. "From some people who know you."

"Who?" Mia said. "And why?"

They moved past the last hall in the university complex and the lake appeared before them, brightly rippled and beautiful. A lone sailboat skimmed past, leaving a silent wake behind. Seagulls coursed overhead and berated each other over some issue only they understood. The oaks along the shore shook their leaves in the gentle breeze.

"How gorgeous," Jack said, something Mia knew he wouldn't normally say.

What's gotten into him? she wondered.

Jack continued, "A perfect setting for what I want to speak to you about."

Mia shook her head and shrugged. "What could possibly be so important that you drove three hours to see me?"

"I spoke with your dad and Pastor Matt," he said, as if this should be the natural conclusion.

"Why?" Mia said, and hoped it sounded as pointed as she meant it.

He'd never taken much of an interest in her parents or her religion before. In fact, the only thing he seemed interested in, ever, was her body.

"Because I've been a fool. I've allowed you to slip away because I'm selfish." He stared out over the water as if allowing that to sink in.

Mia shrugged in agreement, but also in a way she hoped showed just how much she couldn't care less.

Jack looked her in the eye and continued. "I've applied to Bible college." He continued to stare at her. "And I want you to join me."

"No," Mia said flatly. She had no idea what his endgame was, but she wanted no part of Bible college...or him. Especially not considering this new information. Her father and Pastor Matt had practically begged her to go to a Christian school, but she'd made up her own mind on the matter.

Jack tapped the toe of his right shoe. "I anticipated this answer." He looked at her. "But both your father and Pastor Matt told me to remain persistent. To kindly but firmly assert my decision."

"It's not your decision." Mia folded her arms over her torso. "Worry about yourself, and I'll worry about me." Mia felt the shackles of her youth like ice around her body. They felt familiar, something comforting when she'd been younger, but now so constricting. The very shackles she'd come here to escape.

"Doesn't look to me like you've done enough worrying then," he said. "I've only been here a little while and I can see you've already changed. And not for the better."

"What do you mean?"

"Your flippant attitude, the way you dress yourself." He glanced back the way they'd come. "And your new ragtag friends? They're horrible. Why are you hanging out with some scrubby headbanger, a professor who smokes in front of his students, and a slut?"

"Don't judge my friends!" Mia shouted, louder than intended. But she felt furious. How dare him. "Do you have any idea how many people talk about how arrogant you are behind your back? Are you really that blind?"

"I know," he said. "That's why I'm making changes. Because I want to be with *you*. And I knew the only way that would happen is to change who I am."

"I don't want you to change who you are! Not for me, not for anyone. If you want to change, do it for yourself."

"How about for God?"

Are you serious?

He'd gone off the deep end. She needed to end this, now, before things could get any worse. It was great that he suddenly wanted to find God, but that was a very personal journey, not one dependent on anyone else.

"Look," Mia said, hoping she sounded sincere, "I'm super glad you found God. And I truly hope what you said isn't just empty words to try and somehow trap me. If you're sincere, then great, but don't think because you've decided to change your life that somehow obligates me to disrupt my own. Because I've chosen very carefully."

"Your dad and Pastor Matt seem to think your decision to attend state college is rash and petulant. That you need guidance. And since I've relinquished my life to a higher power, they feel that maybe I can make a difference with you. From what I've seen, you need help. You're backsliding."

"Are you kidding me?" Mia said. "You have no idea what that even entails."

But the word stung. Backsliding was a term used by the congregation to shame members of the flock into adjusting their behaviors.

"*They* told me."

"What other Christian jargon did they fill your head with?"

She didn't wait for an answer but turned and ran instead. Mia knew it a naïve move, that he could easily catch her if he chose to, but she couldn't help herself. An escape from this idiot—the words he regurgitated with no real understanding of the devastation they could wrought to a Christian psyche was necessary. Her dad and Pastor Matt were using Jack as their tool, hoping he could herd her back into the fold. They couldn't stand losing control.

Well, I'll show them!

She ran, arms and legs pumping so hard that her heart felt like a piston deep down in her chest. She'd run forever if need be.

"Mia!" Jack yelled, but to Mia's delight, his voice came from far behind her. "I'm only doing what's best for you like the Bible says!"

Best for me, my ass!

He only wanted to control her, like her dad and the pastor. She hoped he would give her some space, a chance to get away and think. If she could get away from him now, she'd never allow him to get so close, ever again. Doubly so in regard to her dad and Pastor Matt. They could burn in Hell for all she cared. Mia thought back to all the times subtle reprimands had been handed out for reading the wrong books, watching inappropriate movies, saying things frowned upon by the church. *I'll show them what backslidden really means!* Anger fueled her muscles with adrenaline.

She hadn't consciously run with any particular destination in mind, but found herself nearing Bruce's campus apartment building. Nobody would know to look for her there. She could hide out indefinitely. Mia hoped Bruce was heading this way instead of staying for the parapsychology group. If not, she hoped he'd left the door unlocked. If not, she'd hide in the lounge and wait for him.

Running around the corner of the Lower Union, Mia reached Bruce's building. She slipped inside the glass doors and hurried down the hall, past the reception desk and down to the next intersection. Mia raced to his door and reached it just as she heard the outer door open. Her mind screamed, *must be Jack!* Her heart raced. Mia heard footsteps coming toward the intersection.

Whoever it was, they would see her if she didn't move. Desperate, she mouthed a silent prayer and tried the knob. It turned. Somehow, perhaps a minor miracle, Bruce had left it open.

Relief flooded her as she cracked the door just enough to slide inside, then closed it softly behind her. Mia stood with her back to the door, chest heaving with labored breaths she'd been holding. She listened as whoever walked in the hall outside the door clomped on past. Mia's heart felt like it stopped whenever those footsteps did, as if the individual knew she was hiding behind the door.

Thankfully, whoever it was moved on.

Thank God!

But her heart continued to pound, because deep down she knew Jack would never give up. Nor would her dad or Pastor Matt. They would pursue her with dogged determination, committed to returning Mia to the fold. This angered her. It was her flesh and soul, her life, and she would allow nobody else to dictate her life. If someone wished to share in it, great, but they would not control her any longer. Angered, she walked toward Bruce's writing desk where Colista's book sat benignly in wait.

The ultimate escape, she thought.

Her anger overrode her fear, and Mia sat in the desk chair. She glanced around the room, heard nothing of wings, smelled nothing untoward. All seemed perfectly safe, as it should, peaceful even. Not a hint of the activity which had plagued her in the past twenty-four hours. Intellectually, she remembered the storage shed, the locker room, and her experience right here in this room, but her rage overruled all.

Mia couldn't imagine what catalyst had provoked Jack to seek out her father and Pastor Matt. Or to give up his football scholarship. And, for what? Just to possess her, to keep her from slipping out of his grasp. What kind of deranged psycho would make up lies about finding God, give up their entire life, just to pin someone else down...

The book sitting before her was key to her success, and a slap to Jack's face, a recrimination in response to his vile behavior. How could he use a religion she pursued fervently for years to justify some endgame he envisioned for the two of them? No, she'd show Jack.

More footsteps outside the door. Was that fumbling at the doorknob?

Jack…has to be Jack! An irrational thought, yes, but one that felt right.

An instinct born from anxiety and experience moved her hand to the book; Mia lay her palm flat on the cover. It's all she'd need, just the smooth feel of the dust jacket to bring her back to last night. Perhaps Jack could have her physical body should he get inside Bruce's room, but never her mind. Or her soul. She felt the pull around her as she looked upward toward the edge of her vision, just like she had before.

A new keyword was needed now, something decidedly not religious, and the first thing to pop into her head was *freedom*. Mia repeated the word over and over. A moment of dizziness, then two things happened. Mia peered down at her body sitting in the chair, just like she had envisioned, and then the door to the room flew open. The air created by the movement pushed Mia away from her body like an astronaut flung away from a space station. She noticed a bright thread-like cord which stretched from her consciousness to her unconscious body down below. Looking the other direction Mia noticed that she was drifting toward the very bright orb in the corner of Bruce's room.

When the door to the room opened, Mia watched Bruce close it behind him and turn the deadbolt with a click. With wide eyes, he rushed to her form which was slumped on the table as if she was asleep.

Mia must have reached the end of her sparkling tether, because she bounced back toward her body and away from the orb that looked suspiciously like a tunnel. She floated in midair as if she possessed the ability to defy gravity.

Not Jack, Mia thought with relief. She really should reenter her body before Bruce got the wrong idea and called for an ambulance. He patted at her cheek as if to wake a sleeping child.

Mia could just make out his words.

"Mia, wake up," he said. "It's just me, Bruce."

With a swimming motion, she tried to move toward her waiting body, but the effort seemed harder than last night. Or, perhaps she had just floated further away. Last night, she'd only needed to leap back in. Right now, however, she not only needed to get back inside her body, but to first traverse the space between. The thrashing of her arms didn't seem to help. Part of the problem was that she could sense an invisible form of her body but couldn't see it. Mia continued to float in place, her movements dictated by the whim of an unseen current of wind or some other form of energy. It scared her.

Bruce shook her body in a gentle rocking motion. "Mia! Mia!"

He looked concerned, and she knew it was only a matter of time before he called someone. Then her parents would come. And Jack! *Pastor Matt.* They'd take her freedom, make decisions for her. *Unacceptable!*

Mia panicked, struggled harder, thrashed what she perceived as her arms and legs in the air as if it were water. She couldn't see her arms and legs, though, only the silverish-gold thread which connected her awareness to her body. What had she done? Would the bright tunnel suck her up into a portal?

Portal? Yes, that's how she viewed it., A tunnel which connected this place with…somewhere else. Mia didn't want to go anywhere else.

Get back inside that body where you belong!

On command, her awareness spilled ever so slightly toward her waiting flesh.

Yes, that's it. Go! Go!

The tether slackened as she floated downward.

Bruce wept. His shoulders shook with emotion. It made her feel good to see him care so much, and that increased her desire to join him physically, if for no other reason than to lessen his worries. But there were other reasons. She stared at him through the shimmering light that was so prevalent in this state of being. Bruce looked almost cherubic. Black t-shirt aside, she realized his heart was nowhere near that dark. She took in his unruly curls, slightly overweight frame and realized that she wanted him. Not because of his physical appearance, but because he would never seek to control her. Would, in fact, look to live side by side with her, to compliment her, but certainly not to change her. She loved him. Yes, even after this very short time, she could admit this.

Mia focused her thoughts on returning to her body. She glided toward it slowly, like floating on a cloud.

Almost there!

The moment she reentered her body, Mia would hug Bruce, kiss him on the lips, and beg him to forgive her for ditching him for Jack out in the quad. Then she felt a disturbance in the air behind her.

Mia glanced over her ghostly shoulder. A black missile of energy shot from the bright orb and grew as it approached. It morphed from long and cylindrical to wraith-like, a black demonic kite. This transformation took only seconds, and Mia braced herself for an impact which never came. The anomaly instead passed through her like a cold dagger. As it did, Mia felt hatred and malice. Not her own, but those of this spirit. The foreign emotion felt like a plague of unwelcome and dark energy which violated her mind, twisted her thoughts.

She felt rage, pure hatred, and if Jack had come into the room right then, she knew she could kill him. Not even just kill, but destroy, rend, puree. Visions of his blood covering her skin, soaking into her clothes, flashed through her consciousness. His eviscerated and bleeding corpse haunted the recesses of her most lurid thoughts. She knew without a doubt that this was the residual energy that had plagued her for so long—since she and a friend played with mom's Ouija board.

A mistake, she knew, a terrible mistake.

The spirit sailed through Mia, releasing her of its hate and malevolence, but jettisoned toward her waiting flesh. The dark shadow hesitated a moment, hovering in place, then darted forward and disappeared into the receptacle of her living body. The thing had passed right through the barrier of her tight young skin and into the place her consciousness should reside.

No...hell no!

Mia flailed toward her body. *No, no, no!* This was far worse than the fluttering of wings, the bad smells, and the threat of malevolent intent. *It's inside me. Like a dark parasite.*

Mia watched as her physical eyes fluttered open and locked on Bruce.

Screw you, Mia thought, then willed her essence toward her body. She'd fight this thing, pummel it from her flesh like stuffing from a pillow. Her energy hurled forward like a missile.

Just before Mia smashed into her own skin, she heard Bruce say, "Mia, thank God!"

Her consciousness made contact with her inhabited flesh. It felt like an electrical explosion, two vast energies colliding. A moment of disorientation, a whirling dizziness, then her consciousness returned. She tried to blink but felt no physical sensation. Instead of her flying in and the black mist pushing out, as she had hoped, Mia realized her conscious energy had bounced off her body like a drumstick off a drum-skin.

Her consciousness hurled outward and toward the bright orb. She could feel the pull of the portal, as if a giant vacuum was trying to suck her out of this realm and into the next. Panic wrapped her as Mia slipped dangerously close to the brilliant aurora. She feared reaching a point of no return. Mia tried grasping at the edges of the portal with ghostly arms, but they slid by, not slowing her momentum in the least. Is this how she would end her life? Did this portal lead to Heaven...or Hell? Mia felt unprepared. She should pray, but the words wouldn't come.

Please, God.

Mia flailed but found no purchase. Her head entered the corona of light. Dizziness overwhelmed her, and Mia didn't know if she was inside or outside the portal. For all she knew, she was on the highway to the great lake of fire...Just like Pastor Matt always preached would happen if she sinned.

Then she felt a tug, and her consciousness reversed to travel toward her body. The silver thread, which had pulled taut, now slackened as the tension lessened. With a herculean burst of energy, derived from God knew where, Mia willed herself to a stop so that she wouldn't repeat the process over and over in a Ground Hog's Day scenario. She hovered in place like a superhero. Then Mia finally noticed what her physical body was up to.

No, no, no!

CHAPTER 14

Bruce watched Mia's arm raise from the armrest as if in slow motion. Her wide eyes seemed to track the motion like she'd never performed the act before. She moved it back and forth, looking at the backside and then the palm in turn, finally raising the palm to her cheek and rubbing with a tentative motion. Then, as if it ran out of energy, her whole arm dropped to her side.

Despite her motor skill problems, Bruce felt such relief that his legs threatened to buckle, as if they were made of jelly instead of muscle and bone. He watched as Mia's eyes fluttered and scanned the room. A small smile played at her lips. Her eyes locked on his, but she didn't attempt to move.

"I-I'm so happy you're here, but I thought you were with Jack," he said. He looked around the room, suddenly wondering if the jock had followed her here. "Did he leave?"

Bruce didn't know why Jack was here, but he'd heard enough to know the guy wouldn't give up so easy. Mia must have ditched him and came here.

When she didn't answer him, he touched her cheek. "You okay?"

Mia blinked, but said nothing. Bruce wondered if she had hit her head. Her facial tics seemed more an involuntary function than a conscious effort. Something was wrong with Mia.

She didn't seem able to speak. Did she have a stroke? Did the stress of her situation with the supernatural and now Jack break her mind in some fundamental way?

A soft breath left her mouth which ended in a phlegmy rasp. A string of saliva slipped from the corner of her mouth to splatter on her right thigh. Gone were the tears that often plagued her eyes. In fact, those orbs appeared more intense than Bruce had ever seen them, the beautiful irises nearly eradicated by the pitch-black pupils. Veins of red snaked through the whites like worms. Her chest heaved with more exertion than Bruce thought sitting in a chair should warrant.

"Mia, are you okay?" he repeated. "Should I call for help?" He was worried about her. He hadn't liked the way Jack had treated Mia out in the quad and hoped this unresponsiveness wasn't due to the douchebag hurting her.

Mia didn't respond. Just the raspy breaths and intense stare.

Now what'd ya screw up, son? You break her? This is all your fault, just like your ma trading up and running out on us. Damn artist don't know how to keep a woman. Should go to tech school, learn some wrenchin'. Mechanics get laid.

"Shut up, old man," Bruce said. "Never asked you."

But he did hope this wasn't his fault in some small way. He could tell by now when Mia became anxious, and Jack had made her so when he appeared unexpectedly. He knew this beyond doubt. Yet he'd only watched as the two walked away, obviously in disagreement about something. Maybe he should have stood up to Jack. He'd felt so helpless, though, not wishing to intrude on a situation in which he wasn't involved. But he was involved, wasn't he? Mia had spent the night with him and had explained her desire to be free of Jack. Bruce put a large hand over his mouth, deep in thought. "Okay," he said to himself. "She came to your room". Hopefully that meant she trusted him and wanted his help. He hoped he could come through for her.

He noticed Mia's left hand still rested on top of Colista's book. He moved closer to Mia, looking her in the eye. Wondered if her catatonic state had something to do with astral projection. Mia had left her body last night, according to her, and perhaps she'd attempted the maneuver again.

"You in there?" he asked.

When Mia only continued to drool and stare, Bruce looked around the room and asked, "Or are you...out there?"

A rumble erupted from deep inside Mia's chest. Her hand flopped back to her lap like a land-locked fish. The appendage continued to squirm as if alive of its own power. A frustrated noise resounded from Mia's mouth as if the action stirred some sentiment within her. Bruce didn't feel comfortable with where the hand lay, as if it were nothing but a tool for pleasure as it rubbed her crotch.

Bruce carefully pulled her hand away and allowed it to hang next to her body. "Pretty sure that's not where you wanted your hand." He shook his head. "I really don't know what to do."

He supposed he should call for help, but if she left her body and this ended up as the result, then a doctor wouldn't do much good. Yet, if she remained in her body...

Mia made a small fussing noise from deep in her throat and then, like a frustrated child Bruce thought, tried to heave her hand back to her middle. The appendage swung next to her, useless to whatever impulse inside her wished it otherwise.

Bruce scowled at Mia's hand, then scanned his room again. "Mia, if you're outside of your body, can you give me a sign of your presence?" He didn't know if that was possible for someone outside their body, but he'd heard the ghost guys on TV say things like that. Bruce wasn't even sure if she would be considered a ghost in that scenario. Maybe they weren't a ghost until they died and their energy became unmoored. "Mia?"

Mia's body rumbled, again, something a bit too close to a growl for Bruce's tastes, and her arm continued to try to hoist her closed fist up into her lap.

Bruce shook his head. "Good Lord," he said, and wished he knew what to do. Her body seemed alive as it tried to move and do things a human would normally do, just not very well, and not like how Mia would do them.

Then two things happened quickly, one just before the other. First, one of his prized possessions, a model of the Millennium Falcon, the only thing he and his father ever built together, fell off the top shelf of his bookcase and crashed to the floor. Before Bruce could process this development, an aggressive knock came at his door.

"Open up in there!" Bruce knew at once who the voice belonged to. A voice that aggressive and confident was hard to forget.

Growls continued to rumble from Mia's human form as if she were a dog, then more pounding from the door. Bruce looked from one to the other, then back to the Millennium Falcon which lay in pieces on the thin carpet.

What to do?

He didn't care to answer the door. Jack would, no doubt, beat him within an inch of his life. The dude looked strong, stood six feet, and possessed the smooth flawless skin only money could buy. Not to mention the chiseled athlete's body, the kind that always made Bruce feel less sure of himself. And the perfect hair, with formed cornrows which appeared as though the guy released them from their bondage every day to shampoo the hair before rebinding.

He's a better man than you, son. He'll be wanting the woman back that you borrowed from him. Bet your sweet ass on that one. Artists don't get laid; jocks and mechanics do.

Bruce supposed avoidance wouldn't work forever, so he may as well answer the door. But he knew, when Jack saw Mia in her current state, he'd go ballistic. Probably work Bruce over like a rabid wolf would a red squirrel.

"I know you're in there, and I'm not leaving until you open up. I know you have Mia in there, too. I just want to speak to her. I'm her boyfriend."

"She doesn't want to talk to you," Bruce said.

Mia responded with a moan and a drip of saliva. Her eyes were a perfect black, her hand still useless at her side, but she continued the old college try. Her fingers waved back and forth as if she tried to feel for something that wasn't there. Bruce thought she'd made some progress with her coordination. As if whatever resided inside Mia had now gotten a feel for how this kind of body-manipulation worked.

"I'd like to hear that from her," Jack shouted back.

"Um, now's not a great time," Bruce said. "She's indisposed."

Was that what people said nowadays when someone was in the bathroom? He hoped it sounded okay, although he held out almost no hope that Jack would consider it a good reason not to demand entry to his room.

"So, she's in there," Jack said with a triumphant blat. He began to pound again, and not the gentle sort one may expect from a stranger.

"Well, yes," Bruce said. He knew it sounded lame. He attempted to bolster his voice, "She told me to tell you to go away."

Even more lame!

The door shook in the jamb as the guy on the other side rammed into it, probably with one of those side-of-beef shoulders.

"Mia!" Jack shouted. "Just come out so we can talk. We can work this out. I know you want your freedom and all that, but let's talk this out."

How could Bruce let the guy enter with Mia in this condition? She couldn't speak to him, yet Bruce had to do something. His choices were horrible at best. Either wait until Jack left, call someone for help and try to slip them into the room without Jack squeezing his ass in, or just open the door now and get the confrontation over with.

Someone might call campus security if Jack kept up, but Bruce doubted it. He'd heard louder parties that never got busted. Most people just tuned this kind of thing out. He could call security himself, but how would he explain Mia's condition even if they did drag Jack off.

Mia moaned like a quiet zombie.

Jack continued to pound on the door.

Bruce finally cracked. A lightning-bolt of craziness hit him, a desire to get this shit over with. He strode toward the door, donned his best pissed-off scowl, then flung the door open without preamble.

Jack, right smack in the middle of a shoulder slam, fell through the doorway like a blind man off a cliff.

Now, what should I do?

Jack lay sprawled on the floor for now, but that would change soon, and then the dude would open a can of the whoop-ass on Bruce. Maybe Bruce should just kick him in the rib cage, maybe even the head. Strike Jack while he was still down, get a head start on the fight. He felt justified in this, because of the inequity in their physiques.

He must have stared too long without action, because Jack scowled as he picked himself up. "I should put my fist through your face for that, dough-boy." Then he looked and noticed Mia sitting in Bruce's office chair. "But I won't. You know, the other cheek and all that." Then he fell silent, mouth unhinged, and walked toward his girlfriend. "What have you done to her?"

"Why would I have done anything?" Bruce asked. "Ironically, she came here to hide from you, who I may add, she was afraid would *do* something to her."

He wasn't one-hundred percent sure, but this scenario made sense. Mia had gotten away from Jack's greedy mitts, then headed to the one place she thought the dude would never look. Too bad she'd introduced him by name, because Jack had probably noticed the direction she headed, then checked mailboxes with room numbers.

"Is that what she said?" Jack asked. He didn't look like he believed it.

"No," Bruce started, "In all fairness, she hasn't said anything."

At that moment, Mia moaned, and a strand of saliva unmoored itself from the corner of her pouty lips and landed on her hoodie. Her eyes appeared glazed and didn't seem to track either Bruce or Jack.

Jack put his hands on his hips and glared at Bruce. The douche even tapped his foot.

"Look, man," Bruce said. "She was here when I got back. Like this."

"Yeah, right," Jack said. "You expect me to believe that?" He looked around at all Bruce's metal and horror posters. "I wouldn't exactly peg you as a quality individual, just saying. Let me guess, you guys smoked a little pot and you laced Mia's with a little something-something extra, am I right?"

"Leave me out of your filthy daydreams," Bruce said and folded his arms over his torso. "I would never do anything to hurt Mia. I care about her for more than her body, or to have someone to control. Like you do."

"You just assuming that, or has Mia been flapping her gums about me?" He frowned, obvious to Bruce that he was trying to determine a course of action that didn't involve making himself look bad, yet that would still get him what he wanted.

"We talk a lot," Bruce said. Then, without thinking the words through much, he blurted, "Right there on my bed." He pointed to the mess of sheets and blankets.

As if in immediate response, the lightbulb in Bruce's desk-lamp shattered into bits of white jagged glass which fell to the desktop and skidded over his laptop.

Jack looked from Bruce to the desk and back, his eyes a flurry of movement. Then he took a step forward. "Who do you think you are, sleeping with another man's girl?" He took another step, fists balled at his sides.

Bruce heard the malice in his voice, the jealousy. "Well, not in the biblical sense…"

"In whatever sense, doesn't matter," Jack said. "I'm finding it real hard to keep my peaceful center here. She must have told you she had a boyfriend, and you decided to pursue her anyway." He looked at Mia. "And to drug her. Is this how you lured her in, with drugs?"

"I did no such thing," Bruce said. "I already told you, I found her this way. Go ahead and call the cops if you don't believe me. They won't find any drugs in her system."

"That what you do, dough-boy?" Jack said. "Take advantage of innocent freshmen and turn them into blithering idiots?"

"Call the cops then," Bruce said. "We'll see what they say. All I know is that I don't think she wants to go with you. And I won't let you take her."

"She doesn't know what's best for herself," Jack said. "The proof is sitting right in that chair. She needs to go back home where she can be looked after by her family and church."

"And you, right?" Bruce asked. "Let's not forget about the fact you enjoy the whole control element, want to keep Mia under your thumb." Bruce felt on a roll and little braver than he did before. "Did you even know she loves to knit, and that sometimes she cries for no reason at all, that she has anxiety issues?"

"Of course, I know; she bawls like a baby all the time. Uses it to get her way. As for the knitting, she'll find out what a waste of time that is once we start building our family. She'll have more important things to tend to."

"You're an asshole," Bruce said and could not think of more appropriate words to describe him. Simple and true.

Just as Jack took another aggressive step forward, the light bulb on the ceiling above him blew and rained frosted glass onto his head. Jack shook the glass out of his cornrows, then looked up. "What the hell is wrong with your electricity around here?"

"You wouldn't believe me if I told ya," Bruce said, arms still folded.

He found himself peering about the room to catch a glimpse of Mia's energy as she flitted about. The Falcon falling, the light bulbs, it had to be Mia trying to communicate with him. He wanted to see her, maybe get on the same page and determine what she wished him to do with Jack.

"What do you mean, I wouldn't believe you?" Jack asked, face scrunched up in a sneer, eyes black, nostrils in a perpetual flare. He looked as though he might put two and two together at some point. "Try me." He brushed the remaining bits of glass from his head.

Bruce sighed. He decided to go with his initial assumption that the exploding light bulbs were a result of Mia's efforts to communicate. The Falcon fell right before he went to open the door to let Jack in. The bulbs shattered when the guy said horrible things. Yeah, Bruce felt he could surmise some stuff, at the very least. But what should he tell Jack?

Then he thought of something.

Bruce pointed at Mia's body in the chair. Whatever consciousness lay within had resumed trying to get her hand in her lap. "Mia is like that because she is no longer inside her body. Thus, the light bulbs."

"You're high, too?" A puff of air passed through his lips that may have been a laugh. "That said...I have no clue what the fuck you're talking about." He pointed at Mia. "Mia is right there. She sure as hell didn't break any light bulbs."

"Her energy is outside of her body," Bruce said, then walked over to his writing desk and picked up Colista's book. "She learned to leave her body."

Another bulb blew out of the lamp over by Bruce's bed.

Bruce realized, too late, that Mia hadn't wanted him to tell Jack about that. But what else could he tell the guy? He couldn't let him keep on thinking he'd drugged Mia.

"See?" Bruce said.

Jack glanced at the lamp which was now reduced to one lonely bulb, then looked back at Bruce. "You're saying Mia broke that bulb? Like with her mind?" He looked at Mia who now attempted to stand without much success. "She looks like a stroke victim, not someone who can shatter glass with her mind."

Bruce watched as Mia's body tried to rise, her ass rocking forward then back in repetitive motions. She did look feeble. This saddened him, because he cared for her and wanted to help. He wasn't sure exactly what the issue was here, but a plan started to develop in his mind.

Jack took the book from Bruce. He read the cover then the back. "Oh, man, her old man and Pastor Matt aren't gonna like this shit." He glanced to Mia, then to Bruce. "I'm not saying I believe any of this, but if she's been messing around with the occult, the church won't like that."

"You go to Mia's church?" Bruce thought Mia mentioned that Jack didn't attend church, that he said he thought it was for suckers.

"No," Jack said as he scratched at the light stubble on his chin. "But I'm going to. I realize now it's the only way to stay with Mia. I need her dad and his wacko pastor behind me. They'll encourage her to marry me if I get all churchy and shit."

"That's manipulative," Bruce said. "Why don't you just go back to your own college and your football scholarship and let me worry about Mia, okay?"

"Not gonna happen. I already dropped out and signed up at the Bible college in our hometown. The plan is to get her to do the same, but right now... I don't know. She's pretty jacked up."

Bruce couldn't believe it. "You would really give up everything, your hopes and dreams, your football career, just to keep Mia under your thumb?"

Jack nodded in what Bruce considered a maniacal fashion. "Yeah, man. I would. See how much I care? Now I gotta figure out how to get her back to normal. Can't bring her home like this." He walked up to Mia and held out his hand. "Can you stand up?"

Mia continued to rock and drool.

"Shit," Jack whispered.

Bruce made up his mind. Only one person could help Mia. And he'd have to tell Jack about it, because the guy just wasn't going to go away and let Bruce take her himself. "We need to take her to Professor Colista."

"What?" Jack asked, eyes wide and white. "You mean the asshat who wrote this book? Are you kidding me? She either needs a chemical dependency counselor or a shrink, not some deranged occult weirdo."

A bulb above the bathroom vanity popped and rained debris into the sink.

Jack snapped his head in that direction, then slowly turned and looked at Mia. He shook his head. Then he looked at Bruce. "So, you're saying Mia did that."

Bruce nodded. "Yes. Her energy, which is trapped outside her body, did."

Jack snapped his head back to Mia who now bobbed up and down, trying to rise. The guy frowned and shook his head. "Then who's that?"

Bruce shrugged. "Good question. A spirit, maybe. Mia's been having some problems with one. It might have slipped inside her." He was guessing here, but Bruce felt it an educated one.

Jack scrunched up his eyes in confusion, and Bruce knew he had no clue about Mia's past experiences. "So, you're saying this spirit possessed her?" Jack put his hands on his hips.

Bruce shrugged and nodded.

"What's a spirit want with Mia?" Jack asked. "Forget it; I don't even wanna know. Man, this is all effed up. Her dad and Pastor Matt are gonna kill me."

"Colista is our only hope," Bruce said. "Let's put our differences aside and help Mia." He held out his rather large hand.

Jack ignored the gesture, then shook his head and let out an irritated breath. "Fine. I'll go along with this for now, but if this dude screws things up even further, I'm calling Mia's folks and Pastor Matt."

"Fine," Bruce agreed, because it was the only way to keep Mia here and not have Jack take her. He just hoped Colista would know how to handle this.

CHAPTER 15

Colista sat in his chair, swiveled away from the desk, elbows on knees. He knew some would say he looked like a gargoyle ready to pounce. It's how he thought best, in this position, the energy in his body more concentrated and focused. He took a series of deep breaths and exhaled each slowly to take full advantage of the life-giving element of air. He would need his wits. He felt it, like one may feel a rather nasty storm approaching. His spirit guide said as much, but he didn't even need the heads-up for that situation.

That strong, he thought. And that could only mean one thing. Trouble with a capital T.

It would come in the form of Mia. The way she slunk off, scolded, boyfriend of old pressed to her side like a yappy, possessive mutt. All that besides the fact she was harboring an attachment. He'd seen it a hundred times. Kid plays with a Ouija board, and that same kid gets an attachment which manifests in the late teen years, once their hormone levels run berserk. Colista could burn the little hanger-on off with little problem. However, in all his years, he'd never run across a student who took to astral projection with the ferocity in which Mia had. She'd seen it rush at her, try to enter her body. No, she hadn't said those words, but Colista noticed it all the same. And now...

Crowley arched and hissed at Colista's feet. The cat gazed toward the door, expectant and wary.

Lovely.

"So, it begins."

He stood and walked to the window beside the door, his large feet gliding over the dark hardwood. A gasp escaped his open mouth. Trouble didn't often come to find him but here it had stumbled right to his front door. All Mia's problems had caught up with her. The haunted young woman alternated between a feeble stumble and being dragged between the old and the new love interests. How they all had come together would make for an interesting story, no doubt.

Good Lord!

Crowley got up off the blanket he was napping on, then made his way toward the spell room by the bookshelves as if the cat knew what would come next. Colista noticed the bushed tail and raised hackles.

"Yes, Crowley," Colista whispered. "Yes, we will have company. Wise to be ready, indeed."

Colista backed away from the window in the small hope they would yet pass his abode by, perhaps stumble toward the lake and try to baptize the girl to rid her of the vermin on their own. When footfalls approached his front door, he took another tentative step backward. Only when Crowley yowled, a reminder of his duties, did Colista reach for the doorknob. Better to appear clairvoyant than ill-prepared. He whipped the door open.

"What took you so long?" Colista admonished. "She looks almost dead, already. Get her in here."

"It's inside, and..." Bruce stammered.

"I know full well what has transpired," Colista spat. He stared at both young men with impudence. "And it's no thanks to either of you, I hate to say. You drove her to this, you know. Selfish boys who fight over a young woman like she's a bone should find themselves ashamed—ashamed indeed. Bring her this way."

"I think she's on drugs," Jack said, voice bold and determined.

"Is she now?" Colista said. "And just what would you know about that sort of thing? You witness a lot of that where you go to college? I surmise this, because I haven't seen you around here."

"Everyone knows what someone on drugs looks like," the young man said, a scowl plastered to his full lips which Colista detested.

Colista knew the archetype: possessive athletic. The ladies should just fall all over themselves to end up with them. And when they didn't, it was the girl who had the problem. He'd seen it so often it almost seemed cliché.

"They do, huh?" Colista stared the youth in the eye. "So, then why did you bring her here? Do I look like a counselor to you? Am I running a halfway house for dimwitted drug-addicted college students?"

A long strand of saliva slopped from Mia's mouth and fell to the ancient hardwood floor, followed by a slur of unintelligible consonants. Colista also noticed the dilation of her pupils as the darkness all but eclipsed the blue. The eyeballs twitched back and forth as if they sought escape.

"Perhaps a stroke," Bruce said.

Colista's eyes snapped to Bruce's. "You, of all people, should know better than that. Get her to the davenport. I shall do what I can for her."

"Yeah," Bruce said. "Just covering the bases. Exploring every contingency."

Colista grunted and took a closer look at Mia's face.

"You're not a pedophile, are you?" Jack asked. "I'm responsible for Mia. I promised her dad...and Pastor Matt." The guy looked to Bruce then back to Colista. "I mean, you're obviously not a quality individual." He then gawked at the shelf of crystal skulls by the doorway to the kitchen. When Colista only stared, he continued, "Just figured you might not hesitate to take advantage of a pretty girl. So, sure, we'll put her on the couch there, but no funny business."

"Colista is a professional educator," Bruce said. "I don't think he's going to hurt her. No need to worry."

Colista scowled and dug a cigarette out of the pack in his pocket. He stabbed the thing between his lips and lit it with a silver lighter with a gold cherub on the body. The smell of flint permeated his nostrils and somewhat reduced the smell of teen angst.

Here we go!

Just as Colista inhaled, the guy said, "Oh, I'm still going to worry. I have too much time invested in Mia not to." A contemplative look spread across Jack's features. "This needs to work out." He looked Colista in the eye. "And just because you don't want Mia sexually doesn't mean you won't fuck her up with your mumbo jumbo." He took an aggressive step toward Colista, raising a fist as if to communicate his seriousness.

With a steady hand, Colista plucked the cigarette from his lips. It made a smacking sound as he inhaled one last time to charge the bright-red cherry. With a quick stroke, as if throwing a dart, he pressed the burning end into Jack's jugular. The scent of burning flesh smelled pungent and sweet. Colista smiled with tight lips. Hopefully that would, as the kids say, slow the asshole's roll.

The young man screamed and swatted the cigarette away like he may a fly. He glared at Colista with challenging eyes, but stayed silent except for a few pain-filled mewls.

Without Jack's support, Mia swung toward Bruce who now bore her full weight. He held tight and walked her teetering form toward the davenport. She fought him a bit, Colista noticed. But not enough. No, whatever resided inside of her, it must still be too weak, because it hadn't taken full control.

"Crowley, on your guard," Colista said in a calm tone.

Jack held a palm over his scorched throat but tracked Mia and Bruce with wide white eyes. Colista noticed how his chest heaved with internal turmoil.

The cat approached Mia and Bruce, its padded feet making soft noises on the floor. It peered at them as if supervising, then mewled in agreement as Bruce lay her on the plush cushions.

Colista pointed an as of yet unlit cigarette at his nemesis. He would never suffer a bully, having endured enough of that in his youth for ten lifetimes. "As for you," he said, less calm. "Threaten me again and you'll receive much worse. Now get over here. Hold Mia still...but not too hard."

Hand still on his neck and a painful wince on his face, Jack complied by walking toward Mia. When out of reach of the cigarette, Jack said, "Being gay is a sin."

"Is it, now?" Colista asked, busy with his work. He collected several colors of sidewalk chalk and two large saltshakers from a wide wicker basket next to the kitchen door. "And where did you read that? Your Bible?"

"Everyone knows that," Jack said.

"Do they?" Colista asked, distracted. "Seems like an antiquated sentiment in today's climate. But I should expect no less from the likes of you." He glared at Jack. "It doesn't seem to appear in the Ten Commandments. Funny about that. Not mentioned in the very document pulled from a burning bush on a very high mountain. God, so we're taught, went through a great deal of trouble to deliver those commandments, yet nowhere does it mention homosexuality within the text."

"He's not really a Christian like Mia," Bruce said, who wiped Mia's brow with a handkerchief.

A loving gesture, Colista thought.

He looked at Jack. "Let me guess. You find Christianity a useful tool for control. Nothing like using a pretty girl's faith against her to get what you want." He pointed the cigarette at Jack. "You are a narcissistic prick. She's better off with Bruce by a long measure."

A beatific smile erupted on Bruce's face. *So easily pleased*, Colista thought.

Mia reacted with a growl from deep inside her throat and Colista wondered which love interest the demon inside her would prefer. He hoped to never find out.

Crowley jumped to the back of the davenport as if on an important mission.

Jack took his hand off the ugly red welt, checked the palm of his hand for residue, and then crossed his arms. "Do what you're gonna do. But if you screw up, just a little, I'm gonna call Mia's family. They'll bring Pastor Matt."

"Not Pastor Matt," Colista said, enjoying the tone of his own voice. He then gathered his supplies and approached Mia.

Mia felt empty and it had more to do with Jack's bigoted behavior than the fact she couldn't reenter her own body. Any sexual preference that didn't agree with his had always seemed like a threat to Jack's own masculinity. She couldn't quite remember why she ever fell for someone like him in the first place. A small town, the desire for a modicum of popularity maybe. Forgivable, she supposed.

She watched as Bruce wiped her face, his gaze loving and pure, the touches tender. *What a guy!* Jack, on the other hand, held her feet in an iron grip and scowled at Colista like a big crybaby.

Colista is right, Jack is a prick.

The entity rebelled against what Colista and Crowley the cat were up to. It writhed inside of her. She could see it jerking about, leaving and then reentering her *flesh*. The silver thread still connected Mia to her body, but the part adjacent to her body possessed a tarnished hue, as if the creature inside had contaminated it. She hoped the corruption wouldn't spread.

The bright orb of light sat above her like a tiny sun. It seemed to beckon to her, and although she'd already learned how to maneuver her energy around, the tether which bound her would not allow her to move too far away. She got the impression it possessed an elasticity, but so far, she found it difficult to summon the strength to stretch it.

"I think Mia might still be outside of her body," Bruce pointed out. "Back in my room, things happened. Several lightbulbs broke. And one of my models fell off a shelf. I think she's trying to communicate."

"Of course she is," Colista said, and continued drawing a chalk circle around the davenport. The antique had been blessed by an archbishop and had proven successful on a consistent basis. "She left her body to escape Jack. This isn't a possession; it's a hijacking. The spirit she encountered in her youth, unless I miss my guess."

"Whadya mean, to escape me?" Jack said.

Colista shot him a look but stayed silent. Mia knew how Colista must feel: there's just no informing the ignorant.

"Give me a break," Bruce said. "If you don't understand by now that she didn't want to see you, then you're a fool."

Right on, Mia thought. *Tell him, Bruce.*

Mia was pleased both Bruce and Colista understood the situation. They wouldn't leave her alone with Jack. Who knew what he would do to her in this state? Jack from the outside, the creature from within. Mia's energy shuddered.

Mia didn't want anyone to have control over her—not anymore. Not ever again. For good measure, Mia willed her energy toward an antique glass lamp on a table adjacent to the couch. As she'd taught herself, Mia reached out with her powers and flicked the bulb. Glass shards exploded and fell to the floor.

"See!" Bruce said.

"No need to ruin the antiques, I'm sure," Colista said as he started another chalk circle just outside the first. "I know you're out there, Mia."

Crowley pawed at Mia's physical neck, then stuck his snout into her mouth. *Ew,* Mia thought. *Good thing she liked cats and trusted Colista.*

Mia watched the shadow beast within her body writhe and thrash as if in pain. It didn't care for the cat at all, and she wondered why. Mia thought she'd heard somewhere cats were the gatekeepers to the underworld, but she thought that was all hogwash. At least, she used to. She'd been taught to stay clear of the occult since she was young. And she had, except for that one time.

"Easy Crowley," Colista said. "No need to crawl inside her. What if she's allergic to you? Then we have more problems."

Crowley backed off, but shot a disappointed look at Colista.

Colista rolled his dark eyes. "They are sometimes, you know."

The cat meeped, ears flat, but remained diligent with eyes glued to Mia's face.

"Keep the furball away from her or I will," Jack said, looking anxious, his eyes bloodshot from the pain Colista inflicted.

Colista shot Jack a look and he shut up.

Both circles complete, Colista scrawled symbols between the two chalk lines. A pattern of shapes materialized as he drew. Mia wondered what purpose they would serve.

Jack took one hand off Mia's ankles and pointed at the design. "What kind of mumbo-jumbo is that? Pretty sure Pastor Matt wouldn't approve. Looks like Devil-worship crap."

He touched his neck and winced as if Colista reached out and flicked the red boil with his mind. Mia wished she had enough energy to scorch him further.

"Nothing could be further from the truth," Colista murmured. "But go call your precious pastor. Having you out of my hair would be a tremendous delight."

No! Mia thought.

As much as she thought herself through with the narrowminded views of her church, the thought of Pastor Matt seeing her in this condition worried her. She could just imagine the church-discipline that would ensue. Pastor Matt had formulated an approach he claimed he pulled from several religious texts. The discipline was meant to shame the individual into modifying their behavior to the liking of the church. He would make them confront her, only three members of the congregation at first. They would speak to her about abandoning whatever behavior they deemed unholy. If that amount of intimidation didn't sway her, they'd thrust her upon the full congregation, so they could all throw their metaphysical rocks at her. Mia could see herself standing at the podium as, one by one, each parishioner admonished her like a woman at the Salem witch trials.

"I am curious," Bruce said as he watched Colista. "Is this like a spell? I mean, you know, I don't say that out of disrespect... Quite the opposite, actually." He continued to mop Mia's brow.

Colista continued to scribble. "If you must know, I am drawing the seventy-two portents of the seventy-two demons mentioned in the Goetia, derived from *The Lesser Key of Solomon*. Mia is a Christian, so we shall use a Christian solution in this case, despite the fact I doubt it is a demon which inhabits her."

Demons? Mia thought. *Oh, God!*

She already knew the thing inside of her wasn't good, but the fact it could be a fallen angel mentioned in the Bible hadn't yet occurred to her. That's not what Colista thought this was, but still. What would Pastor Matt think she'd been up to? She'd never worshipped the Devil, but that's what the congregation would assume astral projection and Ouija boards were all about. Pastor always preached along those lines, and now the church would hold her accountable to her actions. The orb above her burned even brighter, an accusing eye. Her silver tether was now tarnished even further.

"What are you trying to accomplish?" Jack said. "I doubt you even believe in God."

Colista stopped and looked up at Jack. "Do you? Now, watch your tone before I wipe that sneer off your face." He waited for Jack to comply. "But if you must know, this should bind the spirit inside Mia to the confines of this circle until I figure out the best ritual to remove it."

"Hogwash. She's messed up on drugs, is all. You'll see." Jack glanced at Bruce. "Or you already know. Either way, Pastor Matt will know what to do. The rest of this, the lightbulbs and the rituals, are all just stupid parlor tricks. A child could see through them."

"Not your child, Jack," Colista said without looking up.

He kept drawing. Symbols now graced over half the circumference between the two circles. Colista drew with a practiced hand.

Mia giggled, or, at least, felt like she did. Colista was the first person, kid or adult, she'd ever heard talk back to Jack. Most people kissed his athletic ass, told him how good he was. Even her. But Colista could see through his sham, had probably seen it a million times before. Mia hoped Colista would continue to expose Jack as the immature chauvinist he was.

The anti-Bruce.

"That's it," Jack exclaimed. Mia knew his pride had been bruised. This never ended well. "I didn't agree to bring Mia here just to get ridiculed. I'm taking her out of here. I'll take her to a hospital to get her stomach pumped like I should have in the first place. I can't believe I fell for this even for a moment."

Bruce took a step toward him. "Like hell you will."

Mia could see the tremor in Bruce's hands, the involuntary twitch of his eyes, the nervousness poking through his facade, but his intense eyes told her that he would follow through with whatever action he'd decided upon.

Please, Mia pleaded. She wanted to stay here with Bruce. She had never felt so cared about before in her life. Mia also trusted Colista, and his arcane wisdom, to help her. If Jack was allowed to take her to the emergency room, they wouldn't know what to do, perhaps do more harm than good. Then it occurred to her that Jack may not even take her to the hospital at all, but right to her dad and Pastor Matt.

"What you gonna do about it, dough-boy?" Jack folded his arms over his chest so that his biceps bulged.

Mia had seen him use this technique of intimidation before.

Bruce took another step, his chest stuck out in a brave gesture, then more steps until he stood between Mia and Jack.

Mia thought Bruce looked a parody of a hero, but he was her hero, and she'd take it. She would accept his chivalry with all her heart, and if she ever got out of this mess, Mia would tell him as much. She'd kiss him and tell him how much she cared for him.

Jack balled his hand into a fist as he walked. The gleam in his eye told Mia about the violence to come. Jack was only a coward when he thought his opponent superior. "I'm taking her, fats."

"Over my dead body," Bruce said, his right hand a trembling fist.

Colista finished his symbols and stood. "Away from my business, both of you. Go fight over Mia outside, but leave me to my infernal business."

Jack lunged toward Mia, but Bruce pushed his shoulders back.

"Get out of my way," Jack said. "She's mine. Pastor Matt promised me that much."

Mia noticed the hesitation. *He's nothing but a common bully!*

Jack liked to talk tough when there was no one to stand up to him. And until now, no one had. Yet here was Bruce standing firm. She could tell Jack was having trouble figuring out how to get what he wanted. What on God's green Earth did Jack mean about Pastor Matt? She knew he'd spoken to him, that he'd gotten some advice, but did her pastor really tell Jack that she belonged to him, that he could just do as he pleased? Mia knew her church was male-centric to the extreme, but how far would things go?

Mia's physical body watched the altercation with interest. She surmised the entity inside of her wanted Jack to win. Whatever the case, the tarnish near the base of the silver thread hadn't grown in a few minutes, perhaps stymied by Colista's efforts.

"Your Pastor Matt holds no dominion here," Colista said. "I, as an adult faculty member, have taken responsibility for Mia until such time as her parents arrive. Until then, that means I decide what is best. And if you don't both leave, I'll simply call the police. She can't be moved beyond the confines of my boundaries."

Jack grimaced and touched the wound on his neck, weighing his options.

Bruce didn't relax but used the moment to wedge himself further between Jack and her body on the davenport. He looked less nervous, his eyes more confident.

Colista, keeping an eye on Jack, bent down with two saltshakers and poured a combination of black and white granules between the lines, on top of the symbols. Mia's body growled deep in her chest until Crowley smacked her cheek with a clawless paw.

The creature fell silent.

Jack's chest heaved with frustration and uncertainty. He looked from Colista, to Mia, to the door several times as if to decide on a course of action. She could tell he would do nothing. Could see it as plain as his well-groomed cornrows. But he would go call her parents.

So be it.

"Why can't she be moved?" Jack asked, and Mia knew he only asked so he could tell her parents and Pastor Matt. He wanted all the ammunition he could get, so she hoped Colista would keep his answers close to the vest.

Colista looked up at Jack. "Are you still here? If you must know, the spirit inside of Mia, although probably an insipid little fool with zero experience, will eventually figure out how to gain better motor control over her body. When that happens…well, we don't want that. Now go and leave me to my work."

Oh, God! Mia thought. *I'm so dead.*

She just knew Jack would call dad and he would pull her from college and make her return home. Dad, with the encouragement of Pastor Matt, would take all this as a sign of God's will. Mia knew, though, it would just be an excuse to get their hooks in her, keep her in the church, a member of the congregation. Jack would propose and her dad would love it, and hope for her to pump out some *good little cult soldiers*. Mom would stay silent, as usual. In a moment of panic, she wished Colista to make a mistake, to accidentally cut that thin silver cord and allow her energy to drift off into that beautiful orb of light.

So, peaceful…

"I won't leave her alone with you." Jack stared at Colista who didn't bother to even look up.

"Bruce," Colista said as he continued to apply what Mia thought looked like black and white salt to the space between the circles, "call the police, please."

A rush of air came from between Jack's lips. Mia could see he was more scared of the cops than he was Colista and Bruce. If she knew Jack, and Mia did, he probably carried a couple blunts in each pocket of his pants. He always said it relaxed him before big games and what bigger game existed for Jack than this? This was the rest of his life. Jack's competitive nature would never allow him to give up.

"Sure," Bruce said and walked toward the phone on the desk. "Can I stay and help?"

"If you keep your mouth shut," Colista said. "I need a credible witness for whatever lie Jack makes up, anyway."

Jack walked to the door, glaring at Colista over his shoulder. "You haven't heard the last of this. Not by a long shot. You have no idea who you're dealing with here."

"Oh, I think I have a pretty good idea," Colista said. "Bruce?"

Bruce picked up the receiver and looked at the keypad.

Mia smiled from within her energy. It felt so right to see Jack scramble like this, like all those times she'd watched him get flushed from the pocket and run from those defensive linemen like his life depended on it. She'd always secretly relished those moments, and this proved no different.

Jack opened the door and stepped outside. "I'm going, but I'll be back with Mia's parents…and Pastor Matt. They'll get Mia back for me." Then he slammed the door shut.

"Bruce," Colista said. This time he looked up. "If you really call the police, I'll ring your neck. We have much to do and very little time in which to accomplish it."

Bruce hung up the phone with a wicked smile.

Mia relaxed for a moment, now that Jack had made his exit. She hoped Colista could get this thing out of her body and her back in before her parents got here. If they found her in this condition, all would be lost.

CHAPTER 16

Colista sat at his desk with a weathered copy of the *Ars Goetia* beneath his gaze, and Bruce watched with an intense curiosity. He couldn't sleep, anyway, and God knew he'd tried. After an hour, he knew he wouldn't be able to. But Bruce didn't want to disturb Mia's rest, so he glanced in her direction with only a slight turn of his head. The very essence of the kind of fiction he preferred to both read and write lay on that couch.

A Blatty book come to life.

Colista had explained Mia wasn't possessed, only blocked from reentering her body. The professor believed this fact would prove a boon to their cause as he entrenched himself in his readings. This way she'll find a way to help herself when the time comes.

She'd better be able to, boy, because you're a sorry excuse for a hero, his dad said in his head. *If you were half a man, you'd crawl right over to that fancy couch and...*

"Shut up, old man," Bruce said under his breath.

Lotta good your way of handling relationships worked out for you.

He felt bad for this thought. His mother leaving them had destroyed the old man, sent him into a spiral from which he'd never recovered. He drank now, a lot, and spat nasty opinions about his mother and loved to push Bruce so that he would never get hurt as bad as he had. Well, dad wasn't the only one who got hurt when Mom left, and Bruce, despite this misfortune, would never live his life like some bitter old man.

Bruce glanced at Mia lying on the davenport. While he'd never approach her in this condition, the voice of his father hit the nail on the head: *you don't deserve her.*

Mia looked gorgeous, even while possessed or whatever she was. Sure, she hadn't smiled since the thing took control, but she still looked like perfection to him.

However, she did look different. Even her sad eyes looked hard and unreadable, both pupils nothing but large black pits. Her hair was stringy from perspiration, and Bruce could smell the sweat on her body. Despite all this, he already cared deeply for her.

He just hoped she felt the same way. If Colista wasn't sitting a few yards away, he would talk to her energy, so she didn't feel so alone. He glanced around the room in hopes of somehow seeing her essence. If nothing else, he could wink at her, so she knew how he felt. Maybe she could even read his mind! Frantically, he tried to recall if he'd thought anything unsavory by accident. Convinced he hadn't, he continued to look around the room.

The cat sat on the back of the couch like a loaf, paws curled beneath it. It stared at Mia's body with a spooky diligence that shook Bruce. Crowley looked as though he was waiting for something. Dinner, perhaps. For the spirit to fling itself from Mia's body and attack? Something. It didn't even blink, just kept looking on with big eyes, lizard pupils as black as night.

Bruce had read somewhere that a cat was basically a lizard with a cerebral cortex and fur. Yet, it served some purpose in Colista's world. A familiar, Bruce thought. Wasn't that the word? The helper of someone who delved in the occult. Perhaps Crowley was a well-seasoned familiar that would prove an asset in delivering Mia from the clutches of this spirit.

Colista mumbled, then scrawled words onto the notepad beside him. Bruce felt the urge to look over the man's shoulder but fought it. Leave the work to the professionals.

That's right, boy. This man has skill like your old pap. Unlike you. Only difference is he tinkers with spirit manifestations and I tinker with grease and metal. Yessir, mechanics and occult specialists get laid.

Bruce found this internal monologue ironic given the circumstance but decided not to argue with himself. He looked at the clock and realized with a shock that at least two hours had passed since Jack left. He wanted Colista to hurry up, before the jock returned with reinforcements.

"An open portal must still exist," Colista mumbled, then banged his hand on the desk. "It's the only explanation."

"What?" Bruce asked.

Colista didn't bother to turn around. "Don't ask daft questions. It would take me all night to explain it to you. You have time, look portals to other dimensions up on your smartphone, research like a good writer."

"I write fiction," Bruce said to himself as Colista had already returned to his studies. "I make shit up."

But deep down Colista's words rang true. Good writers researched to create a plausible foundation for the things they fabricated. Just what did Bruce know about spirits? Ouija boards acted as portals. At least, that's what some texts suggested. Others simply implied that a Ouija was nothing but a means for an individual to make a connection with a spirit that already existed on this plane. He glanced at Colista and risked interrupting him, "Mia played with a Ouija. Are you saying she opened a portal?"

"An uninspired assessment," Colista mumbled as he flipped a page. "But possibly true."

"Even a blind hog finds a truffle once in a while," Bruce said. Colista had a way of making him feel small.

"Stop sulking because you don't know something. Because then you are a failure."

Ha ha! Damn if he isn't right on the money, boy. You never were much for motivation or detail work. Take after your mother that way, ya know.

"I mean," Bruce started, "sure, I research. So, which is it? Is a Ouija board a portal or just a communication device? I've seen it described both ways." He hoped he sounded competent.

"Which is it, indeed," Colista mumbled. He scribbled something further on the notepad, then turned to Bruce. "I haven't met a non-human spirit yet not associated with a portal, if that answers your question. Not to say the Ouija from Mia's past is the portal, but one certainly exists. And if not the Ouija, then what?"

The last question came out pointed, as if Bruce should be the one to know the answer to this rather loaded query. Bruce ran a hand through his natty curls. "So, you have to close the portal to remove the spirit from Mia's body?"

"Don't put words in my mouth."

Stop with the feeble questions, boy. Let the man work.

Colista glanced past Bruce, eyes squinted in surprise at something he just now noticed. Behind Bruce, Crowley growled, a rumble deep in the ancient creature's chest.

A chill ran through Bruce, and he didn't wish to turn and look at what had garnered both the professor's and the cat's attention in such a negative fashion. When he did turn, Bruce imagined he'd find Mia in some unsavory condition, perhaps vomiting rocks or her head turning around and around like an owl, or Linda Blair.

"Not much time now," Colista mumbled and made to stand.

Bruce didn't care for the look in the man's eye, a suspicious squinty gunfighter gleam.

Bruce turned his gaze to the chalk and salt circle. Perhaps desensitized by recent events, Bruce didn't feel the shock of surprise he'd expected. Mia's body stood erect but motionless by the edge of the ring as if rooted to that exact spot all along. Her balance and overall coordination seemed improved.

The softness that normally pervaded her eyes no longer existed, replaced by a thousand-foot stare and slack facial features. She looked like a strung-out druggie, and once Mia's parents and the great Pastor Matt did show up, Bruce would understand if they admitted her to rehab right then and there.

Who would they blame for all of this? Bruce, of course. Sure, blame the horror writer, as if he'd personally delivered her down the path to unholiness just because he wrote about such.

Colista would come next. They'd report him to the dean, where he'd most likely come under question. Bruce figured the professor was already hanging on by the thinnest thread of academic relevance. In today's day and age of core-competencies and science-oriented curriculum, Colista was probably seen as an indulgence at best.

Mia belched just then, interrupting Bruce's train of thought. She smacked her full lips together as if contemplating speech, but only a growl emanated from deep inside. A probing hand reached out like a wall stood before her instead of chalk lines.

Crowley arched his back, dark hairs along a crooked spine standing at attention.

"Easy," Colista said. "Let's see what the bastard is capable of."

Crowley hissed in dissention as if he would rather scratch the shit out of the thing. Or, Bruce figured, the cat thought some immediate action was required which Colista wasn't initiating.

Bruce tended to agree. If this thing could make Mia stand up, then what else would it do? Could it get outside of the circle and run amuck? Bruce pictured Mia out in the darkness, committing random acts of mischief.

As if in response, Mia's right hand reached up and latched onto her left breast. A long breath cascaded from her mouth as if this were an action long desired. A rather hedonistic action, but what else should he expect from a demon? What was more pleasing than pleasures of the flesh?

"You hold no dominion here," Colista said in a brusque voice. "I command you to loosen your hold or I'll have cause to force you."

Mia growled once, but Colista's words must have found purchase, because the hand at once fell from Mia's chest to her side.

"It worked," Bruce said.

"A battle far from won," Colista said. "I need to act now, sooner than I am prepared. Only a matter of time before this thing figures out a few more things."

The scent of sweat and sulfur poured from Mia and Bruce figured the beast within her must be throwing a minor temper-tantrum. Bruce supposed it'd worked hard to accomplish that one lude act and now would voice its displeasure, or perhaps the absence of pleasure, the only way it could, through stinking and fussing. A rather weak display, a childish, ill-tempered maneuver that would bring it nothing but admonishment.

"Stop with the pity-party," Colista said.

Correctamundo, Bruce thought.

Colista turned to Bruce. "Watch her a moment. Make sure she doesn't leave the circle, otherwise leave her be. Crowley can handle anything else."

"Where are you going?" Bruce asked.

"To prepare." Colista disappeared into a back room without further explanation.

Bruce glanced at the cat. He hoped Crowley could handle any problems that arose in Colista's absence. If shit hit the fan, Bruce didn't have the first clue as what to do. What if Mia's body suddenly stepped out of the circle? What should he do, tackle her to the ground?

Pin her down? He supposed he would get prosecuted at some later date for an action like that.

Stop sniveling like a pussy and make yourself useful for a change. Maybe you'll eventually get into her pants if you start making some good choices.

"Shut up," Bruce mumbled.

Mia continued to stand at the edge of the circle, eyes glued to Bruce in what he could only interpret as malice. He felt horrible for her. Bruce wanted to reach out and embrace her but understood it wouldn't be her essence he comforted. He'd do it, anyway, if he thought it would help. *Probably not.* The embrace would feel only selfish and tawdry under the circumstances.

In an action so quick Bruce could only stare while processing, Mia's left hand leapt to her crotch and her right fist lifted and pummeled her right cheek bone. The maneuver felt personal, as if the thing inside Mia was putting on a show just for him. Two perverse acts of pleasure and pain. Her mouth opened wide and a defiant growl roared from it.

"Don't you do that to Mia," Bruce said.

He'd promised himself, after one of several instances of his abusive father striking him, that he'd never allow another human being to be treated as such. He'd dealt with his dad in the only way he could, by escaping him, but now he'd deal with this without running away. He'd stand strong for Mia.

Bruce raced inside the circle to save the woman he loved from the spirit within her.

"Get your hands off me," Mia shouted, although she knew it must have come out as more of a thought because Bruce couldn't hear it.

She raced toward her body even as the beast made her do vile things. Her cheeks were already bruised from the pummeling by her own fist. Mia reached with ephemeral arms, flying like a missile, hell bent on gaining entrance and control. In a dizzying blur of motion, she reversed direction, Mia's consciousness now racing toward the bright portal up by the ceiling. The silver thread held despite the dark blemish where it entered her body and kept her from sailing out of this world.

Floating between the portal and her body, Mia watched Bruce hurl forward and into the circle. She felt the beast's frustration when Bruce gently knocked her body to the davenport and pinned her arms back.

A plethora of emotions flooded Mia as she watched Bruce: relief that he protected her body from the spirit inside her, joy at the tender and respectful way he touched her, and a deep sadness that she couldn't join him on the davenport.

The spirit forced Mia's body to struggle against Bruce's efforts but could only accomplish a feeble twitching of her limbs. That was until Bruce screamed.

It took a moment for Mia to understand what happened. Then a thin snake of blood squirmed down Bruce's neck. The beast had used Mia's teeth to latch on just below Bruce's jaw, deep enough to draw blood.

Bruce shouted something unintelligible and attempted to pry her jaws apart with spasmatic motions of his flailing hands. Even in pain, Mia noticed how he pried with careful pressure, not wishing to harm Mia's body even while his was under duress.

Mia watched her mouth pull away from Bruce's neck with a mouthful of his stretching skin. Blood bubbled from the tooth punctures and stained Mia's teeth crimson, saturating Bruce's t-shirt. Thankfully, her teeth had missed any major arteries, but blood still cascaded down his throat and dripped onto the antique davenport.

Crowley hissed and then ran yowling back and forth along the back of the sofa.

"What in name of Odin is going on in here?" Colista asked, entering the room on quick strides of his long legs.

He wore the white collar of a priest and a rather gaudy crucifix around his neck. His hair looked slicked back with some wet-style pomade. Colista only wore one black wingtip shoe and his belt flailed about unfettered, which he corrected as he ran. Mia got the impression the screams caught him off guard, left him unprepared for what he found occurring in his home.

"I thought I told you to watch her," Colista said.

Crowley jumped from the back of the davenport and danced around his feet in frantic bursts of energy only a cat can produce, footfalls so loud it sounded like a horse had invaded the small sanctuary. It yowled as if Colista hadn't yet noticed the dilemma. How a cat this scrawny could produce so much noise eluded Mia. Then she looked closer.

A tiny silver thread, much smaller than her own, glinted in the gloom and stretched between Crowley and Colista. Then it disappeared as if it had never existed at all. A moment later, it returned. Mia thought it was some sort of communication, some causal link between pet and owner. Perhaps cats were the gatekeepers between worlds. She thought of old Misty, a cat Mia had cuddled with since she was twelve, how the feline stared at things as if there were something there that nobody else could see. Always, the cat could be seen staring at empty space in the corner of a room or with an eye bent in the direction of the void above the stairwell.

Mia turned her attention back to Bruce. He'd made progress, but not enough. His blood pattered to the cushions of the davenport as he struggled to disengage from Mia's jaws. He'd stopped with the screams but now grunted and moaned as he fought for release from her mouth.

Guilt pummeled Mia. She watched her own body commit this atrocity to the boy she felt deeply for. With fierce concentration, Mia imagined herself a wedge, a slice of energy between her physical mouth and Bruce's jawline. When she could no longer take the anxiety, Mia mustered up as much energy as she could, her consciousness shaking with potential, then flung that energy toward her body and Bruce. Mia momentarily existed in the small space between her own physical teeth and Bruce's puncture wounds. She caught quick glimpses of wet, red tissue and white enamel, but then exploded out the other side of the writhing bodies. Mia's energy collided with one of the bookcases along the wall, bounced back, then hovered several feet above the floor. She felt dizzy and disoriented, but watched as Colista acted.

"What possessed you to go inside the circle?" Colista asked Bruce as he rushed in.

The cat leaped from the floor to the back of the davenport, quite agile for a cat of its geriatric condition.

Bruce gagged out unintelligible grunts, eyes squeezed shut, face pale. He continued to pry at Mia's teeth, attempting to release his skin.

The professor pulled a chain and pendant from a pocket in his robe. The charm reminded Mia of the Star of David, only, at each intersection of lines, a sparkling red jewel rested within the amulet's metal. Instinct warned Mia to remain wary of such things. In her churchy upbringing, pentagrams were synonymous with evil and the Devil, never mind the fact that Catholics wore them all the time. Or that other religions and cultures utilized the symbol in a spirit of hope and peace. Her church only recognized them as occult and Wiccan objects of worship.

Mia remembered watching the Goth kids down at the mall. They always hung outside of Hot Topic wearing their jet-black outfits, wild pasty makeup and pentagrams on chains much like the one Colista now held. She also remembered the day Pastor Matt took the whole congregation out back of the church and burned a pile of wooden pentagrams, fashioned from saplings, at the stake.

Colista held the chained pentagram in front of him in one hand, a crucifix in the other. From the cross, Jesus beseeched Mia with mournful eyes, feet and hands tacked to the timbers with grotesque spikes. Mia felt judged, and a powerful wave of shame swept over her.

She couldn't help but feel this situation could have been circumvented had she been more diligent when it came to her faith. Or if she had just gone to Bible college as her father and Pastor Matt had wanted. She imagined the congregation shaking their heads at her as Pastor Matt roared about blasphemy from his lectern.

"In the name of the risen Lord, I command you to release your hold on this child of God!" Colista shouted from outside the circle. "You hold no dominion here, Satan, and I command you to leave this vessel and return from whence you came." He continued to hold the religious items out toward Mia's body. "Let the crucifix, symbol of your defeat, and this pentalpha remind you of your place. You have already lost. Give this host back to the Lord on High. I command you!" A dribble of sweat started at Colista's temple and ran down his cheek as if the words he had spoken had taken great effort and concentration.

Mia wondered why Colista used Christian words and symbols in his impassioned display of religious will. Perhaps she was in error thinking Colista scoffed at such dogma as Christianity. But hadn't he publicly shamed her at the first parapsychology club meeting for speaking up about things like Heaven? No, actually, he hadn't, now that she thought about it. He had said something about the belief to be neither here nor there or something along those lines.

Colista looked up in her general direction as if he could see her floating there. "Mia, if you can hear me, you must stay diligent and steadfast. Believe in what we are doing and pray to your God. Concentrate on the spirit inside your body and wish it gone. Wish it with all your heart."

He turned back to Mia's body...and Bruce who still flailed about uttering choked sobs. The blood pattering onto the davenport seemed subdued now. "Foul beast, I command you to release your hold."

Mia fired up a prayer as instructed, as she had so many times before at another man's behest. "Dear Lord, forgive me my laundry-list of sins and help Professor Colista remove your enemy from my body."

Looking down she could see the spirit struggle within her flesh, hopefully tormented by her words. Black tendrils flashed when the thing exited and reentered her body with diaphanous motion. It looked like a blob of jelly that didn't quite fit inside the jelly jar.

Colista took a deep breath, chest heaving, then brushed his dark bangs from his eyes. He nodded and entered the circle. A determined look narrowed his eyes and bunched the wrinkles on his middle-aged forehead. He pulled the crucifix away from his body and placed it on Mia.

The immediate release of Mia's jaws sent Bruce sprawling onto the floor. His massive hands flew to the spot on his neck where blood still dribbled from a series of punctures. He rose to his knees and looked to Colista.

The spirit inside Mia used her vocal cords to roar its defiance, which stirred Colista's feathered bangs. Mia could see her bloodshot eyes, bloody teeth and lips, and the crimson splatters that marred the delicate alabaster skin. Small rivulets of blood ran down the same riverbeds usually reserved for anxiety-birthed tears.

With his free hand, Colista handed Bruce a handkerchief. "Press this to the wounds then make yourself useful."

Bruce stood as he grabbed the piece of cloth. After dabbing the torn skin, he stuffed the cloth in his back jeans pocket, then walked up to Mia. "What should I do?"

"Hold her still," Colista said.

It took a couple of tries for Bruce to find a hold on Mia which he found comfortable. She appreciated his modesty but wished he'd worry a little less about her honor and a lot more about helping Colista rip this thing from her.

The spirit inside Mia growled and struggled, spittle flecking on her full lips.

Crowley wound back and smacked Mia across the cheek with his paw, claws retracted, as if this may accomplish even the slightest bit of good. Then it hissed for good measure. The action reminded Mia of a particular western movie she'd watched with her dad before he became *born again*. Now they didn't watch any movies except those approved of by Pastor Matt. In the scene she envisioned, a wizened old cowboy shot a scattergun at an ineffectual distance. Most gun owners knew shotguns didn't do much damage outside of thirty yards, so when John Wayne asked the old fella why he continued to shoot despite the obvious conclusion of his efforts, the old man simply said, "Well, it makes me feel better." It was the same with Crowley, Mia supposed. If she'd been inside of her body, the others would have heard her chuckle. Cats were ridiculous sometimes. So were people.

Colista held the crucifix to Mia's forehead as Bruce held her awkwardly. Bruce's blood still ran from the corners of Mia's mouth, making her look like a rabid animal.

"Release your hold, foul beast! I command you in the name of the Risen Lord," Colista shouted.

Mia continued her prayers even as she took in her ravaged body with its red glossy eyes and blood-covered face and growling maw. God knew she looked a fright now, and anyone who ran across her would think her either crazy or on drugs, perhaps both. She looked positively feral.

A series of fists resonated off Colista's front doorway, accompanied by voices demanding entry. Mia recognized the voices of Jack, her dad and Pastor Matt.

"Shit…Jack's back," Bruce said.

We're out of time!

She glanced at the antique pendulum clock above Colista's desk and noticed hours had flown by like minutes. Panic struck Mia like a freight train.

CHAPTER 17

Colista let out his breath and backed away from Mia's body, leaving Bruce to hold the girl. He was afraid this could happen, that he had taken too much time. He should have known they would spare not a second. That's how these controlling types rolled. When they sniffed out a way to snare a poor soul, they would spare no haste to get them indoctrinated back into the fold.

He had no choice but to let them in, of course. It was one thing to kick out the boyfriend, but there would be hell to pay, perhaps even jail time and dismissal as an educator, if he denied entry to Mia's parents. To hell with Pastor Matt, but he'd arrived with the father, so there was nothing to do but let him in, too.

Glancing at Mia, he wished he had more time to wash off the blood. Colista shook his head. This would prove hard to explain.

As if reading Colista's mind, Bruce took out his handkerchief and made to wipe the blood off Mia's face.

"Don't bother," Colista said. "You'll only smear it around. Better if they see what happened for themselves."

Colista took one last careful look to make sure Mia didn't appear restrained in any way. Satisfied, he turned and approached the door.

Another series of bangs and a bout of shouting erupted.

Without preamble, in part because it had worked to perfection with the boyfriend earlier, Colista whipped open the heavy wood door. When he did, a short, white-haired man, face red, especially around the nose, came stumbling over the threshold like a bowling-ball with stubby arms.

Once the man regained his balance, he looked across the room. "What in the name of the sweet baby Jesus is this blasphemy?" He looked at Colista with distaste.

Colista knew a closet rummy when he saw one but decided now may not prove the best time to bring that fact to light. Perhaps later, when it would work out to his advantage. Instead, he took out his smokes, removed one, then lit it with his cherub-embossed silver lighter.

"This," Colista said after exhaling a plume of pollution, "is a not-so-classic case of spirit inhabitation."

A man who shared Mia's blue eyes, pushed his way inside. "Mia, my God!" He rushed to the davenport but cringed when Mia snarled at him. "What's wrong with you?"

Pastor Matt wiped his sweaty undersized palms on his dark slacks while studying Mia with a practiced gaze. Then he turned back to Colista. "You call yourself a priest? You should be ashamed by this use of occult symbology." He looked around the room. "Just look at this place. A factory of Satan if one ever existed." He snatched the Bible from Jack, who stood in wait like an altar boy, and waved it in the air. "The fiery pits and the lake of fire is the end which awaits you, oh sinner."

Colista noted the pastor's red puffy jowls wobbled as he pitched his fire and brimstone fastballs. He decided not to mention it and took another puff of his smoke, instead. He allowed the smoke to billow up and over his face to speak for him. Finally, he couldn't help himself, and said, "I suppose a cabin on said lake is out of the question."

Pastor Matt rolled his eyes and shook his head.

"Are you on drugs, young lady?" Mia's dad yelled, much louder than necessary since he stood just outside the circle, as if he instinctively understood the protection it offered him.

Mia growled like a rabid dog, spittle flecking her lips and cheeks.

"That'll be just about enough of that," her dad said, but sounded less sure of himself now. "And where did all that blood come from?"

"Me," Bruce mumbled and pointed at his wounded neck. The blood had coagulated but still appeared fresh and shiny.

"She bit you?" Her dad asked.

Bruce shrugged and nodded. "Not exactly her fault, but yeah."

"Why?" Her dad flailed his arms. "Never mind that. Who are you?"

"A friend of Mia's."

"That's the druggie I was telling you guys about," Jack said. "I'm sure he's the one to blame for Mia behaving this way, for the drugs." He sneered at Colista as if he'd won a minor victory.

Colista continued to smoke quietly with his practiced look of ambivalence that placed distance between himself and the situation, even if that distance wouldn't last. He knew how to handle these religious nuts, and he would in due time. They would require his services at some juncture, and he just hoped the moment came before much more damage came to Mia.

Pastor Matt ignored both Mia's Dad and Jack and focused on Colista. "I'm sure you'd like us to believe Mia is possessed by a demon." He puffed out his substantial barrel chest. "Because that would remove the spotlight from your little ring of evil. How much money have you made off these children? How many drugs have you supplied them with? Believe me when I say the authorities will be alerted."

"Please do," Colista said, then took another drag. Damn, he needed the nicotine. Dealing with these fools might even drive him to drink. That bottle of Glenfiddich in the cabinet called to him like a Siren. "But I would encourage you to hurry, whatever it is you plan to do. Mia's future depends on quick action."

"On that we agree," Pastor Matt said. "Douglass, retrieve your daughter and let us make haste back to the church. Once Mia comes down from her high, we can decide on a course of action from there. We need to get her back to her flock." Again, he waved the Bible over his head as if trying to induce a rain shower. Then Pastor Matt squinted his tiny bleary eyes at Colista and shook both his head and his Bible. "And why in the great name of God are you dressed like a priest? It's quite blasphemous, I'm sure you must realize. You're no Christian man."

"I am whatever I need to be," Colista said in a quiet voice.

"A chameleon, then" Pastor Matt said, "a great deceiver." He waved his Bible. "The Enemy is a great adversary, indeed. Beware the snares of the deceiver, for he will drag you to Hell."

"I rather think you have the wrong idea," Colista said, a bit louder now. "I'm a chaos magician, therefore I use the belief systems of my clientele to help solve their spiritual problems. In this case, Mia is a Christian, and therefore a priest was called for."

"Blasphemy!" roared Pastor Matt. Then he spoke more quietly. "A chaos magician. The very title itself rolls off the tongue as a deceit. You, sir, will burn in Hell."

"I'm sure," Colista stated blandly and managed to roll his eyes. He blew out a plume of smoke before speaking again. "Think what you will, however, if you don't allow me to finish my work, the spirit within her will take full control of her motor functions. When that happens, well…the situation will become complicated."

"The deceptive words of Satan," Pastor Matt said.

Colista watched the pastor's eyes rove over Mia's condition and knew what he said would be, at least, considered. Then Pastor Matt spat on Colista's floor in disgust.

Colista barely restrained himself. Such a shameless display of disrespect. Disgusting. Only for Mia's well-being did he hold his tongue and his left fist. Colista would need to disinfect his abode at a later point in time.

Pastor Matt walked toward the ring. "Your deceptions know no bounds. Just look at this ring of shame on the floor, as if such a contrivance could accomplish good."

"Think what you will, but at least I use my spiritual gifts," Colista said. "While you are nothing but a scared sniveling bully, who leads his flock through spiritual fear. You disgust me. You call me blasphemous, but your very existence is such."

"I should slug you," Jack said and took a step toward Colista.

"Mind your place, boy," Pastor Matt said with finger pointed. "I'll handle this."

Jack bowed his head and stepped back to the doorway.

Colista gave Pastor Matt kudos for calling off his dog. At the very least, the guy knew what would happen if things went bad. He and Bruce could easily wind up in jail at this juncture, at the slightest provocation. They were walking on thin ice and needed to use an abundance of caution lest the authorities intervene. In which case, nobody would remain to render aid to Mia—nobody that could make a difference.

Pastor Matt held out a shaky hand. "Come, Mia. We need to get you back where you belong. You had your chance to spread your wings, but enough of this foolishness. It has gone bad for you, as I predicted it would. Now, come with us and stop this."

Mia growled from deep in her chest.

"Don't remove her from the circle," Colista warned. "It is a protection, a border if you will, that the spirit cannot cross. Remove Mia and you free the shackles with which I bound the entity."

"It never ends," Pastor Matt said with a sad shake of his head. He extended his arm further into the circle. "Let us get you home and off these foul drugs in your system. The time for this make-believe nonsense is over. Surely you understand that nothing such as a chaos magician exists. It's merely a ploy to keep you here and addicted."

It became clear when Mia lunged at Pastor Matt that she didn't understand at all. When the pastor stumbled back, Mia pressed forward until she came to the symbolic boundary of salt. Here she stood and growled, blood staining her teeth a dark crimson.

"Sweet Jesus," Pastor Matt said. He looked to Mia's dad. "Doug, see if she'll listen to you."

"Knock it off," Doug said. "Enough of this behavior."

As the words were said, the outside lightbulb above Jack shattered into dozens of pieces and rained down on his head. Jack ducked out of the way with a little scream.

Colista smirked. "Looks like Mia doesn't care for what you have to say, Daddy-O."

"What?" Doug stammered as he stared at where Jack brushed the chunks of glass out of his cornrows. "Mia did that?"

"Are you that simple?" Pastor Matt quipped at Doug. "That you would believe this is anything more than a parlor trick created to deceive the unwary?" He shook his head.

Colista stifled a laugh. *Truth*, he thought. The thought about Doug being simple, anyway. *Simple and weak-minded.*

Jack frowned and parroted the shake of Pastor Matt's head, aligning himself with the man and his actions.

Doug glared first at Jack, then at Pastor Matt but stayed silent.

Pastor Matt walked closer to Mia on stubby fat legs and stood face to face with the beast within. "If you will not come willingly, then we'll have no choice but to remove you and bring you with us. It's within your father's parental rights, you realize."

"She's eighteen," Bruce said, still dabbing at his wound. "And I don't think that's what she would want."

"He has a point," Doug said. "And she's just standing there… Doesn't look like she's high. Just angry. Maybe we should give her time to cool off. I mean, she bit this guy."

Pastor Matt shot his hands up into the air. "Not all drugs affect motor coordination. Now, perform the duty a father should and remove your daughter from the way of harm. Because she is in harm's way, you know. Both physically and spiritually."

"If you choose to remove her from the circle," Colista said after expelling more smoke, "there are some things you should know." He waited until everyone was looking in his direction. "The spirit is a young and infantile creature, jealous and unrefined, even for an elemental." He pointed his cigarette at Pastor Matt. "It'll use her flesh bag for pleasure. That's what all inhuman spirits want, you know— to experience what it means to be human, our emotions and physical pleasure. We've already seen signs of it."

"Truth," Bruce said. "I mean, she grabbed her own breast and that. Even her crotch. Mia would never have done that on her own."

Colista cringed.

Doug's eyes narrowed. "My God," he whispered.

"Stop talking like you know her at all," Jack said. "She would never willingly hang out with you. Her interactions with you were just the drugs talking. Pure and simple."

In a flash, two more lightbulbs in the kitchen shattered and rained to the linoleum floor.

"Would you please stop pissing her off," Colista said around the cigarette that hung from his lip. A strand of hair now hung over his right eye. "I won't have a bulb left in the apartment."

"Enough," Pastor Matt shouted. "Enough arguing and enough of the parlor tricks. It is time to take Mia home. Everything will sort itself out when she returns to the congregation where we can keep an eye on her." He stepped into the circle, then reached out and grabbed Mia's forearm.

Mia exploded. With her opposite hand, the beast forced her to dig her claws into Pastor Matt's offensive arm. Then she hurled her already bloody mouth toward his throat.

With perverse pleasure, in Colista's opinion, Pastor Matt used her own momentum against Mia. Agile for a round, short man, the pastor twisted away, then smashed the side of her head with his Bible. Mia let loose of his arm as she crashed to the floor, blood pouring down the pastor's fingers. He ignored the small wound, bent down, and pinned her to the floor. He wore a scowl which Colista thought would scare the Devil.

"Restrain her," he yelled toward Doug as he struggled to keep Mia pinned to the floor like a beetle in a display case.

"Don't hurt her," Jack yelled but didn't move from the door.

Colista looked toward the ceiling. "Mia, if he destroys your human body, kills you, you'll be released from your tether. If that happens, fly to the bright orb. You'll be taken good care of there. Listen to what I say and don't be afraid."

"My God, Mia. Don't listen to him," Doug shouted as he bent down toward Mia. "Your mom will kill me if you die."

"That's what could happen if you remove Mia while the creature is still inside," Colista said. "It may act as a filter of sorts, and the strain could kill her."

In all honesty, Colista wasn't sure about this, but it was a theory he'd considered on several occasions. He'd never had the occasion to prove or disprove it and he didn't wish the opportunity now.

"Knock it off," Bruce said. "You can't force her against her will. This isn't what she wants. Leave her alone." He took a step in the direction of Mia's body.

"Leave it," Colista said. "Her dad needs to decide. You'll just get thrown in jail."

Bruce stood his ground a moment, chest heaving. His eyes darted to Jack who had taken a step inside as the altercation bloomed. He pointed at him. "You wanna piece of this? Maybe I can't keep them from taking her, but I'm mad enough to beat your ass. And nobody will toss me in jail for that."

"Why, you…" Jack said and stepped forward, a bewildered look on his face. "You can't possibly think you'd win a fight with me."

"Knock it off," Pastor Matt said, out of breath now as he held Mia against the floor while she struggled. "Get down here and help me." He turned to Bruce. "You interfere and I will call the police. Count on that."

"You're making a mistake," Colista said one last time.

Joining the pastor on the floor, Pastor Matt and Doug each grabbed an arm and Jack both legs. Mia continued to twist and turn and snarled like a rabid dog. Her jaws snapped, looking for a target.

Then a ball of fury rained down and came to rest on Mia's back. Crowley, incensed, snarling louder than Mia, took a swing at Jack's arm and drew blood. It hissed and arched his back as it balanced on top of Mia as if to protect her.

"Crowley, come," Colista said, because he could see exactly what would happen. "Down, Crowley, down!"

As cats do, Crowley refused to listen.

Jack wound up with his free right arm and propelled it forward. When he connected with the old cat, Crowley sailed across the room with a squall and landed on his side with a thud. The cat didn't move.

A lightbulb in a lamp next to an overstuffed armchair popped and exploded all over the fabric of the chair.

"Crowley," Colista screamed. He ran to the cat but kept his eye on Jack. "Oh, you'll pay for that, punk." When he approached his cat, he noticed that Crowley's chest was moving up and down. *Not dead, then, thank goodness.* He put his hands on the cat and stroked his straw-like lumpy fur. "It's okay, Crowley. You did your best. Just rest, now."

"Asshole," Bruce muttered but made no attempt to stop the trio.

"Cat got what it deserved," Jack said.

"Never mind that now," Pastor Matt said. "Let's get Mia out of here." He turned and took a step.

When Mia's foot moved over the area above the circle, she shrieked like a banshee. The screams gained in velocity when Mia's body moved further across the salt and chalk.

Doug looked to Colista.

Colista shrugged. "I tried to tell you. You're physically harming your daughter. Hope you're proud."

Mia shrieked louder, body lashing around like a kite in a thunderstorm.

"Ignore him," Pastor Matt said. "He knows not. He's a deceiver. She screams because she knows the congregation will now hold her to account."

The trio continued on until Jack carried the last of her over the threshold of the circle. Just as her feet passed over the line of protection, a giant boom sounded and rattled the curios on Colista's shelves. A tribal mask fell and skittered away. Doug staggered and almost dropped Mia's left arm and shoulder. Pastor Matt looked around as if the Devil might be on the way.

"What the hell was that?" Jack cringed like a whipped dog.

"The barrier between worlds; the break in protection," Colista said as he continued to stroke Crowley's fur. "Good luck to you all." He glanced at Doug when the guy made eye contact. "She's all yours now."

"Get her to the van," Pastor Matt said as they approached the door.

"Remember what I said, Mia," Colista said.

As Mia's dad exited the apartment, Colista heard him mutter, "Mia's mother should be on the way."

"We can't just let them take her," Bruce said. He rushed past Colista just as Jack slammed the heavy oak door shut. "She's so vulnerable. They'll harm her." Tears ran out of the boy's eyes.

"Don't worry," Colista said. "Unless I'm wrong, they'll be back. Just as soon as her parents realize Pastor Matt is an egotistical fraud. When they can't get their daughter under control, despite the oversite of their precious congregation." He hoped Mia's mother was on the way. She would prove to be the key to the matter.

Crowley scrambled to his feet. He appeared unsteady for a moment before shaking a furry head. When he glanced at the closed door, Crowley bowed his head as if in shame.

"It's okay, Crowley," Colista said. "You led the horse to water. You're a good cat. A very good cat."

CHAPTER 18

Mia floated above her body, which was being stuffed into the back of Pastor Matt's windowless conversion van. Mia had ridden in it plenty to church outings, Christian concerts and the like. Now it just looked creepy.

"No one will see her in here," Pastor Matt said. "We can get her home and take care of her there."

Doug checked his phone, then held it up in the air as if Pastor Matt may wish to see it. "We have to wait. My wife's on her way. She'll get upset if we don't wait for her."

"Who wears the pants in your family, Doug?" Pastor Matt said. The leer on his face told Mia he was bating her father into an argument.

Jack watched for Doug's reaction and Mia knew he would align himself with Pastor Matt if a rift formed.

Mia couldn't understand what she'd ever seen in Jack. Worse, she found it hard to believe she used to hang on Pastor Matt's every word. And she would spit right in her own father's face if she could.

The spirit inside of her still writhed, but Mia could tell the line of protections it had crossed had taken a toll. Weakened it somehow.

Colista rocks in the magic department.

The silver thread had grown thin though, and Mia had feared she would have to heed Colista's warning and head to the light. But once her body cleared the salt and chalk, and the big boom sounded, the bright sun-like thing rippled with concentric rings, and the thread had once again grown thick and vibrant.

"Let's just get a motel," Doug pleaded. "You know, one of those outdoor jobs where people don't dig too close into other people's business. I noticed one on the edge of town. My wife can meet us there."

It's a good sign if Dad still cares what Mom thinks.

Mia floated and watched as they stuffed her body into the van. She'd hoped a campus security guard, or a passing professor on the way to class, might notice and enquire as to what they were doing. No such luck. Even at her elevated height, not a soul moved within her line of sight.

They're like common thugs, Mia thought.

They'd seen an opportunity to get her back under their thumbs and taken it. If they thought she was actually on drugs, they were in for a rude awakening. The thing inside of her body would slip away first chance it got and raise hell, would use her body. It wasn't even struggling now, biding its time and waiting for the right moment. Mom wouldn't let them tie her up, so it would wait until they slept, then it would sneak off with her hijacked flesh. God only knew what kind of shitstorm it would get her into.

Hopefully, Bruce and Colista would come up with a plan. Surely, if nothing else, Bruce would come for her! Perhaps with Colista's help he could get her mom to listen to reason. Mom was less inclined to fall under Pastor Matt's spell. In fact, Mom seemed less inclined to look to the man with reverence like Dad always did. Sometimes she and Mom had even joked about how red Pastor Matt's nose got when he preached his fiery sermons, how he would sweat so profusely that his pits grew sodden, and he would smell of sweat and BO at the picnics after church.

Pastor Matt slammed the backdoor to the van. "Let's get Mia out of here."

He started the engine. As the van backed out of the parking space, Mia felt a twinge of concern about how she would keep up and remain with her body.

A sudden urge to see Bruce raged within her, an intense yearning to see him again before things got out of hand. She raced back toward Colista's apartment, the silver thread expanding out behind her like a dog on a retractable leash. She wondered how much leash the thread would afford. Didn't Colista say that he often wandered quite far from his body in his explorations? She wished she had paid closer attention to the man and his book before attempting this all on her own.

She'd panicked in Bruce's room. Allowed her emotions to get the best of her, and that set off this chain of horrible events. If she had control of her body right at this moment, Mia knew tears of anxiety would streak her pale cheeks. In emotional metaphysical shambles, she hurled toward Bruce in a desperate sprint even as the van sped away with her body. Mia wished she understood exactly how this worked, what would happen when something in the physical world came between her and the van. Would the silver thread break and send her hurling into the light? Right now, she didn't care.

With a burst of speed, Mia turned the last corner of the dorms reserved for professors just as Bruce walked out of Colista's apartment. The last thing she noticed before her energy rushed through him were the tears in his eyes.

"Bruce," she squalled but knew immediately that he couldn't hear her, being they were now in different plains of existence. He couldn't even see her.

Bruce kept trudging over the concrete toward campus.

Mia looked around for a light bulb. She'd already shattered Colista's, but his next-door neighbor's remained intact. She reached out and shattered the bulb into dozens of chip-shaped shards. Then she floated in midair and waited.

As she hoped, Bruce's shoulders hunched up, and he slowly turned around in place. He stared in her direction, even though Mia knew he couldn't see her.

"Mia?" he asked in a soft voice.

He looked so sad with his tears, but hope filled his eyes. Seeing him like that broke Mia's heart. Bruce walked toward the remains of the shattered bulb. He looked around as he walked and ran a hand through his careless curls.

An endearing habit of his, Mia realized.

"Are—are you here?" he said.

Mia reached out and touched his cheek, ran what passed for a thumb these days over the moisture on his cheeks. "Bruce, there's so many things I want to tell you. That I love you. That Colista is right about…everything. That I need help." She choked on ghostly tears and added, "That I want to spend all the time in the world with you. You're perfect for me."

Bruce reached up into Mia's energy.

Can he feel me?

A curious look spread across his features, as if he was trying to figure out a puzzle. Mia held her breath. Bruce reached through her energy and touched his own cheek. He looked so confused, his eyes shimmering with emotion.

Mia reached out and touched the back of his hand. When he didn't respond to that, she knew her hope of him sensing her was only wishful thinking.

Bruce spoke, again. "If you can hear me, Mia, I love you. Have since the first time I laid eyes on you. We have so much in common. And I know you're cuter than me, better looking. But I'll work out, lift weights, whatever."

"Just be yourself," Mia whispered and ran her energy over Bruce's hand, again. "I want nothing more than that."

If she were inside her body, Mia would have squealed so loud she might have burst Bruce's eardrums. Without hesitation, Mia pressed her energy to and around Bruce in wispy tendrils, surrounding his body like smoke. Maybe if she smothered him with all the intensity she could muster, then he would feel her. He'd know how she felt.

Bruce stood wide-eyed, then reached out as if Mia stood before him in the flesh. "Mia? I can— I can…"

He feels me!

Mia kissed his cheeks, ran a hand through his curly locks. She looked him in the eye and wished to God he could see her instead of just sensing her presence. How she would love to cuddle next to him in his dorm room. To soak in the scent of his cologne, the softness of his boyish skin, and most important, his kindness. She loved him and wanted to feel Bruce. This ephemeral transfer of energy would never prove enough for either of them.

Just like Ghost.

As much as both Patrick Swayze and Demi Moore wanted it to work, it never could. Mia would not rest until this guy held her in his arms.

Never!

She looked him in the eye and kissed his cheek again.

Then a persistent tug came from behind. It felt like a small child pulling at her shirttail. Only annoying at first, so she ignored this tug like she would a gust of wind. Mia reached around Bruce and rubbed his thick shoulders. She would stay with Bruce for however long it took to solve this problem.

Bruce closed his eyes as if he could really feel her. The expression on his face, the slightly parted lips, quick breaths, indicated such. "Mia," he murmured. He ran his hands through her energy, a lovely gesture.

Too soon, the pull became something she could no longer ignore. In fact, it felt stronger with every passing moment. Her tether had reached its limit. She felt that, given time, the limit could be stretched, but right now she knew it would pull her away from this beautiful man. With a desperate reach, Mia gave Bruce one last ghostly squeeze. She looked around for Colista but didn't see him. Mia cared for Bruce very much but knew only Professor Colista could truly rescue her from this problem—this double-edged problem of her inhabitant and Pastor Matt.

The inevitable happened. She let go of Bruce, then watched him become smaller and smaller. She raced away toward her physical body as if attached to it by a rubber band. The last vision of Bruce came as he reached out with a trembling hand as if something had been taken from him.

"I love you," she screamed.

Bruce disappeared in an abrupt tug, and then Mia passed through a series of blurred rooms and hallways. A stairwell, a lone kid's tennis-shoe, a television showing a program about whales. Faster she went as her momentum built. Faces of people sitting in chairs. A naked couple squeezed onto a couch, making love. A family eating a late dinner. All of it flew by. Then she slipped outside the building, into the open air and raced toward the moving van. When the vehicle stopped for a red light, Mia came to rest directly above it.

Her heart felt broken and sick. She wanted Bruce, yet here she floated, trapped with the three people she hated most in the world...and a demon. She wasn't sure who she disliked more. Just a small act of defiance, but Mia refused to allow her energy to enter the van where her body lay inhabited. She didn't want to see herself stuffed into the back of the van or Pastor Matt's sweaty red face or her own father as he looked on in admiration. Worse would be to see her so-called boyfriend who would most certainly do anything to prove himself worthy of Pastor Matt's praise.

Pastor Matt taught control, but most of all misogyny, exerting that control within a male-centric landscape. Nobody left the flock without permission. Mia understood this now. She couldn't imagine how she'd ever felt safe, comfortable, or happy in the small circle her family enclosed themselves within.

Brush your teeth, Mia, or it'll be the pits of hell.

Don't stay out too late or the fiery lake will claim your soul.

Nothing but lies used to manipulate her.

The van turned left at the stoplight before the freeway and headed down a service road toward a one-story white building with peeling paint and a neon sign proclaiming a vacancy. By the looks of things on the outside, the motel existed in a perpetual state of vacancy, its rooms more typically rented by the hour.

Part of Mia felt dismay at the idea of her body staying in this debacle of a dwelling. The cops probably avoided the place, letting bygones be bygones. Anything could happen to her here. She didn't trust her dad or Pastor Matt to keep her safe. Just the opposite, in fact. The congregational discipline could very well begin tonight. She didn't understand exactly what that would entail but knew enough.

Unpleasant. Yes, it will be most unpleasant.

The van beneath her turned another corner and the hotel office came into view.

The other part of Mia felt a swell of hope that they would remain in the city. Bruce and Colista would find and rescue her. They understood the danger, had seen Pastor Matt in action. All at once, Mia had a plan. *Yes.* Once everyone went to sleep tonight, she would try to expand the range of her silver tether and reach out to Bruce and Colista, guide them toward her body. She needed to escape.

A sobering fact that she felt more concern with the trio of humans in the van than the spirit buried within her flesh. Colista could deal with the spirit. But Mia knew Pastor Matt had nothing to do with God. The thing that possessed her body probably understood the true nature of God better than Pastor Matt would ever hope to.

The van rounded the long, dilapidated building, bouncing off potholes which littered the service road and parking lot like a teenager's acne. From the front, the place looked even dingier, and the cars and bikes in the lot struck even less confidence, a menagerie of rusted hulks which smacked of people who hung to the fringes of life. A few high-priced rigs stood out amongst the rabble like gold teeth.

Mia floated above it all like an eagle, free and graceful, liberated. *Colista was right, after all!*

She took solace that no matter what they did to her physical body, she could remain aloof, free. As evil as it was, the creature inside her had provided Mia with that much. The controlling church of her youth would never do so again.

It's trapped; I'm free. Ironic, yes. It had taken this to open her eyes completely, but the transition had already begun when she refused Bible college.

Pastor Matt maneuvered the van like he'd done plenty of times before, backing the white lump of metal into an empty parking space near the far end of the motel, further from the office and prying eyes. It made sense, because how would they explain the need to carry Mia to a room like a slab of meat?

Pastor Matt got out. He said, "Wait here. Don't move her until I secure us a room. Then we'll figure out a way to get Mia inside without being seen." He appeared to think about something. "And give me your cellphones. We don't need any...complications."

Her dad mumbled something unintelligible but tossed his phone to the man. Jack took Mia's from her pocket, placed his face down against hers, then handed them to the pastor. After Pastor Matt accepted the phones, he slammed the van door and waddled his way toward what made for an office in this dump.

Jack disrupted her thoughts by opening the back door of the van and getting out. He stretched and peered in the direction Pastor Matt had gone, watching as the pastor entered the office.

Inside the van, Mia could see her bound body. While the van moved down the road, the creature within her must have struggled, because her ankles and wrists were wrapped in grey duct-tape. Her eyes were shut, so Mia assumed the creature now lay dormant until such a time that escape would prove advantageous. A trill of fear rattled through Mia's consciousness.

They thought she was on drugs, but she doubted, at this point, they would enroll her into rehab. No, the church would deal with the situation. Looking back, they'd most likely dealt with many situations.

Mia remembered the time Carly Abrahamson went in front of the disciplinary board for getting intoxicated at a party. She disappeared for a few weeks. When she returned, Carly loved the Lord like never before with the glee only a convert could possess. But what Mia mistook for a renewed religious vigor had been fear, plain and simple. Mia's parents told her Carly went to a Bible camp with other kids who struggled with alcohol, but Mia thought that had been a lie. For all Mia knew, Carly had been tied up in Pastor Matt's house, where he scared the Devil out of her. By what means, Mia didn't know.

Jack cracked his knuckles. He peered back into the van at Mia's prone body and smiled. His true colors would come out soon enough, and Pastor Matt would approve. Mia needed to be taught a lesson she'd never forget, something that would keep her submissive and compliant. All the women in the congregation were encouraged to stay home and run the household like good little soldiers.

They shall never have me, Mia thought.

Jack looked to the front of the van, probably to make sure nobody was watching, then licked his lips and reached for her body with a tentative hand.

Mia floated downward, so she could get a good look. She already knew what she'd find.

Sure enough, Jack was running his hand up her sweatpants leg in a way Mia recognized as his attempt to turn her on. He should know by now that it never worked.

He hesitated at her thigh a bit too long, then moved upward to where Mia's shirt had pulled up to reveal her smooth tummy. Jack rubbed her bare flesh. His chest heaved with labored breaths, and Mia knew what he was imagining, how he wanted to do more. Especially once it was dark. How he'd pleasure himself with no regard to her needs, his usual style of lovemaking. Just wild fast thrusts until he lay sated.

Asshole! No wonder Mia never wanted to do it. Never again if she regained control of her body.

For now, she'd have to wait. Mia had tried to force the creature out and knew it was still way too strong to manipulate physically. Colista would know what to do, but he and Bruce had to find her first. She wished she would have left a trail of breadcrumbs like they did in the fairytales.

Jack slid his hand higher, beneath her shirt. His breaths remained heavy and deep.

If you rape me, Jack... I'll kill you! Capital K. Just you wait and see.

"Knock it off." Her father's feeble voice sounded shaky and soft, as if he no longer held any real power, just a faltering illusion. At least he was trying to keep Mia from harm.

"Pastor Matt told me..."

"I don't care," Doug said. "Leave her be."

Jack turned his head sideways as if sizing her father up. "Pastor Matt told me she was mine to do with as I please."

"Not until you're married," Doug said.

"I have the ring in my pocket," Jack whined. "What's the big deal?"

A ring? He still retained the balls to propose to her after what they'd just done? Of course, that's what he'd come for, to propose to her, then bring her back home. Once there, he'd marry her, control her, take from her what he wanted whenever he wanted it. They would melt into the congregation, just another pair of mating couples to populate the future of the church.

Only, it's not a church, but a cult. Mia knew this without a doubt. And this cult existed to exert control. God was used as a means of control, not as a source of love or comfort.

How could I have grown up so blind to it?

Pastor Matt wobbled back to the van. Her dad didn't notice him.

"Yeah, Doug," Pastor Matt sneered, "what's the problem?" When Doug didn't respond, he said, "That's your problem, Doug. You're a sniveling coward who's afraid to do what needs to be done. You can't even rein in your own daughter, so leave that to Jack. He knows what to do, don't you, Jack?"

"Yessir," he said.

His smile looked like a Mack truck could drive through it. Jack had found his calling, something he could believe in. And it was all on the up and up. He'd garnered permission from the pastor of his church. What could go wrong when one had God and Pastor Matt on their side?

Only, Jack didn't have God on his side. He couldn't, possibly. And Mia held out hope that her God would deliver her from evil. She may not be a perfect person, had sinned like everyone else, but she believed. And she hoped that would be enough to elicit His help. She hoped this help would come in the form of Bruce and Colista.

"Grab the bags, Doug," Pastor Matt said. "Jack will carry Mia, but discreetly, understand? We don't need any unwanted attention." He paused. "We're in twenty-one and twenty-two." He stood with small hands on his considerable hips. "And don't think for a moment, Doug, that we're staying tonight just to wait for your lovely wife. No, Doug. Things change tonight—tonight will begin Mia's reintegration into the fold that you so uselessly allowed to be severed. Because you couldn't stand up and tell her no. Just like you can't with your wife. You're mousey, Doug. A shrew." Once Doug lowered his head, thoroughly cowed, Pastor Matt scowled deeper, then walked over the plank sidewalk toward the rooms.

Pastor Matt reached the rooms first and waited as Doug struggled with all the bags and Jack brought Mia.

Doug stopped by the first room and dropped the bags with a thud. "Mia and I will sleep here. I'll speak with her, see if I can make her understand how important..."

"You'll be allowed no such thing," Pastor Matt said. "The Lord has spoken to me." He hooked his thumbs in belt-loops and puffed up with a great inhalation of air. Then he looked at Jack. "You and Mia stay in twenty-two. You understand the expectations of the Lord?"

Jack nodded like a demented toothy bobblehead as Pastor Matt opened the door. Jack couldn't slip inside quick enough—couldn't wait to get Mia alone.

Once the door to twenty-two slammed shut, Pastor Matt turned to Doug. "That leaves you and me in twenty-one, Doug." His smile widened. "You have sins to atone for." His eyes shone as if inhabited by a demon himself. His small pointy teeth flashed white and yellow like sweet corn.

"No," Doug wailed as Pastor Matt shoved him inside with two tiny hands to the chest. He stumbled and fell against the dingy-quilted queen bed. It rocked back and forth on worn springs. "You said we were done with all that. It's not natural. It hurts— It hurts so bad."

"Don't blame me, Doug," Pastor Matt said as he stalked toward Doug like a wrestler on the prowl. "You brought this on. And believe me, I won't enjoy this any more than you. But, as they say, when a job needs doing...and, hey, better to receive your punishment on Earth than spend an eternity in Hell."

"No, please... Anything but that. Anything. Oh, God!"

Pastor Matt reached back and slammed the door shut. Her dad's cries were severed as if by a knife.

My, God! Mia thought. *Would Pastor Matt really assault her dad?*

Would her father allow it? She wasn't sure who needed God's intervention more, her or her dad. He didn't seem like much of a dad any longer, but still. Mia didn't want Pastor Matt to violate him. She kind of felt bad for him. The only chance either of them had was for her to reach Colista. She forced her energy away from the motel, then traveled far away from the sins of Jack and Pastor Matt.

CHAPTER 19

Colista grabbed an ancient Ouija board and planchette off a shelf in the closet and headed back to his office. Not much time to tarry. He laid the board down on the hearth of the fireplace and sat beside it, then gently placed the crystal planchette on the thick wood rectangle and waited, deep in thought. He needed to play this just right.

A knock at the door.

"What now?" Colista grumbled.

With his luck it would be the dean or the cops. Wouldn't be the first time he needed to explain his methods. He walked over with an irritable gait and pulled open the heavy wood door.

"Hey," Bruce said. "I— I think Mia's energy is still around. I just had an experience and…"

"Get in here," Colista said, and he yanked Bruce inside and slammed the door. "Of course her energy is about. She's trying to reach out to us. We're her only hope, you know. I've seen these cult-leader types in action before."

"Right on," Bruce said. "But I don't think her parents will bring her back here, even if they can't get the spirit out of her."

Colista let out his breath as if expelling smoke. He felt the need for nicotine creeping in. "I tend to agree now that I've had time to reflect on this, but explain what happened to you."

"Well," Bruce started, "I just felt it. I could feel her hopelessness, Mia's despair. I think she knows they'll never let go of her once they have her home. We need to help before they get her there."

"Unfortunately, the law is on their side," Colista said. "She's with her father now, and no officer of the law is going to question that, not in her condition, let alone believe that she is inhabited by a spirit. They will buy into her being on drugs and Pastor Matt's plan, whatever that is. Simple as that."

"So, we can't stop this?" Bruce said.

"Don't put words in my mouth," Colista said, then walked back to the board on the hearth. "Now, sit down and watch. You may learn something useful tonight."

Crowley limped into the room and plopped his old ass down next to Colista, as if the creature knew exactly when its master needed him. It bellowed once, then started licking its fur.

"Yes, Crowley," Colista said, "its time."

Crowley meowed, again, in response. A loving cry, Colista knew, born from many an adventure.

"Crowley understands you," Bruce pointed out.

"Well," Colista said, "we've worked together for a long while now. So, one would expect a certain level of cooperation."

"Cooperation?"

"You wouldn't understand," Colista said as he manipulated the planchette, "but Crowley can alert me to the presence of the spirit world better than any person ever could. He knows what to do."

Crowley let loose with a strangled cry, displeased with some action by Colista.

"Yes, Crowley," Colista said, "I know." He glanced at Bruce. "That's not to say he isn't a pain from time to time. Likes things done his way. Like any cat, I suppose."

Crowley licked his butt.

Colista stood and walked to the corner where three gold stands stood against the wall. He carried all three back over to the hearth. "Happy now, Crowley?"

Crowley didn't bother to answer but had found satisfaction in grooming a lump of misplaced fur on its left hip.

"Don't speak with me now," Colista said to Bruce. "This next ritual requires my complete attention, and I don't wish to fuck it up, as the kids say." He took a deep breath, then positioned the three stands equidistant from the hearth. Then Colista patted the right pocket of his vest, removed his phone, then clicked on an app.

The phone began to tick like a metronome.

From the left vest pocket, Colista slid a vile of thick red liquid, removed the cork, then poured the contents into the bowl on top of the first stand. The red liquid wafted up to Colista's sinuses, the scent of iron and rot. Not pleasant, Colista knew, but pig's blood was a necessary ingredient for this particular ritual.

Feeling the need to explain, Colista told Bruce, "Pig's blood, not human."

Bruce nodded but kept silent.

Colista knew the boy probably had questions but credited him with the fact that he kept his mouth shut and watched diligently. A memory seized him. *Pepe*. Yes, just like Pepe used to pay rapt attention, how he'd hang on every step, watch with bated breath, amazed every single time by the simplest of spells. How Colista missed the man, even still. He couldn't have asked for a better life partner and felt cheated that the United States hadn't seen fit to legalize their union until after cancer had ruined Pepe's body and taken him from Colista.

"Are you still a priest?" Bruce asked.

"What?" Colista asked, ripped from his memories. "Thought I told you to keep quiet." When Bruce sulked, he added, "To answer your question, it doesn't matter now. The priest routine was for Mia's benefit. A good chaos magician knows what is needed and when. It all depends on the client's beliefs."

"So, you believe in Jesus?" Bruce asked. "Or do you just pretend?"

Colista glared at Bruce. "It's complicated, now kindly close your trap so I can get back to work."

Bruce nodded.

Colista sighed, then pulled a pack of cigarettes from a pocket and used the silver lighter again. Once he got the cherry going nice and hot, he lit a stick of incense and laid it in the bowl on the next stand down from the pig's blood. The smoke from both the cigarette and the incense wafted upward and collected just below the ceiling tiles.

Crowley rolled upside down, exposing lighter-colored belly fur, and stayed that way.

The metronome kept with its rhythmic tick, and Colista fashioned his movements in time. A mechanical chime dinged from the phone's speaker and Colista reached up to a bookshelf and took down three small animal skulls. He placed these in the bowl atop the third stand.

When the phone chimed again, Colista stacked a pile of three pieces of wood inside the hearth of the fireplace as if in wait of someone to light it. This reminded him of romantic nights with Pepe by this very fireplace again, glasses of wine in hand, discussion deep and thoughtful, the joy of each other's company.

Cancer sucked, and often he wished he could trade places with Pepe. He would, of course.

The phone dinged again, then began a manic alarm.

Crowley rolled back onto his stomach and looked at Colista with expectation.

"Yes, Crowley," he whispered, "it's time."

After Colista pushed a spot on the phone's screen, the screech silenced, and the rhythmic metronome continued. Not as romantic as the old system, but he found the app on the phone more efficient and less prone to mechanical failure. Besides, he always carried the thing with him, unlike the old cumbersome system of chimes and bells meant to keep his rituals at the proper cadence. Pace often proved the most necessary of ingredients in a solid ritual, the spirits able to time their entry accordingly. When the spirits knew what to expect, the rituals were much more efficient. Some spirits would even refuse to interact without the added contrivance. Especially the gatekeeper with whom Colista wished to barter with today.

A chime rang out and Colista lifted his copy of The *Lesser Key of Solomon* off the desk, opened to *The Testament of Solomon,* and walked to the first bowl. He waited, and when the phone chimed again, he began to read in Latin and stir the pig's blood with a silver spoon adorned with a monster's head at the top of the stem. It matched the beast which sat etched atop the crystal planchette of the Ouija board. A set Colista had found at a conference in Romania for a rather good price.

Colista stirred, concentrating on the concentric ripples within the bowl of blood until lightheadedness set in. Just as the room spun around him, the phone chimed once more.

At the next bowl, Colista used an accordion style Victorian fan blessed by a Buddhist monk high in the soaring heights of the Mongolian Alps to waft the spiraled string of incense smoldering upward. As the room continued to shimmy and sway, the fanned smoke coalesced into a multitude of faces, the first a horned creature which Colista didn't care to interact with, but finally a long-faced spirit with soulful eyes and a long neck. It appeared to turn and lock eyes with Colista.

"Gotcha," Colista whispered.

"Got who?" Bruce asked.

"Shut up," Colista said and continued to waft the incense.

Crowley took a step toward Bruce and hissed, back arched like a decorative Halloween cat.

"Okay, okay," Bruce whispered. "Testy."

The phone chimed again, and Colista left the spirit. The smoke dissipated, and the creature along with it. But the incense had already served the intended purpose, and the gatekeeper understood its services would soon be needed. The images of spirits never failed to unnerve him, though. It was as though they could see right to his core, sense his vulnerabilities and exploit them. Colista would have to stay on his toes.

Colista collected himself and stepped to the final bowl and read from *the book* in his left hand. With his right, Colista fingered the three skulls in the bowl until they rattled with a rhythmic beat. He whispered the simple repetitive Latin phrases which would bring the desired spirit hither. And this desired spirit owed him big time from a ritual-gone-bad many years ago. Yes, the gatekeeper would oblige because Colista damn well intended to collect the debt.

He hissed out the words and they seemed to bounce and echo off the walls and bookshelves. He let his anger guide him. Even once the phone signaled the end of this phase of the ritual Colista gave one more defiant rattle of the skulls, just to reinforce that he meant business this time around.

"I beseech you," Colista said in what he hoped was a mocking tone which reflected his demeanor with adequate venom. Finished, he laid the book back on the desk, then waited with the cigarette hanging from his lip as the metronome continued to tick.

He didn't wait long.

The three logs in the hearth burst into flames with a spontaneous combustion. Even though Colista expected as much, the event still rocked him backward a regretful step. If the bastard found him lacking, it would simply go away. Colista needed to show it that he possessed the mettle and fortitude to track it down and make it pay if it refused service.

Bruce cried out, startled, and Colista heard the guy's chair screech backward.

Crowley approached the flames and glared with unblinking eyes. Good old Crowley would never back down. The best familiar he'd ever owned, and perhaps the last. Pepe's loss had stung, but the loss of Crowley would prove unbearable. Perhaps the gatekeeper could also help in this regard.

The flames in the hearth danced as they consumed the wood. Within seconds, the flames morphed into the same face which had manifested in the smoke from the incense. Two flaming red eyes glared first at Crowley then up at Colista. A yawning maw opened within the flames as if it wished to eat both for their trouble.

With a calm demeanor, to show the beast that he harbored no fear, Colista sat down on the stone hearth. He could feel the heat as it licked his skin, but he knew the gatekeeper wouldn't harm him, not if it thought it had something to gain. Besides, Colista had used the proper ritual, so it was bound by duty to listen to Colista's request at the very least.

Colista removed the cigarette from his mouth and held it with one hand while placing the other on the planchette. Then he glanced up at Bruce. "Time to make yourself useful. Place your right hand on the other edge of the glass."

Bruce hesitated for a moment. "Is it safe?"

"Of course not," Colista said. "You could get possessed, your soul sucked into the spiritual realms, or any host of other maladies. But you want to help Mia, don't you?" When Bruce still hesitated, he repeated, "Well, don't you?"

"Yes," Bruce said.

He scooted over to the hearth and laid two fingers on the other side of the glass planchette. He leaned well away from the leering spirit in the flames.

Colista suppressed a laugh when Bruce stared at the beast on the top of the planchette like it might open its foul mouth and bite him. As if it were an extension of the beast in the flames. Colista remembered a time it had made somebody bleed from beneath their fingernails but felt it would behave itself this evening.

"Good," Colista said. "Let us begin, shall we?"

The spirit in the flames danced with what could only be anticipation. He sensed this without looking while Crowley growled deep in his furry chest. Colista now held the spirit's full attention.

Good.

Colista deserved it after the deceit the thing had dealt him some time ago, back when he lost Pepe. Colista laid the cigarette on the edge of the bowl nearest him, then wiped his bangs off his sweaty forehead. Other hand on the planchette, he said, "Gatekeeper, are you there?"

The planchette moved beneath his fingers.

Colista looked up at Bruce. "Don't hang on too tight or move the planchette yourself."

"That wasn't me," Bruce said.

Colista nodded, then picked his smoke back up out of the bowl. A little bit of the pig's blood soaked into the filter. He stared at it a moment, shrugged, then placed it in his mouth and took a hit. After following with a let of smoke, Colista said, "Gatekeeper?"

The planchette flew up to the word "yes" in the upper left-hand corner of the board.

"Good," Colista said. "And let's not forget you owe me."

The planchette flew to the word "no" so fast Bruce gasped. Colista felt the heat from the fireplace behind him intensify.

"Knock it off, ya old stubborn bastard," Colista said. "This isn't our first rodeo, nor do I expect it will be our last. Let's get on with it. And if you deny that you screwed me over with Pepe, then, well, you won't get the offering I've saved just for you."

The flames behind Colista seemed to back off a moment in contemplation before returning. The planchette went to the arch of letters, first a "W" then an "H" and then…nothing.

"You want to know what I have to offer, is that it?" Colista asked. "I haven't even told you what I want."

The planchette moved to the letter "O".

"I see," Colista said. "You're too lazy to use the board. Call me old-fashioned, but I prefer the board to electronics." With a huff, Colista made a show of flinging the board across the room. The planchette flew and bounced off a bookshelf then skittered over to Crowley who looked at it with the disdain only a cat can muster, as if the thing was the bane of his existence. Then Colista walked over to his desk, opened a drawer, and took out a device shaped in the fashion of a black rectangle. Two antennas sprouted from the top like Devil horns.

With the cigarette pursed between full lips, Colista hit the power button and mumbled, "Knock yourself out."

"What?" Bruce asked.

"O is for Ovilus," Colista said in his best sing-song voice. "Our gatekeeper prefers electronics. A rather new infatuation for him. The device will both spell out the word on the screen the gatekeeper wishes to communicate and verbalize it out loud. The Ovilus V is all the rage."

A word flashed onto the glass screen inside the plastic rectangle. "Better."

"I'm sure," Colista said. "Now, shall we get down to business?"

"Terms," the gatekeeper communicated.

"The usual," Colista said. "I performed the ritual. You can keep the blood. And let's not forget the fact that you double-crossed me."

"Survival," appeared on the screen.

"Yes, yes," Colista said, "so you say. You couldn't snag Pepe's soul from crossing over because of a glitch in the system. Some code of honor among demons. A bunch of hogwash. Regardless, I paid you a hefty sum, the blood of a Russian Orthodox priest that cost me two-months wages."

"Happens," the gatekeeper said.

Crowley hissed.

"Yes, shit happens," Colista said, "but then you make amends. Make things right."

"What?" the gatekeeper asked.

"That's better," Colista said. "I rather like your spirit of cooperation." When the heat didn't rise and the device stayed silent,

Colista added, "That was a little joke there. A pun. Anyway, I want a gate closed, a board-opened portal shut down."

Then Colista felt the heat intensify on his back. Two words formed on the screen of the Ovilus: "Simple" and "Which".

"We shall see," Colista whispered. "This one has remained open for twelve years, at least. A spirit uses it and now inhabits human flesh."

"So."

"No problem for a gatekeeper, aye?" Colista said. "We shall see."

Colista smiled when the heat increased behind him, which meant he'd sufficiently reeled the spirit in. He knew it wanted to settle this blemish on its credentials and earn itself a fat reward in the process.

"Tell."

"Yes," Colista said. "I shall. It's a board upstate and the spirit inhabits one of my students, a Mia Hollenbeck. I'm afraid her family has fallen afoul of a rather nasty cult."

"Wait," the gatekeeper said.

As always, the gatekeeper would need to confirm the open portal or gate. This could take anywhere from thirty seconds to all day. It depended on the gatekeeper's workload and the obscurity of the open gate.

Colista took a drag on the cigarette, expelled the smoke, then looked at Bruce. "Now, we wait. If the gatekeeper can close the portal, then that should end the inhabitation of Mia's body. The spirit will be pulled back to the spiritual realm."

Bruce nodded with tired eyes. "She'll still be with her old man and that pastor, though. But at least she will have a chance to get away."

Colista smiled. "This is the only way I know of to help. The rest is up to her...or you."

Bruce closed his eyes a moment, then locked in on Colista's. "Tell me about Pepe. You know, while we're waiting."

Colista took another toke. When he finished, he closed his eyes in a drowsy gesture and then opened them. "I don't often speak of him."

Bruce shrugged.

So did Colista. "Well, physically, he was a demure man, thin but possessed an uncanny athletic strength. A scratch golfer, he also excelled at tennis and pickle ball. But he was more than that, of course. Much more. He was the yin to my yang, kept me balanced, the light to my darkness. He accepted my...gifts. But he also kept me honest." Colista smoked for a bit before continuing. "Met him in the Caribbean. He ferried boats, and I was there on sabbatical. I leased one of his boats and the rest is, as they say, history. Even after he developed a cancerous growth in his lungs—we both smoked, you know—he remained unchanged, his joyful enthusiastic self. Until the very end. That's when I tried to make a deal and things went bad. Took me a long time to get over it. Hell, I'm still not over it."

"What kind of deal?" Bruce asked. "Immortality?"

"No human body can last forever, Bruce," Colista said. "But in Pepe's case, he was young and strong enough to survive a spiritually-manipulated remission from cancer. But I was betrayed."

"By this gatekeeper?"

Colista nodded, wiped his bangs out of his face, then smoked again. "I paid, and the gatekeeper failed to deliver. Simple. Brutal, but simple. It is what it is, but he will atone. Not that we'll be even-steven, but it's the best I can realistically hope for."

"Wow," Bruce said. "I've learned a lot in the last twenty-four hours. Things I didn't even know existed. But whatever it takes to help Mia; I'll do it."

"Fictionalize it, Bruce," Colista warned, understanding the kid may want to write about the matter. "I learned long ago not to ever post about actual rituals and spirits. People abuse the hell out of that shit. No, just give them a flavor, a hint if you will, and they'll fall all over themselves to buy your wears." He allowed smoke to drift up and over his face, deep in thought. "Spirits are bastards," he whispered.

"But Pepe isn't why you got into this field," Bruce stated. "You were already teaching and practicing. What made you want to be a ...a chaos magician?"

Good Lord, this kid sounds like a reporter! "I suppose it started when I was a child, as most things do. My parents divorced. I lived with mom. Mom couldn't afford much, however, so found the proverbial deal one can't refuse."

"I know about that," Bruce said. "Mom ran out on dad and me some years back. Haven't heard from her since. Luckily, she left us the house. We couldn't have afforded a new one. How did your mom get by?"

Colista let out a plume of smoke. "As is usually the case, the deal included one helluva haunted house. Got it, of course, on the cheap."

"Holy crap!"

"I found I was a natural magnet for spirits, and I soon learned that I needed to take control. I possessed a gift, but it needed refinement. I educated myself, but that kind of training never extrapolates to the real world, so to make money, I entered academia and earned a PhD in psychology. As you may imagine, it has been a lifelong struggle to combine both into a reasonable career. But I managed. And…here we are."

"Yes, here we are," Bruce said, "saving Mia. I sure appreciate it, because I'm pretty sure I have momma issues and, well, girls who dig my style aren't exactly lining up…" Bruce scrunched up his nose and covered his mouth. Colista took this as unstated emotion and felt the sentiment would come in handy during the ritual.

A wicked stench permeated the room as if a thousand demons had just walked in.

Crowley stood, hissed, and ran to the hearth where the fire still burned, yellow and orange flames licking the wood. Deep inside the pile, blue tendrils danced like the Northern Lights.

"This can't be good," Colista said. Then he picked up the Ovilus and peered at the screen. "Gatekeeper, what is the meaning of this?"

"Wait," came the reply.

Colista sat and stared at the screen for what seemed an hour before the stench abated. Then the Ovilus read, "Visit."

"From whom?" Colista asked. "Anything that smells that bad can't be good. A higher-up, I would imagine."

Then the Ovilus rattled off a series of words: "Correct. Dangerous. Elemental. King. Father."

Colista scrunched up his brow, then raised the cigarette to his lips and inhaled. Sometimes he wished he could have a real conversation with spirits on the other side, but limited means existed for communication, even in today's day and age of consumer and professional grade electronics.

"Let me get this straight," Colista said after expelling a rather large cloud of smoke. "An elemental king came through one of your gates. He's dangerous because you were sniffing around a gate that he would appreciate staying open. A gate that one of his progeny is using. Which means…"

"Sensed. Yes."

"Did he discover you?" Colista asked.

"No. Will."

"What does he mean?" Bruce asked.

"Quiet!" Colista demanded, then turned his attention back to the Ovilus. He knew this gatekeeper all too well—knew him well enough to realize the spirit would stall for something more. "What more do you require, gatekeeper? Let's keep in mind that you owe me!"

"Protection."

"You're scared of this elemental?" This surprised Colista. He'd never known the gatekeeper to fear using the skills given to him. His job was to open and close the gates and portals between the realms. His kind had held these keys for eons.

The fire behind Colista roared to life in anger.

"Testy," Colista said. "So, you're not scared but need to buy protection. Is that it? And the pig's blood won't cut it."

The fire lowered and the Ovilus blipped. "Correct. Much. Protection."

"What does that mean?" Bruce asked.

Colista looked up at Bruce with a weary glance. "An elemental king possesses enough clout to make life miserable for the gatekeeper, so he requires a protective spell to thwart the elemental should the gatekeeper proceed with the deal we offered."

"Because the elemental doesn't want the gatekeeper to close the portal in Mia's mom's Ouija board…"

"Perceptive," Colista said. "Most wouldn't catch on that quick. The spirit using the portal, the one inhabiting Mia, is this elemental king's kid. That makes the kid a…"

"An elemental prince," Bruce finished.

"Yes," Colista said. "Nothing more than a privileged brat with nothing better to do than raise hell. The gatekeeper doesn't like this kind of thing, wants to help, but…"

"Needs more green-backs," Bruce said.

"Something like that," Colista said and turned back to the Ovilus. "How much more do you need?"

"Human," the Ovilus chirped.

"What?" Colista said. "You never need human."

"Much. Protection."

"There must be another way," Colista said. "You can't possibly expect me to sacrifice a human being. There's not enough protection in this world to save me from jail." Colista felt goose bumps form on his neck and arms despite the heat of the flames. In all his days, Colista had never harmed a live person or animal in his rituals.

"Cat."

Crowley hissed, ran to the table and swatted at the Ovilus.

"No, no, no," Colista stammered as he moved the device out of the cat's reach. "You most certainly can't have Crowley. His energy is worth any two humans."

Since the day a trembling cold kitten showed up on his doorstep, a bond had immediately formed. They were partners who anticipated each other's needs, especially in matters involving the spiritual realms. Sure, Crowley ate a lot, required constant cleaning of its infernal box, perhaps enjoyed grousing more than Colista cared for, but no way he would trade the cat for anything.

"Boy."

Colista looked up at Bruce.

"Hey," Bruce said as he stood. He edged toward the door. "Don't even think about it!"

"Fine," Colista said. "But I have an idea."

He felt in his bones that this would prove the correct choice, even though he had never involved a human in his rituals before. This situation felt different. The karma contained within this particular sacrifice would easily fuel whatever protection the gatekeeper required. It would then free Mia's body for a return and rid the world of a monster. Two of them. And the universe would help Colista cover the whole caper up, because that's the way of things. Yes, perfection. Maybe the big man himself would even get involved.

Doubt it, he thought, but one never knew. And, if Colista were lucky, which he rarely was, there would remain enough collateral leftover to reunite he and Pepe in the afterlife. Yes, a win-win of mass proportions.

Colista mashed his cigarette out on a clay plate next to the Ovilus. "Deal," he said to the gatekeeper. "Human."

The fire roared behind Colista, then died to nothing but a few pieces of charred coals. The Ovilus squawked using the audio feature, "Waiting."

"Soon," Colista answered. Then he turned to Bruce. "Let's go. I have much work to do if we're gonna pull this off." Colista's heart beat rapidly. This would require planning and perfect timing. Never had the stakes been this high.

Crowley grumbled, but then relaxed enough to sit and groom his singed fur.

CHAPTER 20

Mia floated outside the door to her and Jack's room, frustrated and angry. She'd attempted to stretch the silver thread far enough to reach Colista's rooms back at campus but could not manage it. It felt like a tight muscle that, given time, could stretch and elongate, but time was a commodity she didn't possess. By the time she negotiated a longer tether, her body would have run afoul of any number of circumstances. Not least of which laid next to her body right now.

She considered peeking inside to see what Jack was up to with her. Or her dad's room. But she didn't out of fear for what she might see. Either violation would prove too much for her to handle. Yet, she needed to know. And apparently Colista and Bruce were unreachable, so she would have to help herself.

She stared at the room which her dad shared with Pastor Matt. Something vile was going on in there. She could feel it, as if it were a disease creeping up her silver thread and into her essence. But her dad had made his bed; now he could, quite literally, sleep in it. She, on the other hand, hadn't agreed to what could be going on with Jack behind door number one.

With a burst of energy, Mia approached the door. It offered zero resistance as she went through and slipped into the room. Mia came to rest and floated above her body, noticing several things. One light bulb shone next to the bed which, surprisingly, was not occupied by Jack. On the bed, Mia lay alone, flat on her back, hands behind her head, legs slightly parted. Thank God she was still fully clothed in her light-gray sweatsuit. Her eyes, dull and lifeless, seemed to consider Jack who stood next to the bed. He'd taken his shirt off to reveal large pecs and biceps but otherwise remained clothed. He had tried to clean Bruce's blood off her, because the resulting crimson-stained towels lay on the floor in a wet heap.

Jack's mouth moved as he spoke in a quiet whisper. "Pastor Matt said I should rape you if you wouldn't have sex willingly. He said that's how real men keep their women under control. I don't want that, Mia. I want you to give it up to me willingly. I mean, it's not like we've never done it, but Pastor Matt says it's a woman's duty to please her man whenever he wants it. And it's a man's job to keep his woman accountable to this. Do you understand?"

Mia felt sick. As a kid, she'd remained sheltered from a great many things. She felt bad for her mom who must have had to endure torment from both her dad and Pastor Matt. She'd spared Mia any hardships, but now that Mia was of age, it would be her turn for enlightenment.

Gross! She wouldn't willingly fuck Jack ever again if he was the last man on Earth.

Yet, she knew the evil spirit existing within her would want that end—would want to experience the feelings and stimulations that humans experience. That's what Colista had said. Spirits that were never human were jealous creatures and would stop at nothing to experience what this spirit sat poised to experience at her body's expense.

You dirty, gross thing… Get out of me!

Jack ran his free right hand over Mia's belly, like he had in the van. "I'll become a better lover; I promise. Pastor Matt explained that was part of the deal. That orgasms would keep you happy and content."

Gross, gross, gross!

She didn't think she could hate Jack or Pastor Matt more, but if she had to pick which she hated the most right now, she wasn't sure she could. They were both viler than the spirit who had hijacked her body. Her entire childhood had been a lie. She knew this now. If she wanted something better for her adult life than what her mom had, then she needed to do something about it.

The bed bounced when Jack flopped onto it and crammed his right hand into his jean's pocket. It took a little work, but he finally pulled a box from the depths of the material. Once secured, Jack rolled toward Mia and held the box out toward her waiting body.

"I want to do this the right way," he said.

Mia's body continued to stare at him through dull orbs. Not even a twitch to indicate that she'd heard him. For this, Mia felt gratitude. The last thing she wanted was to become engaged to this prick, giving him an excuse to climb on top of her for a little pleasure-ride.

Jack opened the box and smiled.

The ring within shone with brilliance. It looked to Mia, at least in the gloom, to consist of a white-gold band with a rather nice diamond set in the middle. A beautiful, even tasteful, ring that under different circumstances may have made her heart leap out of her chest.

Mia thought of Bruce.

"You like that?" Jack asked, voice soft. "You wanna get married? What do you think? We can have kids and raise them as part of the church. It'll be perfect. Pastor Matt says we have an obligation to be fruitful and multiply, and I intend to multiply a lot."

No, I won't marry you!

Mia's body remained still, only the rapid twitching of her lifeless eyes bearing any indication of awareness.

Jack sighed. "I know this is sudden."

He lifted her left hand and slid the ring onto her ring finger. When he let go, her hand flopped back down to her thigh as if no muscle existed beneath the skin. Jack stared at her hand as if he expected her to lift it and peruse the ring.

"Well, what do you think?" When she didn't answer, he continued, "Come on, Mia." He sounded exasperated. "You've always known it would be you and me together forever. That Bruce guy can't possibly mean anything to you."

He means everything!

"Well," Jack continued, "the ring is on your finger, and I don't see you taking it off. So, I'm going to assume you're down with all this. I mean, even if you're not, Pastor Matt says it doesn't matter."

He leaned toward Mia's body and kissed her neck, then slid his hand part way up the front of her hoody.

Get off me! In her panic to stop him, Mia hurled herself toward the lightbulb on the stand next to the bed and swatted at it.

The bulb exploded like a glass grenade, shards bouncing off the nightstand and onto the floor.

"What the hell?" Jack whispered. He turned his head and looked over his shoulder, his hand sliding back down to Mia's stomach. "What is with the lightbulbs in this town? The electricity must suck." He looked around the room for a moment. "Bunch of crap what that professor said." Then he returned his attention back to Mia's body. "No more stalling. Time to consummate this engagement. Just think, Mia. This is the first night of the rest of our lives together."

Joy of joys, Mia thought. Her energy flashed with anger.

"You're gonna enjoy this," he whispered.

Mia's body exploded into action beneath Jack's touch. First, it rolled sideways so her eyes met Jack's. Then, defiant, she removed the ring from her finger and threw it across the room where it banged around and came to rest beneath the counter that held the white porcelain sink After slapping Jack across the face, her body crawled on top of the stunned young man and rocked her curvaceous hips. Grunts fell from Mia's lips as if she were feral.

Mia didn't know how to feel, nor what to think. She had enjoyed watching her body dispatch the ring from her finger. That had been sweet. But now the demon inside of her wanted to experience sex. Mia could see the darkness of the thing leak outside the borders of her body as it ground her hips into Jack's midsection in a lewd pantomime. The shadows dancing in and out of her body reminded Mia of a roiling bank of storm clouds.

Jack sputtered, "Mia, stop it. I mean, I'm supposed to be in charge." He tried to grab Mia's hands but the creature inside used her body to slap Jack again, a solid fleshy smack. And hard, too. So hard that Jack closed his eyes and gritted his teeth.

Damn right! Mia thought, and just for a moment felt at kin with this creature. After all, it only wanted to experience what it felt like to be her. Maybe she should feel honored by this. Especially if it was going to beat the living shit out of the man who was now squirming beneath her inhabited flesh.

"Mia," Jack sputtered. "I want this, too. But I really think you should put the ring back on. And a little bit of tenderness would feel good, you know?"

Mia's body growled, then she slapped Jack twice more, a palm to the right side and a backhand to the left. Her hips continued to piston back and forth, and the grunts from her mouth came more quickly.

A trickle of blood wormed out of Jack's nose like a crimson thread. He swiped at it with the back of his hand and stared at it. "That's enough of that!" He attempted to push Mia off of him.

Using Mia's long arms, the creature possessing her pinned Jack to the bed and continued with the lewd display of sexuality. The base of her silver thread of energy, where it met her body, turned blood red as if angry about the current state of things.

It's using my body! That's it!

As much as Mia enjoyed the pummeling of Jack, she would not allow the beast to use her body for pleasure. Mia hurled her energy, anything to stop this violation. When she smacked into her body, she expected a firm resistance, but instead sailed through untouched.

Nothing happened.

Then her body slumped to the side, off of Jack, and slid to the seventies green-carpeted floor in an uncoordinated tangle of limbs. The creature lay with Mia's back on the floor, legs spread, and a sheen of anger in her eyes. It tilted Mia's head upward and growled at Jack as if he'd done this. Her tongue bled, turning her lips and teeth crimson.

"What's wrong with you?" Jack asked. "What kind of drugs are you on?" He wiped more blood from his face and looked around the room. "You've lost your damn mind." He sat up, then looked down to the floor. "You're a fucking mess. Look at you. The Mia I know wouldn't be caught dead in a sweatsuit...or lash out so violently." He shook his head. "Pastor Matt thinks we can rein you in, but maybe you need therapy or something."

A fierce growl bubbled from Mia's mouth.

"Shit," Jack whispered, then climbed off the bed and stood above Mia.

Mia knew a mistake when she saw one. Before she could intervene, her body's right foot rocketed up and slammed into Jack's junk like a runaway train.

Jack screamed and fell to the floor, hands clasped to his crotch as if trying to hold everything together. "You bitch!" he wailed, and rolled around on the green shag.

Her body stood and planted a wicked kick to Jack's forehead. The force bounced his head off the floor like a melon and ended his screaming and ranting. Mia couldn't help but hope he was dead. But she also wondered why the entity would want to take Jack out in the first place?

What's your end game, asshole?

Jack's chest rose and fell. *Not dead.*

Her body looked at the door. Mia shivered at her own appearance: the filthy and stained sweat suit, the sweaty, stringy hair, and the blood.

So much blood!

All she wanted was to have her body back, a long shower, Bruce pressed beside her, and a knitting project in her hands.

Heaven.

Her body stumbled for the door, arm outstretched.

The creature living inside her must have accelerated the old learning curve somehow, because it turned the knob, opened the door, and staggered out into the cool night air. The sound of traffic on the freeway, even at this hour, roared inside.

Mia floated out behind her flesh like a balloon on a string. Once outside, Mia glanced toward the door to the room her dad shared with Pastor Matt. She knew the kind of thing that must be playing out inside that room. She wasn't naive. Maybe she should feel bad for him, but he was the one who enrolled his family in this Godforsaken cult. This church family wasn't the nice kind of community that worshipped together and enjoyed Sunday picnics.

With a rueful smile, the beast within her turned to look at Mia using her own eyes.

You— You can see me?

The creature laughed with a rasp. It pointed toward the door to the next room and nodded. It wanted to give Mia this, a gift of sorts for the use of her body perhaps. It would revel in the delight of exposing her dad's shame. What else did it have in mind?

But it was something else that Mia wanted. She nodded at the spirit in her body. *Do it!*

On stick-tight legs, the spirit manipulated her body well enough to walk to the door of her dad's room, raise a hand, and bang three times. When nobody answered, the creature commenced with three more knocks.

Mia recalled from a television ghost show that evil spirits enjoyed knocking in sets of three because it mocked the Holy Trinity of God, the Father, Son and Holy Spirit. *Perfect*. She just wanted a piece of that asshat Pastor Matt. Better yet if the demon did the work for her.

From inside, a bed squeaked. Several moments went by before quiet footfalls padded toward the door. Pastor Matt would assume it was Jack seeking guidance on what he should do with Mia.

Mia's suspicions were confirmed when the door opened a crack and Pastor Matt's round head poked out like a turtle from a shell. Mia didn't think she'd ever seen his face so crimson, even after an energetic sermon. His white hair stuck out from his dome in messy little white tufts, eyes so full of broken blood vessels he looked like an insane demon. The odor of booze and sweat and horribleness wafted out, and Mia felt a swell of surprise that she could somehow smell these things.

"Mia?" When Mia didn't respond, he continued. "Is everything okay?"

Pretty much nothing is okay! Mia thought. *But it will be soon.*

Her body twisted back and delivered a punch to Pastor Matt. It held a lot of force but lacked direction. The haymaker caught the door before it hit Pastor Matt's bulbous nose, causing too-little damage.

Pastor Matt covered his nose and stumbled back into the room. He unfolded his hands and saw no blood, and a triumphant smile erupted across his power-crazed features.

Mia's dad shouted from behind the closed bathroom door, "Mia, don't come in here. I'm— I'm showering."

Funny that I don't hear any shower!

She figured he needed one, but was now attempting to hide his shame. He wouldn't want his daughter to see him after receiving cult discipline.

Yes, she thought, *a cult and not a church. Hide, daddy...go ahead and hide while your daughter takes care of the situation.*

Pastor Matt let his towel drop from his waist. His tighty whiteys were dingy and yellow with age. He stalked toward Mia's body like a predator ready to grapple.

Mia's body looked curious.

Sticking with the tried and true, Mia flung her energy toward the nearest lightbulb. It burst all over the rumpled queen-sized bed.

That got Pastor Matt's attention. "Interesting," he said, and rubbed his chin. "Maybe that dimwitted professor was actually on to something." He seemed to consider this. "Yes, I would rather think that you, Mia, are trapped outside of your body." He looked as though trying to catch a glimpse of her essence. "And I'll rather enjoy the atonement of your body as you watch."

He stalked toward her, a jiggling bulge growing inside his underthings.

"Run," her dad begged of her. "Please...run!"

"Much too late for that," Pastor Matt said, voice mean and tight. "Maybe if you were more of a man, you'd march out here and do something about it. Stop me from exacting punishment on your daughter like I did you, even though it's my right to do so as your pastor." He continued to stalk forward.

Daddy! Mia thought.

She'd heard the tenderness from her youth in his voice just now, from before he became *born again*. Back when he'd been concerned with being a father and things like compassion rather than control and punishment.

"Your father bowed to my authority just a short while ago, Mia," Pastor Matt said. "Now, so shall you. It's for the greater good, you know."

Mia stared at Pastor Matt's short, red body. His sweaty love handles shook as he walked toward Mia, arms outstretched, ready to hold her down. He slicked his white hair back in a misguided attempt to appear presentable.

"It needn't be all that unpleasant," he said. "Just a submission of control, an acknowledgement that I am in charge. It can still feel good, enjoyable, pleasant even."

Mia felt ill. *What a horrible little man.* She watched as her body relaxed, as if the beast within would submit to the man.

You'd better not, Mia thought and tried to project those thoughts to the beast within her. *This is not an option.*

The beast smiled, just a small upturn of the right side of her lips. One lone incisor shone through like a tiny glacier inside a dark cave. A small gesture, but one Mia knew was intended for her benefit. It might not wish to give her body back, but Mia didn't think it intended to allow Pastor Matt to provide the human stimulation it so desired. No doubt, that frustration would be dealt with later. For now, the creature would sate its lust with a good fight. Savor the emotions of human anger and hate.

Mia sprang forward like a gazelle, with a grace and coordination Mia didn't know the creature possessed. It feigned another blow to the head, but at the last minute pulled up and delivered a kick to Pastor Matt's groin.

Pastor Matt backed away and laughed, then patted the crotch of his stained underwear. "I'm not that big. Don't tell. In any regard, you'll need to do better than that." He sprang toward her.

Mia's body ran from the room.

"Douglass," Pastor Matt screamed, sounding out of breath. "Get your clothes on and get out here. We need to round up your wayward daughter. She's rebelled against God and the church and must receive punishment. It's the only way to save her soul."

He laughed like a madman, head raised to the heavens.

Mia forced her energy out the door, away from Pastor Matt, and watched her body run and disappear into the growing darkness.

Run, demon! Get away! Words she never thought she would utter in her lifetime.

How things change.

CHAPTER 21

Colista laid down on the davenport inside the ring of symbols and salt, then started a chant in a language Bruce couldn't understand. Latin or some such, he figured.

"I thought you had a lot to do," Bruce said in a panic. "You know, to save Mia. No time for a nap, is there?"

Colista stared at him with a withering expression. "Oh yes, nap time. Nighty night, Bruce, see you in the morning." He paused for effect. "Don't be an imbecile. I need to figure out where they've taken her. I'm hoping they haven't yet left town, because we need to find out where they are for two reasons. First, we must keep the creature from harming Mia's body, of course. Priority one. Second, I need a sacrifice. Now, shut your pie hole and let me work."

"Yeah, fine." Crowley crawled up on Colista's lap and curled up. Bruce said, "Sorry."

With wavering eyelids, Colista's eyes rolled up in his head, yet his lips kept moving with the special words he needed to accomplish whatever he was trying to do while lying on the davenport. Soon, Colista's body relaxed and he and the cat both fell into quiet rhythmic breathing. Colista's eyes moved under his lids. The cat whimpered in its sleep.

Bruce's thoughts drifted to Mia. *Good Lord.* He tried to reach out to her with his mind, even without a clear understanding of what that meant except the emotional connection he shared with her felt strong enough to accomplish the feat. No go, but the effort did make him feel closer to her. Bruce tried to imagine the terror she must feel. He'd never been so worried about another human being before, but then he'd also never met a girl like this.

He imagined bringing her home to meet his father.

What's a fine piece of ass like you doing with my boy? He's an artist, you know.

Shut up, Bruce thought as he explored Colista's home. He rather liked all the ancient relics. On the south wall hung decorative masks from various cultures, some tribal, some Renaissance, and some others even looked Elizabethan masquerade quality.

Bruce looked away from the masks. Somewhere out there, Mia was struggling, her energy trapped outside her body. Maybe he should have followed the group when they took her. Colista said not to, that there were other ways to track her, but Bruce felt like he'd failed Mia.

Just like he'd failed his father so long ago, making mom go away and never come back.

That's not true! He'd play neither the villain nor the victim anymore. Mia needed him confident and strong, free from his own negative thoughts. He couldn't help her if he was drowning in his own horrible memories from his childhood.

Time to grow up, Bruce! And this time it wasn't his dad's voice but his own.

Okay. Yeah. Bruce paced, hands behind his back. *I need to acknowledge I care about her.* That seemed a given, but he felt good thinking it. Bruce would also tell her this the first chance he got. When this was all over. *I want her as a girlfriend.* He tossed this thought around. Yes, he would do whatever needed doing, all toward this eventuality. Bruce imagined their future, perhaps cohabitating in a nice apartment downtown, he clicking at his laptop, she knitting out on the patio.

Bruce nodded as he walked about the room. Colista had taught him one thing: anything was possible. Just hours ago, Bruce would never have thought any of this remotely real. Sure, he enjoyed getting Colista's signature and all that, even writing about the supernatural. But he never put much faith in God or any other deity. Now he'd experienced the spiritual realms for himself and wondered what the implications of such a realization were.

Did he have a responsibility to acknowledge it? Maybe he could ask Mia about it sometime. After all, she seemed churchy and in the know. Yet, he felt a difference existed between what Mia believed and what Colista had shown him. Then, again, perhaps it would prove one in the same. Maybe Mia would have some new insight now that her body had been inhabited by a spirit-energy other than her own.

Bruce worried, picking at his cuticles and smoothing his shirt over his stomach. He hoped she was okay. He didn't trust the demon inside of her, or her dad, but especially not the white-haired dude who claimed he was a pastor. Bruce had a bad feeling that guy would bring Mia the most harm.

Bruce stopped in front of a glassed-in cabinet harboring a set of antique syringes. Some appeared to contain the remnants of ancient rusty blood, while others looked empty. They all hung from fastener-hooks drilled into a cork backing. He wondered if the ones with blood had been used in a ritual such as the one he'd just witnessed.

Rituals.

With a burst of anxiety, Bruce wondered if this gatekeeper spirit could be trusted. What if this elemental king offered up a more lucrative deal? This seemed likely to Bruce. Nothing against Colista, especially given that the gatekeeper apparently owed the guy because of poor Pepe, but wouldn't a king whose kid was hiding inside Mia know what a gatekeeper, who was also a spirit, would want more than a human being would? Albeit a very knowledgeable human, but still.

Another thought occurred to Bruce. Perhaps Colista, a human, could deliver the one thing a gatekeeper really wanted…a human sacrifice. This thought turned Bruce's blood cold. He didn't know if he could go through with sacrificing a fellow human. He guessed it depended on the human, but even a truly evil human would prove troublesome for Bruce's moral compass. He couldn't think of any circumstance in which he could see himself slicing open somebody else's throat and bleeding them out. He didn't think he could live with it. Or could he, if for Mia?

Oh, Bruce! What have you gotten yourself into?

This situation felt too much like a horror novel come real, and it made him uncomfortable. He imagined himself sitting at his computer, working on a fictionalization of this whole conflict.

What a plot device! A very true man versus the supernatural.

That would equate to a most magnificent horror story. He could even envision movie rights, foreign rights, hardcover releases, the paperback on every bookstore shelf, and perhaps the need for an agent to navigate him through the literary minefields.

Then guilt hit Bruce like a hammer. This was Mia's story he was considering here. He didn't even know yet how it would end and here he was already cashing in on thoughts of royalties and such.

Not good, Bruce. Not good, bro.

For once you were making some sense, son. Don't ruin it by getting all mushy, now. Write the damn story!

Shut up, dad!

He would put Mia first. Not himself, or some story and for sure not his old man. Bruce worried about Mia. Pins and needles poked at the interior of Bruce's stomach, the result of his anxiety and feelings of helplessness. *A demon inside her, Jack and the pastor harassing her from the outside.* These thoughts made his skin crawl. Anything could happen to her. He paced around these rooms, waiting for Colista to find things out. Bruce yanked at his curls in frustration.

Part of him wanted to be proactive, rush back out into the darkness and find Mia, wherever she was. Bruce imagined finding her and asserting himself, taking her and her problems away with him. *Deep breaths, Bruce. You'll never find her by yourself.* He looked at Colista who still seemed to sleep on the davenport. Bruce didn't exactly understand how this was helping, but he had no choice but to trust the man.

Colista mumbled something that Bruce couldn't understand, then fell silent. The man's brow remained creased with what looked like a worried expression. Was Colista astral projecting right now, trying to find Mia? It was one of his specialties. He wrote a whole book about the subject. If so, where was his awareness roaming right now? Bruce wondered if he could see Mia. His heart sped up thinking about it. Bruce wished he would have made Colista explain himself.

But who are you to demand anything?

Grow a spine, boy! Take control of the situation. You've always been a coward, son. Afraid of your own shadow. And now that pretty lass is out there unprotected.

Shut up! His old man could fuck off.

But this time he couldn't help but feel his dad was right.

Colista moved at a steady pace, his feet a good six inches above the ground. He preferred this to flying high where everything looked different than his normal perspective. Sure, sometimes it proved entertaining to fly, but he found he'd outgrown that kind of thing long ago. The pure joy of his energy roaming free of his flesh had become, he supposed, old hat.

He'd stopped astral projecting for fun long ago and only used the technique nowadays when it suited the situation. Just like he no longer investigated hauntings for fun. He had a spiritual gift that he didn't want to abuse for the sole purpose of sated curiosity.

It'd been Pepe who proved most influential in this regard. He'd encouraged Colista to live his life while alive and worry about the afterlife when dead. This rang true with Colista, and he found that during his time with Pepe, he did indeed experience life…and loved it. But it'd been Pepe who snuck off first, and Colista assumed his energy only concerned itself with the activities of those now past.

Pepe's energy had never visited Colista, and he wasn't sure how he felt about that. During the process of death, which drug on much longer than either Pepe or Colista had felt comfortable, he'd often wondered if Pepe would linger. He'd warned him not to, of course. Encouraged him to shoot into the light the very moment he could. This realm was not a healthy place for spirits. Non-human entities could use human spirits for energy. Besides, without a brain to store memory, spirits relied on a stream of consciousness for information that proved tricky, at best. Everyone involved needed to remember this for the good of all.

Thus, most of Colista's work outside of the university centered around this premise, crossing spirits over and the like. In this case, however, he hoped for the opposite. He needed to get Mia's energy back in her body. But to do that, he needed a human sacrifice. He knew who he wanted. However, getting them to his place would be a challenge. But Colista thought he knew of a person who could get the mark there with no problems.

Colista remembered Doug Hollenbeck say his wife was on the way. In fact, according to Colista's hasty calculations, she should be here by now if she was the woman he imagined. The reasonable parent who Mia confided in when the men folk were controlling and abusive. And where would she go? Maybe her husband would call again and tell her where they were, but Colista didn't think so. If Pastor Matt got his way, the woman wouldn't know where Mia or her husband were. So, in that case, she'd hit the only spot she knew of. Mia's dorm room. Colista would confirm her presence there and then he and Bruce would go fetch her.

He realized the woman may not climb right on board with his scheme, but Colista would play it safe and not tell her everything. Not until he confirmed his suspicions that she would turn on her church. In his albeit limited talks with Mia and Bruce, and having met the man in the flesh, Colista found it likely she'd suffered at the hands of Pastor Matt. *No way Mia was worried enough about her so-called boyfriend being aligned with her childhood church that she escaped her own body without that same fear being noticed by an observant mother.* This is the premise on which he would operate, anyway.

With practiced ease, Colista glided toward the women's dorm, up the cement steps, and then hovered near the wall of rectangle mailboxes. He found the names from the Parapsychology Club roster: Fallon/Hollenbeck. Room three-thirty-one.

He raced up the stairwell, turned right at the third-floor landing, raced over puke-green striped carpet, and finally floated before Mia's oak dorm-room door. He could hear a loud conversation in progress.

No desire to walk in on an interlude—he'd never had the spine or craving for voyeurism—he listened at the door. The voice of two women speaking in loud tones wafted through the solid oak.

Seems safe enough to risk a peek inside.

Passing through solid matter always felt wrong to Colista, although his head and shoulders passed through the material with ease. He didn't understand the science of how such things worked, but they did, seemingly well thought out long ago by a power much smarter than he.

Chastity stood with her hands on her hips. An older woman stood with arms folded and a scowl of distaste on her face. The woman looked an awful lot like Mia. Same blonde hair, same height. The only difference were the brown eyes as opposed to Mia's bright blue gems.

"Where is she?" folded-arm woman said. "I know you're covering for her. Not that I blame you, considering what you've probably heard. It's important I find her."

Chastity looked at the woman with a strange tilt of her head, probably sizing up what the woman just said. "I told you," Chastity said slowly. "Her boyfriend...you know, the one with the cornrows...showed up at a Para-psych meeting and they walked off together. That's the last I saw of her, and that was this morning. She hasn't been back to the room." She glanced up at the round stainless-steel clock on the light-blue wall. "Probably twelve hours ago by now."

A boy—Brody, Colista knew—peeked from beneath the covers on Chastity's bed. "Whoa! Can you two keep it down? I'm nursing a sweet buzz here and you're making me lose it. I'm like, you know, right on the razors edge and I don't wanna waste it. Shits expensive."

Chastity walked over and flipped the covers back over Brody's head. "Give me a minute."

Brody mumbled something unintelligible.

The woman scowled but didn't say anything about Brody being in the room or the fact he was intoxicated. "It's really important I find her. My husband called and said he was going to bring her home because she's having some problems."

"Problems?" Chastity said. "Not that I know of. In fact, she's the last person I'd expect to have a problem. Straitlaced, if ya know what I mean."

"What we as a family consider a problem might vary from your definition," the woman said in a careful tone.

"Right," Chastity said. "You're all churchy and stuff." She seemed to consider this a moment. "I guess I should tell you about Bruce. Now, I think it's a good thing, but Mia said you guys were pretty set on that Jack fella for her. Anyway, you might want to try his room." Chastity gave her the dorm and room number. She shrugged. "Mia wasn't as set on Jack as you all."

"I was referring to Mia's social anxiety as the issue." Mia's mom shifted her weight. "For the record, her *father* is set on Jack," Mia's mom corrected, arms still folded, scowl still on her lips. She turned for the door and came face to face with Colista, who unfortunately could now see right up her nostrils. She, of course, couldn't see him. "Thanks for your help." She turned back to Chastity. "My name is Renee. If Mia happens to come back here, please tell her I'm looking for her. Please tell her to call my cell."

Chastity nodded. "For the record. Mia seems to be coming out of her shell, socially speaking. Maybe getting away from home helped that."

Renee's shoulders bunched, but she didn't turn back. Instead, she opened the door and stepped out into the hall.

Colista was already on the way back to his body.

CHAPTER 22

Mia followed her body while it sprinted through a hole in the chain-link fence which surrounded the motel complex. Pieces of trash littered the edges, discarded refuse: a milk jug, a white sock, an old bald bike tire, and—*Gross*!—was that a used condom?

Past the fence and its collected debris, they approached a quiet backstreet lined with dilapidated clapboard homes. Well behind, Mia could hear Jack calling for her. Hopefully, by the time he made it this far, her body would have moved on into the shadows.

The spirit inside wanted to avoid being caught so it could conduct itself in whatever manner it saw fit. Mia could feel its presence surge just beyond the silver tether. Not so much an evil essence as a wild one. Reckless abandon. It had granted Mia the satisfaction of tormenting Pastor Matt, disrupting the man's plan, but now it would concentrate on its own.

A noisy house behind a high-wall pine fence caught the demon's attention, and it trotted in that direction. Loud voices shouted into the darkness, laughs floating off into the branches of the surrounding oaks.

Drunk revelers, Mia knew. She'd never been drunk, but Jack had often tried to talk her into it. He thought it would loosen up her inhibitions. His needed no such help.

An intoxicated man stumbled out through a gate, put hands on knees, then puked onto the cracked and pockmarked concrete sidewalk. Back spray spattered the toes of his black shoes.

Mia's body took advantage of the entry point and slipped by the dry-heaving drunk and into the home's backyard.

"Hey," the drunk guy slurred, staring at Mia's body through beer-goggled rheumy eyes. "You here with anyone?"

Mia watched her face manage a flirtatious smirk. Much to her relief, her body moved on into the relative darkness of the backyard trees.

"Catch up to ya later," the drunk guy mumbled.

Mia found herself alone in a backyard with the spirit inside of her. Straight ahead, just beyond the trees, Mia could see a cedar deck. People held red Solo cups and visited in hushed tones. As she floated closer, Mia noticed some of the people were kissing. Others were sprawled on cheap patio furniture in various states of repose...and dress. Three kegs sat inside a series of three rusty garbage cans, ice spilling over the edges. Three college-age guys pumped the taps in a brisk manner to alleviate the problem of a weak stream of beer while others waited to fill their cups.

Mia felt the spirit's excitement. It wished to interact with the people at this party in diabolical fashion, experiencing intoxication and sexual pleasure. These things didn't exactly scare Mia, but she wanted to be the one in her body enjoying them if she chose of her own free will.

A staircase on the right side of the deck allowed her body access to the party. Now Mia could see bowls of snacks, popcorn and chips, scattered across glass patio tables. In equal supply were small bowls of white powder.

"Hey," a guy said. He'd just come out on the deck from inside the house. "You need a wristband. Nobody rides for free, if ya know what I mean." He looked around. "Say, where'd you come from? Pretty sure I would have remembered a face like yours."

Mia's body took a step forward.

No, no, no! Run, run, run!

Mia didn't like the look of the guy. His voice possessed a pleasant quality, but she could tell he'd grown accustomed to achieving whatever ends he wished. He'd expect no less now. The nice-guy smile and civil façade would fall away on a moment's notice. Mia further understood that the demon inside of her would not exactly say no. Mia felt a surge of panic.

Mia's thoughts oscillated between trying to focus her energy and wanting to sack-punch this douche. She'd stretch the pretty silver cord as far as she could, because she couldn't bear witness to what would come next. The violation of her flesh would break her psyche.

The guy stuck out his hand. "Never mind the wristband. I'm Jeb. And you are?" He turned his head sideways and smiled, dimples forming by the corners of his lips.

Jeb? Give me a break!

Mia's arm and right-hand thrust forward and clasped hands with...*Jeb!* Mia felt like a spectator, someone watching two other people interact, with zero control over the situation. She couldn't even butt in and make a nuisance of herself.

"A quiet one, huh?" Jeb asked. He dropped Mia's hand but took another step forward. "I like quiet ones." He wrinkled his nose. "Are you homeless? You look a bit disheveled...and have a little BO going there. Is that blood? Geez, you're a mess." He chanced a finger on her lips, then parted her upper to see her teeth. "Holy shit."

Of all the nerve! Mia thought.

But she looked down at herself, and could see why Jeb may think that. Her gray sweatsuit appeared ratty, areas of dirt and red rust mixed with dried blood smeared across the front. She didn't even want to think about her hair. When was the last time she showered? After yoga and that seemed like forever ago. And her teeth must still be red with Bruce's blood.

"You're welcome to use the shower," Jeb said. "And I think an ex left some clothes about your size. Interested?"

Mia's body didn't move—didn't even appear to blink, wavering back and forth as if trying to balance properly.

Jeb put hands on hips. "Must've gotten into the blow a little too hard. Tried to tell them to keep it discreet, but they rarely listen. Kids." He smiled and chuckled at this like drugs were a big joke.

Mia's head moved back and forth as her eyes scanned the immediate area, as if looking to score some of said powder.

Don't you dare!

If her body took drugs when she was not inside it could she go to jail? She found this quite likely, because she thought most cops didn't believe in things like spirits and possession. They'd bust her, then when they found out she couldn't speak, or wouldn't, they'd send her to a shrink amongst other unsavory things. Just like in the movies, they'd probably throw her in the loony bin, either for the rest of her life or until the spirit got bored and left her body. Only then would she be able could communicate again like a normal human being.

"This what you're looking for?" Jeb asked with a crooked grin. "You coming down a little... Wanna fly high again?" He pulled a baggie containing white powder from his back pocket and shook it with a slight up and down motion.

Mia watched in horror as her head bobbed up and down. *Oh no.* The demon and her body were going to get loaded on cocaine. Oh shit, now Mia would get addicted. Scum. Her parents...and the church would...well, after what she knew now about Pastor Matt, they could all go hang, but still. No, she refused to worry about the church or what they thought any longer. She would repeat this line of thinking until she completely accepted it.

Jeb stepped closer to Mia whose hand twitched as it went for the powder.

"Nobody rides for free," he said. "You understand what I mean, right?"

Mia's head bobbled up and down again.

No! You will not pay with my body!

Jeb took Mia by the hand and led her down a dark hallway, stopped at a closed door, then opened it. They both entered. Mia found she didn't want to follow her body yet, so she stayed in the living room. For the first time, she truly noticed the house. The tan carpets were stained, and the beige painted walls were chipped and scratched. A stale stench of old beer, sweat, and other unmentionables wafted to her ghostly senses.

A den of sin if one ever existed, Mia thought, anything to distract herself from her predicament.

A harsh demonic screech sounded from down the hallway, what Mia knew came from her own vocal cords.

No!

The thing would sleep with douchebag Jeb and then take the drugs, or vice versa. Either way, it was an unacceptable situation. She needed to think of something to stop this, and fast. She wished she'd never met Colista or learned about astral projection. Of course, then she would have never found out about Pastor Matt until things were well beyond a point where she could do anything about it.

"Mia!" a voice yelled from somewhere far away.

Sounds like Jack.

He must have caught up with her in time to see where she went. She couldn't decide which would be worse, a douchebag like Jeb or that jackass Jack. Neither was a great option, but at least Jack would do what he could to get her body out of here. Even if it was just to defile her himself.

She left the living room and floated back out to the deck. Several people still milled about, but she didn't see Jack.

"Mia!" the voice came again.

Mia looked down toward the gate from the deck. Jack stood in the opening in the fence, two big dudes with tight t-shirts blocking his entry. She watched while he visited with them. Jack pointed in her general direction, probably telling them he was here looking for her. He nodded casually and smiled, trying, in all likelihood, to put the guys at ease and allow him access. Mia watched as they shook their heads.

Jack threw his hands in the air and yelled something at the smaller of the two men. This didn't seem to be going as Jack planned. The bigger dude, who looked to be at least two-hundred-twenty pounds of muscle and sinew, pushed Jack until he stumbled back out through the gate and into the alley.

Mia found she didn't care what happened with Jack. If he couldn't get in, great. If he did, maybe he could help her body get away from Jeb, even if it would be out of the frying pan into the fire. Panic seized her. She needed to get to her body and start breaking some light bulbs.

Without much effort, Mia flowed back across the deck and into the house. The silver thread wavered in the air between her and where her body resided down the dark hallway. Partiers walked right through the slice of energy without effort—without an inkling.

Mia tried to decide what to do but didn't arrive at anything reasonable. She would play things by ear after entering Jeb's room based on what she witnessed.

She approached the door then entered.

Mia stood just inside the door, confused and a bit stunned by what she saw. Her face looked ghost-white from the powder covering it, her eyes blinking, lashes frosted with cocaine.

Jeb knelt in the corner coughing. He didn't look good, face flushed, eyes red from the burst blood vessels in the whites. "You're gonna pay for that one."

Mia realized the spirit, in its haste to ingest the drugs, must have given Jeb quite a dose as well.

The empty baggie lay on the floor, a telltale smudge of white powder leading from it to where Jeb knelt. His extremities trembled and Mia wondered if this was caused by the coke.

"If I OD, you'll never make it out of here alive," Jeb wheezed.

The demon didn't appear to care one way or the other, allowing her body to sit and enjoy the effects of the coke. Mia didn't appear near as strung out as Jeb, so she surmised the entity had been somewhat smart about dosage or else coke affected demons differently.

Jeb stumbled to a dresser and, using shaking hands, pulled out another baggie with pills. He popped a fistful of pretty ones into his mouth and swallowed them dry. "Soon as I recover a bit, we'll have a little talk about manners." After putting the pills on the dresser, he mumbled, "You're lucky that wasn't Fentanyl. We'd both be dead…"

Nothing in Mia's body's demeanor denoted the spirit cared about that threat. Although, either by chance or design, the thing seemed to be looking out for her flesh to a small degree. Perhaps jumping into another body would require more effort than the entity cared for. Mia could see it now as it flashed in and out of her body, exhilarated by this very human experience.

Oh, God, I'm so screwed.

Jeb stumbled back toward the bed and stood before Mia on shaky legs. He shook his head. "How in the hell are you still standing? Only longtime users your size could take that much coke and still hang in." He reached out and brushed the white powder off Mia's long dark eyelashes. The powder rained down and onto the floor as her eyes continued to blink. "Don't look like a speed freak…"

Horror filled Mia as—much to her surprise—her hand reached out and grasped Jeb's junk. Not hard, just a tender squeeze and a light bounce. A heavy breath left her mouth which came out as a wheeze of air, then a deep raspy laugh.

"Are you kidding me? You're one funky bitch. Three grams of blow and you still wanna fool around." He shook his head with a smirk plastered to his full lips. "Unreal."

Mia could still see the clean-cut academic athletic type beneath the shaggy hair and the beer belly that had only just begun to form. Yes, he'd probably been an athlete at one time, but somewhere along the way, Jeb found drugs. She'd read somewhere this could happen because of an athletic injury. First the pain killers, then harder things, until finally they turned to what was affordable.

Mia laughed, again, that creepy low-pitched moan, like a smoker on steroids.

"That's creepy as fuck," Jeb pointed out. He scrunched up his nose. "And you really do stink. Geez, what are you?" Then he laughed, despite Mia's body continuing to fondle him from outside his jeans. "I mean, you're not like a vampire or something...are you?" He looked uncertain for a moment, brow wrinkling, head turned sideways, before laughing his comment off.

Mia didn't answer but a tight smile spread across her lips exposing white teeth still smeared with splotches of blood.

"Shit," Jeb whispered. "You better be worth the investment. That bag cost me almost a grand." He pointed at the baggie which now lay on the green shag carpet.

Mia doubted the demon cared about his investment. Much to the contrary, she supposed. Jeb's blabbering about the difficulties of life would get him nowhere with it. Jeb was nothing but a sack of meat for this spirit to pleasure itself with.

Jeb extended his long arms and shoved Mia backward onto the bed. Her body bounced until the bed finally came to rest. The creature inside her flesh spread her legs open.

"I really should make you shower up first," Jeb said, hands on hips. He sat on a corner of the bed, making Mia's body bounce again. "But you're so fine, I'll just hold my breath."

He reached over and ran a hand over Mia's exposed flat stomach and up under her soiled hoodie toward her breasts. Then he glanced at his nightstand. "But first, a little mood lighting."

In what Mia considered a corny gesture, Jeb reached over and turned on the lava-lamp. The light within revealed a congealed lump of lava that bubbled upward as the liquid heated up.

"There we go." Jeb pulled the waistband of Mia's gray sweatpants down just far enough to kiss her left hipbone.

Gross, Mia thought. She wanted Jeb to be Bruce so bad. A tender kiss on her hipbone like that from him would be wonderful and even exhilarating. Her heart fell. How would Bruce, Colista or even her mother find her now?

The beast within her spread Mia's legs even wider.

"Ready to go, huh?" Jeb said. He patted her belly.

Mia could see the goose bumps erupt over her own neck.

Jeb edged himself closer to her, so he sat between her legs.

"Not real big, but I bet your nipples…"

The pig never got to finish his utterance, because Mia went out of her mind, feeling a tempest of energy revolve around her.

No, no, no!

She wouldn't allow a violation of her body. Mia focused her energy on the lava lamp as she had the various lightbulbs. Enough of men who thought they could take what they wanted when they wanted it. First Jack, then Pastor Matt, and now *Dime-bag* Jeb!

A loud electric pop and the lava lamp exploded into a cloud of clear viscous liquid and a thousand sharp shards of glass. Her aim was improving.

No way… Hell yeah!

Jeb screamed, grabbed his face and fell from between Mia's spread legs and onto the floor. He writhed on the ground like a giant white grub. He finally looked up in disbelief. Mia saw blood dripping from his left eye, both lips, and from his cheek where a large, ragged chunk of glass had imbedded itself. It must have gone through and sliced his tongue, because blood poured from his mouth and covered his lips in bright crimson.

"Motherfucker," Jeb moaned, barely intelligible.

Mia wondered if he could see out of that mangled eye. A string of blood spiraled from Jeb's lips and onto his lap. The bulge there had receded considerably.

Mia's body growled in frustration and sat up to get a view of the carnage below.

Then gunshots and screams erupted from outside the bedroom door, and Mia wondered how the situation could possibly get any worse.

CHAPTER 23

Colista reentered his body and sat up. He turned to Bruce who seemed fascinated by his curio cabinet filled with syringes. "Let's go."

Bruce whirled. He appeared wild and surprised. Then he blurted, "I'm going to find Mia! I should have never let them take her."

"Bad idea," Colista said and rose from the davenport.

Crowley leapt down with a squall, disturbed from its slumber on Colista's chest, then peered at Bruce.

"You have a better one, then?" Bruce said as if he'd suddenly grown a spine.

Colista considered him with suspicion. "Go ahead if you want. But the likelihood you can track her down now is next to zero. If you even did, you would need a plan. Or hadn't you thought that far into the future yet?"

Bruce crossed his arms and a scowl crept across his facial features. He actually looked more determined than Colista ever remembered seeing him over the last couple days.

With arms outstretched, Colista waved appeasing palms. "We both want the same thing," he explained. "We just have two different plans." Once Bruce visibly relaxed, he continued, "If you'll be so good as to come with me, I require your rather elementary way of explaining situations."

"To explain the situation to whom?" Bruce asked.

"Mia's mother, of course," Colista said as if this tidbit should have proven self-evident. "She's here on campus, and we need her on our side."

"That's where you went?" Bruce asked. "To look for Mia's mother?"

"Yes," Colista said slowly, as if talking to an imbecile. "The only other person in the world who can legally take and keep Mia if she were ever determined to not be of sound mind."

"Don't talk to me like I'm a douchebag. I may not have a PhD, but I'm smart. I was just thinking that Mia's eighteen and can make her own decisions."

Colista nodded. "I appreciate that you finally found your balls—believe me, I do—but we don't have time to quibble. If we hesitate, we'll miss Mia's mother. You'll just have to trust me. You with me on this?"

Bruce raised a hand to his stubbled chin and looked over his shoulder as if to ponder Colista's words. When Bruce turned back, he possessed a bright gleam in his eye. "You better be right about this. Because I really want you to be."

Colista nodded. Something had gotten into Bruce, and Colista rather enjoyed it. While Colista was out and about, Bruce had grown up somehow. Where that came from with such suddenness, Colista had no idea, but he would use it to his advantage.

"Then let's go," Bruce said and walked toward the door. "Where is she?"

"Headed to your dorm room," Colista answered. He turned to Crowley. "Crowley, stay. Soften up the gatekeeper if you would."

Crowley stalked to the fireplace, tail whipping back and forth in a display of defiance.

"Stop grousing," Colista said. "The gatekeeper is fond of you, even if he joked about a cat sacrifice. A joke, Crowley." Then he turned to the door. "Off we are."

But Bruce had already opened the door and exited the apartment. Colista could see him moving away, so he hurried out the door to catch up. Despite the thirty-year difference in their ages, Colista caught up to the young man with just a few strides of his long legs. Pepe had always told him that he loped like a baby giraffe when in a hurry.

"On a mission," Colista said in a friendly tone.

He liked the way Bruce was stepping up to the plate. This kid enjoyed Mia's company and would do what it took to get her back. That was a far cry from the nerdy wannabe writer he'd met some days back. All to the good.

Bruce glanced at Colista over his shoulder but kept on the move. "Yeah. If we need Mia's mom, then let's get to it. I can't stand the thought of Mia being out there, in danger, for any longer than necessary." He slowed. "I still don't understand what we hope to accomplish. I mean, if she knew where Mia was, the woman wouldn't be here looking for her."

"Fair point," Colista said. This next part would prove tricky to explain, he knew. "But I have no intention of using Mia's mom to find Mia."

To Bruce's credit, the guy didn't stop walking, but he did allow his mouth to drop open. "What the hell are you talking about? Wait. Don't tell me you plan to use Mia's mom as the sacrifice to the gatekeeper?"

"No," Colista said as he walked beside Bruce. It had been a long time since he'd felt the urge for a good old-fashioned belly-laugh but refrained.

"I see that smirk. What's so funny?" Bruce asked, a serious look plastered on his mug, eyes squinted, nose scrunched until his dark eyebrows met.

Colista got himself under control. "Well, nothing, except no, Mia's mom won't wind up being sacrificed to the gatekeeper. I'd never give it the satisfaction. No, but Mia's mom will make the best possible bait for the gatekeeper's human sacrifice."

"What…who?"

"Who will act quickly to get her under control and not let this get out?" Colista said. "At least, not outside of the church family."

Bruce smiled. "That's right. Do you think she can pull it off? Can she manipulate him without Pastor Matt catching on?"

"Yes," Colista said. "I do. At least I'm willing to bet on it. Pastor Matt is just egotistical enough to not believe any harm could ever come to him. I've seen the type before."

They headed out across the quad, Bruce leading, and a building which must be Bruce's came into view just over a hundred yards away across the greenspace filled with benches and fountains. A few students lingered around the lawn, despite the late hour. It was quite warm, and he couldn't blame them for taking advantage of the nice weather. One day, long ago, he and Pepe would have done the same. It occurred to him that perhaps he'd stopped living, that he had buried himself in his work to either forget Pepe or, more likely, to never move on from him.

He examined Bruce's determined gait. If this awkward college kid could change in such a short period of time, for a girl nonetheless, then so could he. And he would, just as soon as he wrapped this little assignment. Making the gatekeeper pay for its mistakes regarding Pepe would go a long way toward Colista moving along with his life.

Bruce reached the steps that led to his foyer just ahead of Colista and bounded up quicker than he thought the kid capable. "Whoa!" Bruce stopped midway through the foyer where the mailboxes sat. "Is that her?"

Colista peered past Bruce and down the hall. The woman he'd seen in Mia's dorm room, Renee, stood in front of an apartment door. He assumed it was Bruce's. Her hand reached out and rapped on the hardwood with a steady beat.

"Yes," Colista said. "Her name is Renee. Go ahead and greet her. Tell her who you are and how you know Mia. I'll jump in when the time's right."

Bruce nodded and walked toward the woman. His feet barely made a sound on the newer green and gold striped carpet.

Colista could tell the guy was running through what to say in his head because of the way he kept running a trembling hand through his curly locks. He followed behind Bruce, giving the guy time to break the ice before he jumped in with the weird stuff. It wouldn't do to scare the woman off. Most likely, she'd spent a fair portion of her adult life in a place which promoted an overabundance of caution when it came to the paranormal. Pastor Matt would have made damn sure of that.

Renee turned to Bruce. She folded her arms across her midsection, then tilted her head sideways as if to size the student up. Face stoic, she bit her lower lip, revealing her own nervousness.

"Can I help you?" Bruce asked. Colista heard the attempt at lightheartedness in his voice. "That's my room."

"Bruce?" Renee asked, a tentative waiver in her voice.

Colista wondered if she may suffer from the same social affliction as Mia. Did that trait have something to do with getting suckered into a cult? Did social anxiety make one more vulnerable to control?

"That's me," Bruce said. "You look just like her, so I guess you're looking for Mia."

Keep her talking, Colista thought. He liked the tone of Bruce's voice, friendly, calming.

"I am." She didn't yet unwind her arms to shake hands, ever reserved and cautious. "I'm told you're a friend of hers." She seemed to make a mental appraisal of him. "She has some social anxiety issues, so I'm glad she has made friends, but I would really like to find her."

"Sure," Bruce said. "She does, but she's been doing really well. I mean, you know, a few tears, but she knows what she needs to do. She loves the knitting...she knit-bombed her roommates band equipment." He paused. "Anyway, yes, Mia and I are friends." He reached out with a beefy hand.

Slow but sure, Renee unwound her right arm and grasped Bruce's hand. She gave it one pump and then reeled her arm back in and around her body as if she might just fall apart without the support. Renee looked confused about what to say next. "My husband came here to get her because her boyfriend called about some trouble. I was supposed to meet them, but I can't seem to find anyone now. And nobody will answer their phone. You know how it is."

"I'm sure it's frustrating," Bruce said, "but my professor and I may be able to shed some light on the situation."

For the first time, Renee leaned out and noticed Colista waiting down the hallway. Sensing his cue, he approached. Renee's jaw set, lips a thin line and she ran a hand through her shoulder-length hair. *Nervous,* Colista thought. He didn't want to alarm her, but things needed discussing.

"Why do I feel like you two knew where to find me?" she asked.

It was Bruce who thought the quickest. "Oh, Chastity called me. And I told Professor Colista here and, well, here we are to fill you in."

Colista glanced at Bruce, allowing a small smile to play on his lips. *The kid is resourceful.* He turned to Renee, allowing his smile to morph into something less edgy. "Yes, good old Chastity. She has her flaws, but she's a real gem, deep down."

"She was sleeping with another student when I got there," Renee quipped, as if that said everything about Chastity.

"That'd be Brody," Bruce explained with a bright smile.

"I don't care who it is," Renee said. "I just can't believe Mia lives in a room with someone who sleeps around and didn't tell me." She shook her head. "You know what? Never mind. Who am I to judge? Just point me in the direction of my daughter and I'll be on my way.

Out of your hair. I'm sure the two of you have better uses for your time."

"On the contrary," Colista said, edging closer now. "There's nothing I'd like more than to help Mia. She's a remarkable young woman, independent and strong."

"Are we talking about the same person?" Renee asked.

"I'm assuming," Colista said. "Not too many Mia's running around."

"Mia's awesome," Bruce said. "She's really fun to hang out with."

"That's what I'm afraid of," Renee said. "I live in a constant state of fear that she'll either have a complete breakdown, or that she'll turn feral." She tried to make it sound like a joke but Colista heard the true concern in her voice.

"So much fear," Colista said quietly, almost a whisper.

"What about fear?" Renee asked.

"It just seems both you and your daughter share some fears," Colista said as he probed the edges of a tender subject. "It seems she constantly worries about something back home that she doesn't wish to share or talk about. And now, it seems like you have your share of worries, as well."

"Who wouldn't worry about their daughter?" she asked.

"Worry, yes," Colista said, "but, in my experience, most parents are excited to see their children taste some independence."

Renee let out a breath. "Well, call us unique, but we would have rather seen Mia go to Bible college instead of state. Mostly because of her social anxiety. Kids at Bible college tend to…"

"Mostly?" Colista interrupted. He needed to keep her on track—keep her talking about the situation at home. He'd probe until he found something useful.

"What do you want me to say, Professor Colista?" she asked. "Our family is a bit conservative. We try to follow the values our church sets forth. Is that so strange? We just want the best life possible for our daughter. A biblically positive one."

"Is that what she would have gotten if she stayed home and went to Bible college?" Colista asked, allowing a tone of disbelief to filter through the words.

"Why are you so curious about Mia's home life?" she asked.

"You used to own a Ouija board, didn't you?" Colista needed to keep her just the slightest bit on edge now. He needed her to speak the truth, not some blurring thereof.

"That's none of your—" Renee stared at Colista, face white with a slight blanch of blue forming under her eyes.

"Mia blushes blue, also," Bruce said in a jovial tone. He smiled. "And it's okay about the Ouija board, but it is important. Kind of key to what we're about to explain to you."

Renee wiped at her cheeks as if they were wet, then looked to Colista as if he would have the answers. "What is this about? Is Mia in trouble?"

"You could say that," Colista said. "Not with the law or anything like that, but trouble nonetheless. Trouble that will require your assistance to overcome."

"Well, of course," Renee said, "I'm her mother. But what's this have to do with our homelife...and my past?" She sounded suspicious now, as if Bruce and Colista may know more than they were letting on.

"It seems Mia got a hold of your Ouija board when she was young," Colista said. "Is this true?"

"It may be," Renee said, "but that happened before I was born again. Mia doesn't know I know. I would never touch one now that I understand the risks—understand that it's an instrument of the Devil."

Colista thought she sounded more desperate to explain herself, as if she were used to defending her position to this Pastor Matt fellow.

"No need to explain to me," Colista said. "As you remarked earlier, who am I to judge? That said, Mia seems to have encountered a bit of a hanger-on from her experience with the board. That, as you say, is part of the trouble."

"Part?" Renee asked, the first hint of panic in her tone. Her chest heaved in and out, and when Colista didn't immediately answer she asked, "Hanger-on?"

"Hmmm, yes," Colista said, wanting to appear as if he needed to ponder the next round of discourse. "By way of warning, this next part may sound foreign to you, but rest assured it's actually quite common and…a relatively easy fix under normal circumstances."

"Normal circumstances?" Renee stared at Bruce and Colista like they may very well be out of their minds, but things were beginning to come together in her mind.

"Yes," Colista said, "your pastor arrived at the most sensitive of junctures."

Renee winced. "Pastor Matt's here?"

"In all his glory," Colista said.

"Dude's an asshat," Bruce included.

Renee nodded, but Colista wasn't sure to which comment.

"So," Colista continued, "I mentioned Mia's hanger-on issue. Now, that's simply a manifestation from the open portal that is your Ouija board."

"But," Renee said, "I threw that thing out years ago. In fact, I burned it."

"Oh my," Colista said. "Always a bad idea to burn a board without first binding it, because then, yes, the board is destroyed, but the portal is still wide open. We're probably fortunate that nothing else has wandered out of it." Colista scratched his chin. "Hmmm…the entrance must be well hidden on the other side."

"What?" Renee asked.

"Oh, nothing," Colista said. "It doesn't matter. What does is that I was a hair's breadth from relieving Mia of her problem when your Pastor Matt so kindly showed up with your husband and Jack in tow and ferried Mia off beyond my influence."

"So you're saying Mia is possessed by a spirit from my old Ouija board?" Renee asked, sounding panicked. "And now she's with Pastor Matt?" Now she sounded even more unnerved. "He'll punish her!"

"Yes," Colista said. "I do believe he will. That's why we need to act fast, before anything…unfortunate can occur. And Mia isn't possessed, precisely. She would need to be trapped inside of her body with the spirit for that to happen."

Renee shook her head and held out her hands. "I— I don't understand."

Colista sighed. "Now, I want you to take this in the best possible way, but Mia was experimenting with astral projection. While she was projecting and out of her body, this spirit slipped in." Renee's body went rigid. "So, as you may have already guessed, she's trapped outside of her flesh bag."

Bruce scrutinized him or, what Colista assumed, using the term *flesh bag*. It had indeed been a severe use of language.

"Gross!" Renee quipped. "And just how did she get introduced to this projection rubbish? She wouldn't have looked it up herself."

"I will take full responsibility for the matter," Colista said. "She learned it from one of my books and took to experimenting on her own. To my defense, she kind of took to it behind my back, so to speak…without any guidance."

"So, now you can see why her father and I preferred Bible college," Renee said.

"With all due respect," Bruce said, "her curiosity started with your Ouija board." He shrugged as if it were no biggie, that everyone made mistakes now and then.

Renee huffed at this but remained silent for a moment. "So, this thing is…inside of her body. Okay. What is Pastor Matt doing about it?"

"Very little, I'd presume," Colista said. "He's deemed that she is on drugs and in need of rehab through your church. Although, I would guess that his form of rehab may deviate from normal protocols for such matters."

Renee turned even whiter—and bluer—then hung her head.

"Don't let him do it to her, too," Bruce said.

Colista whipped his head to the boy. *Brilliant!* The boy was bloody brilliant when he put his mind to it hard enough. The words represented a risk, but a calculated one.

Tears in her eyes, Renee looked at Bruce. "Don't judge me."

"I'm not," he said. "But Mia went away to college to escape Pastor Matt and the church, to avoid the things that happened to you."

The boy was doing some guess work here, but still a smart display of deductive reasoning. Colista couldn't help but smirk.

"What did Mia tell you?"

"Everything," Bruce said with a straight face.

"But-but, she wasn't supposed to know until…until…"

"Until she was an adult?" Bruce asked. "And then she'd get fully initiated into the cult, which involves sex with Pastor Matt."

Renee remained silent.

"The boy is quite right," Colista said. "And don't you think it's time for this all to come to an end. Nobody else, especially Mia, need get hurt."

"I don't know how this all fits together!" Renee wailed.

Colista leaned against the wall next to Renee. "What if I was to tell you there existed a way to relieve Mia of her inhabitant and get rid of Pastor Matt forever at the same time? A win-win situation."

Renee sniffed, then wiped her eyes. Then she looked Colista in the eye with such ferocity that he thought she might bite him. "Is it guaranteed to work?"

"Yes," Colista whispered quite close to her ear.

"In that case," Renee hissed, top lip raised, teeth exposed, "nail his ass to the Goddam wall and save my daughter!"

Colista understood they were now seeing the old Renee, a reversion back to her earlier years before hubby and the pastor. The anger and pain reflected on her face would prove useful in the hours to come.

CHAPTER 24

Mia looked from Jeb to her body, then toward the closed door, trying to decide on a course of action.

Jeb moaned, then leaned over to rest against the bed. He was bleeding but not as hard as she would have liked.

With a groan, Jeb sat up, then grabbed a hold of the chunk of glass still imbedded at the edge of his left eye. "Oh, damn that hurts like a bitch." He pulled at it with an ineffectual tug before screaming. "What the fuck." He didn't seem completely coherent to Mia.

Mia supposed he wouldn't die. He wasn't bleeding profusely, and she wondered if the drugs in his system would keep him from going into shock. But he did look lethargic and in pain. She wasn't sure how to feel about this. The Christian girl in her didn't want him to die, but the part of her on the receiving end of his attention sure as hell did.

Jeb moaned again, but quietly. He rested his head against the dresser wearily but stared at her. "Did you do this?"

Mia's body looked at him through curious bloodshot eyes. Mia got the impression the beast inside her would enjoy the situation whichever way it played out.

Then another gunshot blast from outside the room, closer this time.

A man screamed and a thud resonated from just outside the bedroom door.

"Help," Jeb moaned, then fondled at the chunk of glass, until a solitary bloody tear leaked down his cheek. "Ouch...damn!"

Mia's body broke into motion as if the spirit had waited for this particular moment to act. Perhaps the thing grew tired of watching Jeb piss around with the chunk of glass or it was bored and wanted to stir things up a bit. Either way, it sat up, crawled to its knees, and before Jeb realized what the hell it was up to, plucked the jagged knife-shape piece of glass from the bloody socket. It sounded a little like a plunger.

Oh my, God!

Jeb shrieked, a distinct sound from his earlier cries. Both hands flew to his left eye just in time to stop something white and runny from glopping out of the socket and onto his lap.

It looked like a big white grub in a sea of red!

The demon waived the six-inch chunk of glass around as if attempting to slice the air into little pieces. A horrible sounding chortle fell from its lips. With a quick motion it reached out and made a small slice across Mia's forearm, then had the audacity to cry out as if it didn't realize it would hurt.

Stupid bastard! You're gonna harm me...or give me a bloodborne disease.

The thing stopped wailing and smiled, understanding now the kind of feeling its little glass knife could inflict upon the human nervous system.

You're nothing but a toddler with a new toy! Not impressed! Mia flung her energy at the chunk of jagged glass.

Perhaps the glass was a better conductor of energy, or maybe Mia had just improved her abilities, but the glass wavered and then exploded into fragments.

The creature fussed at this and punched at the air as if to punish Mia's energy for ruining its toy.

Mia supposed the beast thought of her as a thorn in its side and probably didn't know what to do when a victim's energy remained trapped outside the body rather than within. A dilemma for it, Mia guessed, but one it may find a way to deal with given enough time. Something would need to be done in a hurry, but she was too busy keeping her physical body from harm to contemplate much else.

Jeb rose to his feet, legs shaky, one hand over his ruined eyeball. Blood oozed out between his fingers. "You're insane," he muttered to Mia and turned toward his dresser.

He pulled a drawer open with his right hand and rummaged around inside using his good eye. A pair of light blue undies fluttered to the floor and then a pair of black socks.

A loud series of knocks on the door pulled Jeb's concentration away from the drawer. "Jeb, man, get your ass out here! Some dude took Sal's gun and shot him. I got some lead in him with my own piece but he's still coming!" More pounding on the door came.

"Oh, shit," Jeb said. "Rog, hurry up and get in here. Be careful, though..."

But Rog didn't heed the advice, or he didn't hear it. The moment he opened the door and slipped inside, his concentration still on the area outside the door, Mia's body leapt from the bed, grabbing another chunk of glass off the bed, and pounced at Rog.

"Look out!" Jeb said.

Rog turned to Jeb, still not aware. "Holy shit, what happened to you?"

Mia clasped hold of Rog's back and hooked one arm around his neck, the other plunging the glass shard into the guy's rib cage through his red and black checkered flannel.

The thick glass clacked off rib bone.

"Get this crazy bitch off me," Rog screamed.

He gyrated to dispel Mia's body from his, his shoulder hitting the open door and slamming it shut. Rog spun around in circles, Mia firmly planted on his back like an angry cat. The demon wrapped both legs around the guy's middle and continued to jab at him with the glass shard. The gun in his waistband came unmoored and met the carpeted floor with a thud. A dime bag of weed fluttered out of his back pocket and met the gun on the brown shag.

Jeb rummaged through his drawer like a desperate lunatic. More underwear, socks, and bags of drugs dropping to the floor. Finally, he let out a grunt of satisfaction when he pulled an ugly black pistol from the bottom.

Oh no, Mia thought, *they're gonna kill me.*

She glanced up at the tiny sun which followed her everywhere. If they shot her body, Mia would need to escape through there. She hoped it didn't come to that, but her options were limited. Too bad Jeb didn't keep more lava lamps around.

Another series of bangs pounded at the bedroom door. "I saw you run in there! Mia! Mia, are you in there?"

Jack! Out of the frying pan and into the fire.

Mia couldn't honestly decide which was worse, being trapped inside this room with the two druggies or Jack.

She thought of Bruce and prayed he would somehow find her and intervene. Mia concentrated on his gentle nature, his care and tenderness. If she had to die, she wanted to do so thinking of pleasant things.

"That's him, Jeb," Rog whispered as he wrestled with Mia. "That's gotta be the guy who wasted Sal."

Jeb grabbed Mia from behind and secured her arms, pistol now tucked into his waistband. "I'll shoot him through the door; give me a minute." With Rog's help, he dislodged Mia's struggling body and threw her on the bed. The glass chunk flew from her hands and over by the dresser. "Now, stay there."

Mia's torso bounced a few times then came to rest near the headboard. More blood and gore now spackled her sweatsuit, the byproduct of Rog's deposits to the collection.

Rog cursed beneath his breath as he lifted his flannel shirt. Several lacerations leaked crimson, none of the gashes likely lethal. "I think she broke a couple ribs." He patted them and winced.

Most men were babies, Mia knew. Rog was no exception because no way did that glass break a rib. That said, Jeb seemed different. He'd been stabbed in the eye and still managed to wrestle Mia's body to the bed. The deflated white orbital now hung from the socket on his pale-skinned cheek. The empty socket wept red puss, but the major bleeding had subsided.

Perhaps some of this pain management was attributable to the menagerie of drugs he had consumed, but still.

More bangs came to the door.

"I hear you in there!" Jack screamed. "Give her to me! Mia belongs to me!"

With a roll of his lone eye, Jeb grabbed the black pistol from his waistband, lifted it, then turned it sideways. "Back off, bro, or I'm gonna start raining lead."

Jack grew silent, so Mia's essence stuck her head through the wall. Jack had moved off to the side and knelt as low as he could get. Blood dribbled from a wound at the edge of his left thigh where Rog must have winged him. "I'm armed," Jack yelled.

Someone from down the hall screamed, but Mia couldn't see who. She hoped they would call the cops, even if she didn't know what that meant for her physical body. She'd most likely get shoved into a squad car with everyone else.

Jeb sent a round through the door. A bullet hole formed in the sheetrock across the way, pieces of chalky debris raining to the floor. A picture crashed down.

Jack fired back, a small hole blown through Jeb's bedroom door. He must have missed because nobody shouted out immediately.

"Whoa," Jeb said after a moment. "Cease fire, bro. Let's talk this thing out. I'm sure we can reach a favorable outcome for everyone."

"As long as that outcome involves Mia and me walking out alive," Jack yelled.

"Yeah, sure," Jeb said. "Now holster that piece and open the door. Slow, now. No quick movements."

A moment passed, then Mia watched Jack stare at the doorknob across the hallway. He was evaluating the risks, although thinking situations through to their conclusion had never been his strength. Too many years of getting his way by throwing some muscle around. He took a tentative step toward the door. When nothing untoward occurred, Jack closed the remaining distance in one step. He reached out for the knob but made sure to keep his body to the side, just in case the druggies were lying.

The door clicked, then creeped open. When nobody from either party let loose with a barrage of gunfire, Jack said, "I'm coming in."

"Okay," Jeb said.

Jack peeked around the corner and then entered the room.

As one would expect, Jeb shot him. Mia gasped. Jack just found out the hard way what a real altercation was like. Sure, he'd engaged in some pushing and shoving, a fistfight or two after a ballgame, but nothing life-threatening.

Rog slammed the door shut when Jack fell to the floor, cradling his hand to his abdomen. Mia didn't see any blood, but Jack was making little fussing noises and rolling around on the floor.

"Stop whining," Jeb said. "I don't think I even hit you like I wanted. Got the gun instead looks like. Couldn't do that again if I tried." He'd probably meant to shoot Jack center-mass and missed. Whatever the case, he held his fire now.

"Why'd you shoot me?" Jack hissed, still in a great deal of pain. "I think my wrist is broken."

"Why do you think, genius?" Jeb said, then put the pistol back in his waistband.

"Yeah," Rog said. "You shot Sal, man. In cold blood." He reared back to deliver a kick to Jack's midsection.

"Hold on," Jeb said.

Rog delivered only a slight blow to Jack's hip, but it was enough to make Jack yelp.

"Knock it off," Rog said. "I barely touched you."

Jack glanced up at Jeb. A disgusted look crept over his face, but Mia saw the relief there of knowing he wasn't going to die. "Shit, man, your eye. It's all, you know…"

"Yeah," Jeb said in a withering voice, "I know. I have your bitch girlfriend to thank for that."

Jack glanced over at Mia's body, which lay propped up on both elbows, legs slightly spread, sweaty hair splayed over thin shoulders. The spirit seemed willing to wait and see how things played out before making another move. A growl came from her lips as if to reinforce the fact that trifling with her body could prove dangerous to one's physical well-being.

"I mean," Jeb said, "just look at her. She's a fucking mess. And what's with all the growling?"

Oh, great! Mia also recognized this look on Jack's face. After fighting and scrapping with other jocks after games, he would then get all buddy-buddy with them. *Sickening.*

"Yeah," Jack said. "She got into some shit she shouldn't have. I don't know." Then he glanced up at Jeb. "Doesn't that hurt?"

"Sure, it hurts," Jeb agreed. "But I have enough blow in me to kill a bull…and enough downers to stop a rhino. I'll have to remember that combination, because this is the best high I've had in a long time." He shook his head, and the deflated eyeball swung back and forth. "Not just a great painkiller, but a helluva rush, too."

"Nice," Rog agreed. "Maybe we can combine it into one pill. It'll be the new Ecstasy, the latest and greatest party drug. Either one, alone, would kill ya, but together…"

"This is why I love you," Jeb said. "The business mind to my experimentation."

"I like how you guys think, man," Jack said. He shook his sore hand. "Look, I'm the kinda guy always looking for an angle. I have a whole system up where I was going to college. Plenty of weed and amphetamines. But can I trust you?"

Jack might be lying, trying to get in their good graces, but she doubted he was. That was the truly sad part. She knew he used occasionally, but a whole system? If that was true, he'd jump right in with these goons.

Jack continued, "If you're interested, I have a group we can make some money on. They're ripe for the picking."

"Keep talking," Jeb said. "I'm starting to smell the sweet aroma of cashola."

"Cashola," Rog repeated, then nodded.

"You see," Jack said and pointed at Mia, "she belongs to a church that, well, let's just say they like to do things the wrong way. Got themselves an old white-haired pastor who likes to diddle the congregation and keep them under his thumb. I get the distinct impression a few drugs in the old goblet with the blood of Jesus wouldn't be unwelcome, if you get my drift."

"Oh, I'm getting it," Jeb said with a smile. "Read ya loud and clear, bro. You pull this sale off, you get twenty percent. Fair?"

Mia would never have guessed that Jack understood what fair was in the druggie world, but she'd been wrong about everything else. And he was right about Pastor Matt.

"Yep," Jack said. "Right as rain, man. As much as that old fuck collects in the plate on Sundays, he'll jump at the chance for this stuff. Anything he can use to increase his hold on his precious congregation. All for the man upstairs." He winked and pointed at the ceiling, ironically, not far from where Mia floated.

Then Rog added, "Perfect! They think they're giving their money to God, but they're really giving it to a couple of druggies. Ha!"

"They're suckers," Jack said. "Pure and simple. It's a sweet situation."

Mia wondered if Jack ever loved her. What of her parents? Her whole childhood was a lie.

"What we gonna do about her?" Jeb said, pointing at Mia.

"She belongs to me," Jack said. "She's part of the church community, and if we're gonna keep this business proposition afloat, I need her by my side. She's my connection. Know what I mean?"

"She don't seem too cooperative," Jeb said.

"Oh, I wouldn't worry about that," Jack said. "That bastard Pastor Matt taught me one useful thing. That's how to keep people cooperative and submissive."

The spirit inside Mia growled.

Jack stood and walked toward the bed, still favoring his right hand. "Might as well start her education right now."

"Now we're talking," Jeb said. "I call seconds. Rog, you'll have to wait."

"Whatever," Rog said.

OMG! They're going to do to me what Pastor Matt did to Dad! No, no, no! Mia raced around the room in a panicked circle, just above the three men's heads.

"You feel that?" Jeb asked.

"Yeah," Rog said. "Feels like someone turned on a fan or something. The air's moving pretty good." He looked around as if something might bite him.

"I'll have to call the landlord after we get the place cleaned up," Jeb said. "For now..." He took a step in Mia's body's direction.

"Hey!" Jack said. "My girl; I get to go first."

Jeb nodded, but now all three guys approached the bed at once.

Mia's body leered at them with a solicitous grin. A quiet half-growl/half-moan escaped its lips.

Nose wrinkled in distaste, Rog said, "Maybe...I mean, not to be picky...but *maybe* we ought to get her cleaned up first. You know, like rinse her off. She don't smell too good and she's got blood and what not all over her."

Jeb smacked Rog in the side of the head. "Don't be a dick."

Jack said, "It's fine. She's not clean inside or out, according to…well, some professor at the college."

Jeb turned to him. "Whadya mean, inside or out?"

He looked nervous, like Jack was about to flake out on him just when Jeb thought he'd struck gold.

Jack lifted his shoulders in a gentle shrug. "You know, like possessed or some shit." When Jeb frowned at him, Jack added, "Hey, I thought it was bullshit, too, and Mia was just on drugs, whatever. But now… I'm not so sure."

"She ingested so much blow earlier she ought to be dead," Jeb said. The narrowing of his eyes said everything now made sense. "That and the fact she stuck a chunk of glass in my eye. Yeah, I'd say possession is as good an explanation as any."

"Possessed?" Rog asked. "You mean, like spook stuff, like *The Exorcist*? Or *The Amityville Horror*? You know, the dude who shot all his kids."

"More or less," Jack said. "Pastor Matt thinks she's on drugs, but I think Mia was into some badass stuff. Besides, Pastor Matt doesn't know his ass from a hole in the ground."

"Yeah," Jeb agreed. "But he knows how to control people. That's all that matters. If he wants to think Mia's on drugs, all the better. Then he'll want some of ours…lots of ours."

"I think she wants it," Rog said, getting the trio back on the track. "I mean, look at her."

Get your legs back together! Mia screamed to herself.

She was never one to slut shame anyone. What anyone did with their bodies was their business, but this was her body, and she didn't want group sex. That didn't stop the thing on the bed from spreading her legs so wide that Mia worried her legs might pop out of their joints.

"Holy crap," Jack said. "She must be possessed. The Mia I know would never…"

Damn right, dick!

If he hadn't already, Jack had officially crossed over from hapless punk to the worst person in the world. She hated him. Mia wished him dead.

Jack reached out and ran an experimental hand along Mia's ribs. When she didn't shriek with displeasure, he let his hand slide up a bit higher.

Mia had seen enough. She built up her energy, then propelled herself like a bullet. Mia aimed for Jack's earhole and passed through it, her energy flying out the other side of his head. Reversing direction, she did the same with Jeb. While they batted at their ears and hair, Mia's energy flashed as she entered between Rog's eyes and exited the back of his cranium.

"Spiders!" Rog screamed. "It feels like spiderwebs. Everywhere! They're everywhere!"

Mia kept at it. She could feel the energy enter her as she drained it from the atmosphere and used it to fuel her rage.

"But I don't see anything," Jeb said, continuing to bat at his head.

"The temperature just dropped," Jack added. "Maybe the breeze, the spiderwebs, and the cold have something to do with Mia."

"Yeah," Rog said. "For sure. I watch *Ghost Adventures*. This place is haunted. Whatever's possessing your skank there is haunting us. It's getting after us, wants to drag us to Hell."

Rog rose from the bed, then ran from the room, the door slamming behind him.

Jeb glanced at Jack. "Good riddance. More for us." He winked.

"I ain't scared of no ghost," Jack said. He grabbed at the drawstring of Mia's soiled sweatpants. "Let's get this done."

No, no, no, no!

CHAPTER 25

Back in Colista's apartment, Renee dialed Pastor Matt's phone number using the landline rather than her cell. Doug hadn't answered, so perhaps the combination of calling Pastor Matt and using Colista's phone would net a better result.

Bruce watched Renee with interest. *Just an older version of Mia...with brown eyes*, he thought. *Lovely.* He knew his feelings for Mia made this comparison important to him. He wanted to like her mom and wanted her to like him, because he still hoped for a real relationship with Mia and her family.

"It's ringing." As instructed, Renee pressed the button for speaker so they could all hear. She looked nervous; hands shaky as she flipped the left through her hair.

"Relax," Colista said. "You'll do just fine. Just say what would come natural if you were at home."

She looked to Colista just as Pastor Matt picked up and the ringing stopped. Labored breaths poured from the speaker. Renee looked frightened and Bruce felt for her. "Pastor Matt? Thank, God! I'm so glad I got ahold of you. I-I need you."

"Calm down, Renee," Pastor Matt said. He sounded pleased to hear from her. "I'm sure you're concerned about Mia. I can assure you that all is under control. We'll have her home before you know it and I'll…I'll take care of everything." He paused. "Am I on speaker phone, Renee?"

Renee's head snapped up in panic.

Colista smiled and shook his head.

"No, of course not," Renee said. "I'm just in a tight space and everything is echoing." She breathed hard in and out. "So, um, it's not exactly Mia I'm calling about, although, I am concerned, of course."

"Not Mia?" Pastor Matt asked. Bruce thought his voice held a note of intrigue.

"No," Renee said. "I'm frightened, and I need you. I need your strength. Your soothing."

Pastor Matt remained quiet for a moment, until Bruce thought he might have hung up. Finally, he said, "What are you frightened of, Renee?"

Renee breathed heavily above the phone. Bruce couldn't tell if this was unintentional or a ploy to reel Pastor Matt in. "A professor named Colista frightened me with his words." Then she looked at Colista with a smile and Bruce knew the woman was clever and knew just what to say. "You see, I came to find Mia, and a young man told me to speak with the professor. Of course, I did." She paused for obvious effect.

Pastor Matt breathed heavily from the other end of the line. Bruce imagined the guy, face and nose beet red, sweat stains marring his armpits.

Renee continued. "He frightened me. He spoke of things only you can explain to me. He told of blasphemies to our risen Lord! Please-please come to me." An octave higher, she said, "I need you."

Bruce cringed at the high tenor of her voice, not sure if she added it for effect or if real fear birthed it. Talking to this man, trying to deceive him after all these years, had to be nerve wracking.

"I understand," Pastor Matt said, voice husky and low. "I shall come and soothe you, provide you with comfort and ease your questioning mind. You only need but tell me where you are."

Colista gave Renee the thumbs up.

"It's so cold here," Renee whispered in a seductive tone. "I require the touch of God's love, Pastor Matt. To feel warmth."

"And I shall give it to you," Pastor Matt cooed. "Just tell me where to find you."

Pastor Matt gave Bruce the creeps. The thought of Mia being in close proximity to him made him feel sick in the pit of his stomach. How were men like this made? Born or finely crafted from the atrocities of life? Perhaps he'd been abused as a child. Perhaps he was just a sadistic sociopath.

"I-I'm in Colista's apartment," Renee whispered, pulling Bruce from his own thoughts, as if she needed to remain quiet so the professor wouldn't hear. "He's in the bathroom, but I think he'll come out soon. I-I just wanted to find Mia."

"I understand," Pastor Matt said. "I shall arrive in less than ten minutes. I'm not far. Then we can…observe God's sacraments. And find Mia, of course. I do believe she is safe with Jack as we speak."

Bruce watched Renee's mouth turn up in a snarl. She hated Jack, that much was apparent. "Praise the Lord," she managed through clenched teeth.

"Praise Him, indeed," Pastor Matt said softly.

"I need to go," Renee hissed quickly. "He's coming." She hung up with a clack of the receiver into the base.

Colista clapped. "Excellent work, Mrs. Hollenbeck."

"Don't call me that," Renee said. "I'll divorce Doug the minute this is over. And I'll move as far away as I can from the church. I don't know if Mia will come." A tear slid down her cheek.

"After tonight, you won't need bother yourself about your...church," Colista said. "I made a promise that I intend to keep. Now, we have much to prepare in very little time."

Colista stalked over to the fireplace and put three more logs in the hearth and lit them, then tinkered with the three bowls on the three pedestals. As he did, he said, "When Pastor Matt arrives—and perhaps Doug will come with him, but I doubt it given that conversation—it's imperative we get him near the fireplace." He looked from Renee to Bruce with a serious scowl. "And this next part is especially important. Neither of you must shove him directly into the fire. The gatekeeper must do the honors. Am I clear on this point?"

"Sure," Bruce said, "but why? Is it a rule of magic or something?"

"No," Colista said. He turned to Renee. "It's a rule in your Bible. I believe it reads something like *Though Shalt Not Kill.*"

"If he's done anything to Mia, I'll kill him myself, sin or no sin," Renee said. "I'll send him straight to Hell."

"Along with yourself, in due time," Colista said, then poured more salt around the circle surrounding his davenport.

"Do you even believe in God?" Renee asked. "I mean, you're a practitioner of magic."

"True," Bruce said, and couldn't wait for Colista to explain. The guy could speak the truth like nobody he ever heard before. And not in a manipulative way like Pastor Matt, but to help others without any regard to what he could get out of it.

Colista looked up at Renee. "Yes, on both counts." Then he turned back to the salt ring and began a second swath around. He continued, "All things spiritual are about conviction. We are destined to follow the path in which we feel convicted to tread. For some, such as you Renee, that's Christianity. It's a different path for others, but we needn't bother ourselves with the muddying of those waters."

Renee leaned forward, elbows on knees.

"As for me?" Colista asked. "Well, let's just say I'm destined to perform as a chameleon of sorts."

"But what do you believe?" Renee asked.

"What my clients require me to believe."

"But isn't that dishonest?"

"Not at all," Colista said. "Because I do believe. Every time, without fail. It's how chaos magicians make their hay. We are trained to believe in all faiths as that faith becomes necessary for a resolution." He added, "Explaining further will jeopardize your salvation, I am afraid. Now, when Pastor Matt arrives, I need you to answer the door and invite him in, Renee. Tell him I'm in the kitchen." He turned to Bruce. "You'll be with me. If I give you an instruction, I require you to follow it without question."

Bruce saluted. "You can count on me." And Colista could, because Bruce would do whatever it took to help Mia. First thing that needed to happen, according to Colista, was to pay the gatekeeper. After that, the portal would close and relieve Mia's body of the demon. Then she would be easier to find, because she'd be herself and looking for them. Simple.

"Yes," Colista said. "That's what I'm afraid of."

"Who are you, exactly?" Renee asked Bruce. "I know you said you're a friend of Mia's." She smiled with a polite upturn of her lips. "How good? Be honest. I think you'll find me more open to possibilities than Douglass."

"Pretty good," Bruce said. "Good enough to risk my life. I'm pretty sure I love her, to be honest." He bowed his head. He knew how that may sound to a mother. She probably would tell him to never see Mia again.

"I see." When Bruce looked up, her lips were pursed, but a twinkle of light had erupted in her eyes. "I feel like any boy who would risk his life for my Mia is the very best kind of friend. No other man in her life has done as much." She left it at that.

Bruce felt a swell of emotion so strong he couldn't respond beyond that simple gesture. Then something meaningful leaped to the forefront of his mind. He blurted, "When I find her, I'm going to hand her yarn and needles; she'll need it."

Renee smiled, friendly crow's feet forming at the corners of her dark eyes. "Yes, I believe she will." Then she looked to the fireplace. "I'm worried about her. She's so fragile, and if there's an evil spirit inside her…"

"She's stronger than you give her credit for," Bruce said. "Since she's been at state—well, at least since she's hung out with me. I've watched her excel at dealing with her emotions. Sure, she cries uncontrollably sometimes, but she's learning how to overcome it with her knitting."

"Her social anxiety…"

"Shrinking," Bruce assured her. "Becoming much less frequent."

"And you have something to do with this?"

Bruce turned his palms out.

Don't get full of yourself, punk. Mia's out of your league and so is her family. They'll never accept you. You're a joke, kid. At least your old man can get laid.

Shut up!

Bruce looked up at Renee. "I'd like to think so."

Renee stood and stretched. She said simply, "She'll need a new life after this —new friends." Renee looked nervous and glanced at the door as if Pastor Matt might stand right outside it.

Bruce's heart leaped into his throat. He felt sure Mia's mom just gave him permission to date her. He wouldn't take this for granted. He'd treat her right. Maybe he couldn't believe everything she and her family believed in, but perhaps he could believe in enough. If he could believe in spirits and gatekeepers, he could believe in a lot.

Don't get your hopes up, son.

Knock it off!

For the first time in a while, Bruce felt optimistic. If they could free Mia from both the demon inside her and from the clutches of the pastor, perhaps both their lives could change for the better. Dare he imagine that they could help each other heal from this debacle and limp into some kind of life together? *Maybe.* What mattered was what he did moving forward. Even if that entailed leading a man to his doom. No man deserved it more—a man who abused his parishioners under the guise of their own dogma.

Bruce glanced at Renee and wondered how she'd hold up under pressure. She seemed okay, but her eyes harbored bags beneath and she stared into the middle distance, probably thinking of the encounter to come. The restraint it must have taken to not scream at Pastor Matt to give her daughter back immediately must have been overwhelming.

Colista fiddled with a clay jar that appeared suspiciously like an urn and sat it next to the hearth. It harbored an acrylic design of a yacht on a calm ocean. He mumbled something about a "*Vessel of the Diablo Si.*"

"A what?" Bruce asked.

Renee took a step back like it might bite her but kept an eye on the urn and Colista; and the cat as it sniffed about at the decorated vessel.

"A *Vessel of the Diablo Si,*" Colista repeated. "It's capable of harboring or imprisoning a spirit." He looked up at Bruce. "It would have contained a revenant of Pepe's energy if the gatekeeper hadn't double-crossed me. Now it only serves as a place for ash." Colista scowled. "And a little reminder to the gatekeeper about its promises."

Something else Bruce would need ask about later. How did an urn become this *Vessel of the Diablo Si?* An intricately laid spell, Bruce supposed, just like the offerings in the three stands. So many things he had yet to learn in this world.

A light knock came at the door.

"Show time," Colista said. He left the vessel sit and bounded toward the kitchen door, Crowley at his heels. The cat appeared to understand the importance of the whole thing, because it kept quiet. Over his shoulder, Colista said, "Bruce, come on. Renee, get the not-so-good pastor over by the fireplace."

Bruce took Renee by the arm with a gentle hand and asked, "You okay?" Only after the steely glint in her eye gave Bruce answer did he follow Colista into the kitchen. He picked a place behind the double-doored fridge and listened.

The door opened and Renee said, "Thank God you're here. I think the professor will come out at any moment. Please."

"Not to worry," Pastor Matt said in his low, soothing voice. He sounded like a predator to Bruce. "This shouldn't take long."

A long silence drew out before Renee spoke. "Can we please sit by the fire? I'm so cold, Pastor Matt. The professor's words chilled me to the bone." In little more than a whisper, "He said Mia has a demon inside her."

"Of course, we can sit by the fire. And, rest assured, it will be the fires of Hell which will warm the professor, for the words he spoke to you," Pastor Matt said. "As for you, I shall warm you with the blinding heat of the living Christ."

"What of Mia, Pastor?"

Pastor Matt let out a rather loud breath. "Yeah, touch me there. Hold it, please. Can't wait to get you back to the motel and..."

"Mia," Renee said rather stern.

After a moment, Pastor Matt said, "The only thing inside Mia is drugs. We'll get her home and..." Then Pastor Matt croaked out a choked shriek. "Stop squeezing it so hard!"

"Crowley, move," Colista said as he bolted for the library.

Bruce took off right behind him. Just before Colista got out of the kitchen, Bruce heard Renee say, "That better be all that's been inside of Mia or I'll squeeze so hard your unborn children will scream."

Another choked cry from Pastor Matt.

Holy shit! Bruce thought. Renee and Pastor Matt sat on the hearth, and she had his dick in a hold so tight her knuckles were white. Bruce stood by Colista's desk, not sure what exactly to do. Colista ignored it all and sat at the desk before the open grimoire.

The front door burst open, and Bruce watched Doug stumble inside. He appeared unable to comprehend what the situation entailed and what, if anything, should get done about it. Then he seemed to catch on. "Honey...why are your hands around Pastor Matt's penis?"

Pastor Matt screamed and attempted to pry Renee's fingers from his most private of places.

"Good Lord," Doug said, but did nothing but stare at his wife hurting his pastor.

Then Pastor Matt found his words through what looked to Bruce like excruciating pain. "Kill them, Doug, for God's sake. Kill them all!"

Mia's dad looked from his wife and Pastor Matt to Colista and then finally to Bruce. "What are you doing still hanging around? Why is my wife here? Pastor Matt told me to stay in the car while he spoke to the professor, but I thought he might need help."

"I wouldn't know," Bruce said. "I just got here." He tried to think of something meaningful. This was Mia's dad, after all. "Look, to her credit, it appears as though she's trying to harm him, not screw him. Know what I mean? She's trying to help Mia!" At the mention of his daughter's name, Doug recoiled as if slapped.

Pastor Matt shrieked, gave up on trying to remove Renee's hand and tried to reach her throat.

"Mia," Doug said, seemingly to himself. "I don't know where she is." He took a step in the direction of Renee and Pastor Matt. "What's going on here?"

"She's fed up with his abuse, maybe?" Bruce suggested.

"Yes," Doug said. "Abuse. You may be on to something there."

Bruce couldn't believe this man had sired Mia. Perhaps Renee had slept around a bit back in the early days of their relationship. Mia didn't look much like her dad—not in the least. Nor did she harbor his personality traits.

"You move, even an inch, and I'll rip it off," Renee screamed.

"My God," Doug said and grabbed his hair between the fingers of both hands. Bruce knew the man's allegiances were conflicted.

Colista began to read from the book on his desk, a mumble at first, then his voice gaining strength. Crowley stood and faced Pastor Matt where Renee held him captive. A low rumble resonated out of the cat.

"Gatekeeper," Colista began, "your payment is nigh. Come from the nether and claim your prize, keep your commitments." The fire roared upward with a ferocity which heated the entire room. Then Colista said, "Renee, run!" before initiating a mumbling Latin chant.

The chant resonated and seemed to course about the room of its own volition, first soft and then rising into a fury pitch.

The fire behind Renee and Pastor Matt intensified and rose, appearing as a solid wall of flames. Bruce could feel it from where he stood across the room. A fiery mouth and eyes materialized within the orange and yellow bank of fire. He also noted that the flame avoided the *Vessel of the Diablo Si.*

Pastor Matt tried to pull away like a scalded cat, caught short by Renee's hold. Her hand slipped off the pastor's sweaty flesh, but she caught the leather of his unbuckled belt as if walking a pudgy white-haired dog.

"Unhand me, woman," Pastor Matt bellowed without much conviction. His eyes were transfixed on the face in the fire, not on Renee. He pulled for escape from Renee and the fire but seemed to lack the strength.

"Good Lord," Doug said. "Pastor Matt, what's happening?" Bruce didn't understand why Mia's dad would still look to the man for guidance when the pastor so clearly held no answers.

Pastor Matt grunted like a pig as he attempted to pull away from Renee. His face looked a mess of sweat, grime, and grim concentration. The blood vessels in his eyes looked ready to burst. He looked like a man fighting to avoid the eternal fires of Hell, just as he had said would happen to Colista. *Ironic.*

"Murder," Pastor Matt screamed. "They plan to murder us. They are evil, Doug. Can't you see that? Kill them! It's self-defense. You won't go to jail if you kill them in my name."

He continued to struggle and finally managed to gain some headway as his belt tore free from his waist. Renee fell over, tripping over the bunched rug, belt still in her hand. Pastor Matt lunged forward and fell onto his stomach and crawled away from the monstrous fire on his elbows.

Crowley hissed, then reared its paw back and scratched Pastor Matt's cheek. The pastor looked stunned by the sudden blow and stopped crawling. That's when Crowley leaped on his head and dug its long claws into his scalp, holding on as if its life depended on it.

"Get this infernal beast off me," Pastor Matt wailed.

Doug took a couple of steps in Pastor Matt's direction.

Bruce made to stop the man, but Colista's head snapped to him. "Do not interfere!"

Bruce stepped back to the wall. Truth told, he didn't want anything to do with whatever lurked in that fireplace. Even though he knew the gatekeeper was here for Pastor Matt, Bruce wasn't so sure the thing wouldn't steal a couple collateral souls if given the opportunity. Only if Mia needed him would Bruce willingly go near the gatekeeper.

Renee rolled away from the heat of the flames. She came to rest against a chair near where Doug stumbled with tentative steps. Bruce watched Renee, her chest heaving with exertion, staring at the man in disgust.

Pastor Matt got a hold on Crowley and threw the cat into the air. Strands of his white hair went with.

Crowley screeched as he flew, hit the edge of the davenport, then dropped to the floor. He lay panting, eyes closed.

Bruce took a stride to help Crowley, but Colista gave him another look which stopped him. He stayed frozen as the professor returned to the text, reading in Latin. The words buzzed around the room like angry bees in a windstorm.

Pastor Matt managed to shove himself up to his knees, blood streaming from his scalp. His pants, sans a tightened belt, lay wrapped around his knees. He wore stained white underwear. He glared at Doug with eyes so red he looked like a rabbit in headlights. "Don't just stand there; help me, fool." He reached out for Doug as if trying to escape quicksand. Then he pointed at Renee. "This is her fault. She betrayed us. This is what you get for running a loose household, Douglass!"

Mia's dad shook his head. "You-you were trying to mess with Renee."

"I was trying to exert control," Pastor Matt screeched. "Something I wouldn't have to do if you were a real man and fulfilled your obligations. Now help me up and we can get this all under control."

Doug looked to Renee, who sneered at him with an upturned lip. He turned back to Pastor Matt. Slow enough it seemed to take a lifetime, Mia's dad made his choice and reached to grasp the pastor's hand. After all of this, Bruce was shocked he would still side with this madman. But he supposed that's what cult life consisted of.

Colista's eyes were closed, his lips moving in silent prayer. Crowley remained where he'd fallen, watching. Renee pinned Bruce with her eyes, seeming to ask him to do something so the pastor wouldn't get away.

Doug's fingertips touched Pastor Matt's open hand, then a large tongue of fire shot from the fireplace and wove itself around Pastor Matt's torso like a flaming lasso.

Doug retracted his hand as if the fire bit him and took a small step backward.

Pastor Matt pulled away from the flames, eyes narrowed with stubborn refusal. Even as the fiery rope caused his clothes to smolder, the pastor stood, strove forward, jaw set, determined to simply walk away.

Bruce watched in fascination as the pastor and the flames both fought for purchase. The mouth within the flames opened wider even as Pastor Matt set his own mouth in grim determination. The harder the flames pulled, the more the man dug in as if he thought the Lord would still save him from this fate. The outcome seemed inevitable, yet Pastor Matt fought on.

Pastor Matt grunted with exertion but never wavered in his effort. He kept one foot in front of the other as if walking in slow motion. "Someone help," he wheezed. "Douglass!"

Another whip-like strand of fire lashed out and wrapped itself around Pastor Matt, this time around his waist. The area in which it adhered itself smoldered upon contact.

Like an old bulldozer, Pastor Matt bulled forward. For the first time, the strain caused his legs to tremble. Between cheek-puffing grunts, a low whine squeaked out from between his clenched teeth. His eyes, while still narrowed, had turned an even starker crimson, as if his orbs may explode into bloody missiles of pulp.

A third fiery strand shot out of the hearth, this time lacing around Pastor Matt's neck.

This finally stopped Pastor Matt's forward momentum, but he had yet to give up any ground. He turned his head toward Doug. "Help me," he wheezed as the third fiery brand burned a black ring into the flesh of his jowly neck.

Doug took a step backward.

Pastor Matt trembled with fatigue, his muscles straining. He wet himself. "You coward," he said.

A pained noise passed Doug's lips, as if the act of defiance physically hurt, but he didn't move to help.

A breaking point must have been reached because Pastor Matt looked to the sky, like he expected help to come from above. Then, with fists clenched, he wailed, "Nooooooo!" Seconds later he was hurled backward across the room as the three blazing ropes of fire yanked him into the waiting mouth within the fireplace. He thrashed within, thin slices of the fire breaking off and swarming his flesh like a school of flaming piranha.

Crowley finally lifted its head, looked over its shoulder where Pastor Matt suffered, then allowed its head to plop back onto the floor, exhausted.

Colista continued to chant, taking no chances it seemed. Bruce figured the guy worried the gatekeeper would rip him off again, if he didn't stay diligent.

Pepe's vessel remained unscathed.

Within the devouring flames, Pastor Matt's white hair went up, turning his scalp black. Bruce could smell the singed hair, that scent quickly becoming overpowered by the greasy meat smell of barbeque. The man seemed to open his mouth to scream, but all that came out was one of the wriggling brands of flame. His eyes burst next, the whites disappearing in twin vortexes of swirling orange, yellow and blue.

The mouth within the wall of flame opened wide to encapsulate and devour Pastor Matt. Bruce thought the maneuver looked a lot like a garbage truck raising a can and dumping. Pastor Matt's head and shoulders went first, then the rest of him disappeared into the maw. Seconds later the wall of fire went out as if it never existed. Pastor Matt now resided with the gatekeeper in whatever capacity that may entail.

Doug turned to Renee. "It's over, honey. We're free."

That didn't take long, Bruce thought.

Renee stood. She walked up to him with one hand extended—an olive branch, Bruce thought. Her brown eyes sparkled, and her gaze softened as if she felt sorry for her husband. Then her other hand shot forward and punched him so hard in the forehead he stumbled backward all the way to the fireplace.

Doug investigated the dark fireplace like Pastor Matt might still be in there somewhere. When nothing presented itself, he turned to Renee. Bruce could see the red bump which had raised on his forehead. His mouth opened then closed. No words, Bruce supposed. Finally, he said, "Renee, please. You have to understand. Let's just go find Mia and go home."

"I'll find her without your help," Renee said, her eyes flinty with anger. "You won't be getting anywhere near her. Or me. Not ever again."

Colista made eye contact with Bruce. He shook his head. *Wait!* Bruce nodded his understanding. Bruce turned his attention back to the argument.

"Be reasonable. It was Pastor Matt. He held me in thrall. My eyes are open now. We—we'll start a new life together."

Renee looked like she might vomit, eyes strained, a hand over her mouth. "Not a chance. Mia and I have a lot of healing to do. You have no place in it."

Crowley lifted his nose high, as if sensing something.

"Renee," he pleaded. He raised both hands toward her.

Then a blossom of heat and light ignited behind Mia's dad. The man tried to move away, but a large burning effigy reached out to him from behind. Despite eyes, mouth, and hair fashioned from fire, Bruce recognized Pastor Matt. The apparition laughed low and dark as it grabbed Mia's dad by the neck.

For a moment, Bruce thought the gatekeeper had double-crossed Colista once more, but when he glanced at the professor, a smile graced his alabaster lips.

Pepe's vessel seemed to quake with an unspoken fervor.

The ephemeral version of Pastor Matt drew Doug up to its burning face. It said, "He wants you too, Douglass. He wants you, too."

Renee's eyes caught the light from the apparition, and Bruce could see the glee within them. He couldn't blame her. Bruce just hoped they were all safe. The look of amusement on Colista's face gave him the answer he needed to extinguish that line of thought.

Mia's dad fought Pastor Matt's fiery grip, pushing with his legs, his hands trying to peel away the phantom's flaming arms from his neck. He continued to struggle with wild thrusts of his legs when Pastor Matt tipped Mia's dad backward and into the flameless void of his mouth. They morphed into one giant ball of intense flame and then…simply disappeared, leaving behind a cold empty fireplace once more.

Pepe's *Vessel of the Diablo Si* stood victorious, a lone sentinel to the unspeakable carnage.

Crowley went back to sleep.

CHAPTER 26

Mia hovered above her body. No more lightbulbs existed and her attempts at breaking their craniums resulted in only one desirable result. Now she felt rundown, like a battery out of juice, without any way to recharge.

Jeb palmed his damaged eye socket. "I think I'm coming down. Shit. Hurry up so I can have a go before I black out from pain."

Jack unbuckled his belt and slid his jeans off, exposing his dark toned legs. Then he looked at Jeb. "Um, bro, you wanna, you know, turn your back or something?"

Jeb shrugged and turned around with a huff of air. "We should just two-hole her, you know. That'd really consummate our deal, bond us. We'd be like blood brothers—brothers from another mother."

"Later," Jack said. "Right now, I just wanna get my groove on."

Jack's groove, Mia considered, never lasted longer than thirty seconds, so Jeb wouldn't have to wait long.

The bed jiggled as Jack crawled onto it without his pants. He pulled off Mia's sweatpants to reveal red underthings. The spirit inside Mia waited with a less-than-patient gaze for Jack to get his crap together so it could experience the *Big O*.

Good luck, Mia thought. The only *Big O* she ever got from Jack was a ride on the Octopus at the county fair.

Just as Jack squeezed his skinny ass between Mia's thighs, she felt a wave of pure energy ripple through her. She watched a dark shadow wriggle out from inside of her flesh, hovering in the air for a moment, kicking and thrashing like a displeased infant with red eyes. Then it was sucked into the bright orb like lint into a vacuum.

Mia felt her energy glide toward her body through no effort of her own. She entered it like wind into a burlap sack. It felt like a balloon inflating as her awareness filled her body and before she knew it, Mia stared straight into Jack's dark eyes. She smelled his sour breath and felt where he pushed against her down below. Mia decided to end this madness.

Jack recoiled when Mia slapped the side of his head with an open palm. When her thumb entered his eye socket, he pulled away, slapped a hand over the hurt eyeball and then fell to the floor, writhing in pain. Mia stood, then leaped off the bed, her feet coming down hard on Jack's privates. His mouth opened and closed like a fish without water.

"What the fuck?" Jeb turned toward the commotion just in time to catch a fist from Mia right in his already-destroyed eye. He crumpled to the floor with Jack.

Mia ran for the door. Part of her didn't trust this reinsertion into her body. The demon would probably return and then she'd end up trapped inside of her body with the thing this time—full possession. She ran through the party house, past people who stared at her instead of asking if she needed help, then out into the night. Her feet pounded the pavement until her side ached.

She didn't know where anyone was, but knew she wanted to get to Bruce. She didn't need Bruce—didn't need anyone. But she wanted him. When together, they seemed to bring the best out in each other. Everything else in the world faded into the background as she made her way toward state college.

Mia didn't need to hide any longer.

PROLOGUE

The chartered fishing boat rocked over the three-foot rollers like a toy in the bathtub. Mia opened her mouth and accepted the grape offered to her, then continued to knit. *Knit pearl two.* The *Stalking Jack the Ripper* novel she scored from the library lay next to her, three-quarters read.

Bruce popped a grape into his own mouth then pounded the keys on his laptop. He'd been at it all afternoon, and if the pleased smile was any indication, his writing was going well.

Or he's happy to be here with me.

Mia gazed down her long body wrapped in a bright yellow two-piece with a sheer cover-up. Then she allowed her gaze to make its way to the front of the boat where Colista stood out on the harpoon deck, wind blowing his dark hair back off his neck. He looked stoic but at peace for the first time since she'd known him.

After she made it back to state and found Bruce, he'd first held her tight, then filled her in on the fate of Pastor Matt and her father. She also had a frank conversation with her mother about what their lives would be like moving forward. Much different, of course, but a vast improvement. Mia told her mother in no uncertain terms where she would be staying for her education. Many questions remained unanswered for all of them, but time would heal and, perhaps, render the answers inconsequential.

Mia had no idea what had happened with Jack and Jeb, not a single phone call to try and woo her back, or to even chastise her for her behavior. Part of Mia wished he would try so she could explain a few things to him about how two people should treat each other. But it didn't matter. She had Bruce, and he had her.

Colista decided on an immediate sabbatical off the coast of Bermuda, inspired by both Mia and Bruce, and took them with for a vacation. He figured he'd pined away for Pepe for long enough, and since the gatekeeper had kept its promise this time, Colista found closure. Or he would in short order.

"Check it out," Mia said and pointed at Colista.

"Finally," Bruce said and placed his hand in Mia's.

Colista carried Crowley awkwardly in one hand and an urn marked with an acrylic design in the other. He laid Crowley on the deck where the thing promptly tipped over and licked its butt. The professor smiled with affection at the cat, mumbled something unintelligible at this distance, then held the urn in the air.

When Colista removed the lid, a small bit of white ash blew up and into the sky. "What you always wanted, Pepe," Colista yelled into the heavens. He tipped the urn and a cloud of white dispersed into the air. Where it settled into the water, the liquid took on a hazy white suspension for a moment before the remains of Pepe spread out and dissipated into the deep. "For you, Pepe!" Colista yelled, urn raised above his head.

Mia hugged Bruce then, her face buried in his neck. She just knew everything would be okay now. For all of them.

ACKNOWLEDGEMENTS

To the entire Silver Shamrock Publishing team. Not just folks who publish my work and make me look good, and who have made me a better writer, but awesome peeps who I now call friends.

ABOUT THE AUTHOR

Author of the novel *Seven Cleopatra Hill*, the three-book Bruised series, and numerous short stories scattered about the nether. He also investigates the paranormal and plays a mean match of volleyball. Justin lives somewhere on the Mississippi river with his wife, a crabby Bengal, and an easy-going Danetiff, where he's busy writing the next novel.

ALIVE, YET DEAD...

The bloody War Between the States and a harrowing confinement in an enemy prison camp had turned Joshua Wingade into a broken man. His nerves and spirit shattered by the barbarity of battle, and demoralized by a cause that his heart secretly despised, Wingade returns home in hope of finding peace and healing.

But, upon his arrival, he discovers that Hell had come to call. His beloved wife had been violated and transformed into a horrid bride of the undead, and his only son abducted by a band of diabolical outlaws led by the renegade vampire, Jules Holland. Along for the ride are three demonic henchmen from the fetid bowels of Hades and the dark witch, Evangeline.

Aware that he is no match for the gang, Wingade rides across Georgia and Tennessee nonetheless, intent on rescuing his child from imminent disaster. During his journey, he witnesses the horrors and atrocities Holland and his evil confederates have wrought. Eventually, he finds himself at the outlaws' mercy. An instant before death, he makes a final pledge to his stolen son.

"I promise, Daniel! I will come for you!"

DEAD, YET ALIVE...

He awakens to discover that the cold finality of the grave has been thwarted. With the help of the Louisiana mojo man, Job, he has been resurrected. But, the frail and fearful man named Joshua Wingade is forever gone. In his place is the stoic, steel-nerved Dead-Eye with his blind eye aglow and a gun hand as swift and deadly as greased lightning.

Together, they vow to pursue the vampire and his minions, and deliver
young Daniel from his bondage. However, they know that time is their worst enemy. If Holland and the others make it across the Mississippi River to the Western territories beyond, their vengeance may never come to fruition. For they are entering a new purgatory known as the Devil's Playground... a vast wilderness rife with violence and terrors unleashed from the Hole Out of Nowhere.

A place where death and evil are dealt freely, without atonement to anyone... including God himself!

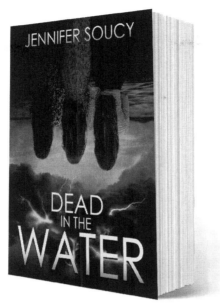

58171928R10163